THE MASTER OF BRUGES

Terence Morgan taught English for thirty years, in England and Singapore. He has worked as a freelance editor and journalist and has written many educational books for children. He lives in Lincolnshire. *The Master of Bruges* is his first novel.

THE
MASTER
OF
BRUGES

TERENCE MORGAN

PAN BOOKS

First published in Great Britain 2010 by Macmillan New Writing

This edition published 2011 by Pan Books
an imprint of Pan Macmillan, a division of Macmillan Publishers Limited
Pan Macmillan, 20 New Wharf Road, London N1 9RR
Basingstoke and Oxford
Associated companies throughout the world
www.panmacmillan.com

ISBN 978-0-230-74413-4

1 3 5 7 9 8 6 4 2

A CIP catalogue record for this book is available
from the British Library.

Typeset by Ellipsis Books Limited, Glasgow
Printed in the UK by CPI Mackays, Chatham ME5 8TD

Visit www.panmacmillan.com to read more about all our books
and to buy them. You will also find features, author interviews and
news of any author events, and you can sign up for e-newsletters
so that you're always first to hear about our new releases.

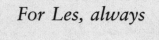
For Les, always

PART ONE

On the Mixing of Colours

Begin, then, with the imagined colour, the colour that you see in the eye of your mind, and then work towards it, taking what steps you may. I warn you now, at the outset, that you will never achieve it. Never. Take yellow; for example – the yellow in your mind will be the most yellow yellow that imagination can conceive; it will be brighter than a sunflower, warmer than the sun, richer than the yolk of an egg, but you will never see it before you in reality. Take a sunflower, dry it, crush it to powder and mix it with oils, but you will not have the yellow you want. Mix egg yolk with oil and paint it onto your surface, and as it dries it will crack and that gorgeous vibrant colour will fade to a hideous brown. Take any thing you like of yellow, and the work of moulding the hue takes away the essence of it.

I have spent my life in the pursuit of a blue, a particular shade of blue. It is a vivid flash of the bluest blue imaginable, the blue of the moment of creation. You can see it, briefly, and then you lose it again. It occurs at sunrise over water; just at the moment the sun reaches over the horizon, there is a single instantaneous flash of blue light, the purest blue in the universe. It is there, and it is gone, and if you are lucky you can wait twenty-four hours and hope that you will see it again. It is the clearest blue of the sky commingled with the blue of the Virgin's robe, the blue of the cornflower mixed with the blue of cobalt, the essence of blueness, and yet it can never be captured. The eye of the mind can remember it, but not reproduce it, but it lives to see it again. It is an orgasm of the eye. But no man can make its pigment.

This is what you will face in your role as a painter of portraits. What you put on the prepared surface may be beautiful, but it will never be accurate; it may sometimes be even more beautiful than you had imagined, more attractive than you had ever dared to wish for, more exquisitely rendered than the scene or sitter you see before you, but it will all the same be different.

Nothing is as it appears. Nothing ever can be as it appears. Everything is different from the imagining of it.

That is the first lesson to be learned. Reality is the first victim.

Although truth may remain.

Of the Workshop of Rogier

(December 1460 to January 1461)

The boy and his easel came clattering to the floor behind me. How insignificant and trivial they seem at the time, these accidents that are of themselves nothing, but that change lives and bring down princes, transform a continent and condemn good men to Hell.

I had been resident in Brussels perhaps three years. By then Rogier was old, and was beginning to suffer more badly from the arthritis which eventually stopped him from working at all. In the process it was worsening his temper, which was already volatile at the best of times.

That day in the workshop, we knew there was a big commission in the offing because Rogier turned up in his finest robe and began to berate the youngest of our number, a mere boy whom he had taken on to fetch, carry, sweep, bear the brunt of Rogier's anger and accept frequent clouts when he didn't move fast enough. It didn't bother us; it was Rogier's way and we'd all been on the end of it at some time or other. A man of little conversation and even less affection, Rogier seemed to substitute hitting people for normal social intercourse; even when greeting someone he would indulge in a burlesque wrestling match, for his few intimates, or a hearty clap on the back for a new acquaintance.

This day the youngest of us, the boy Joris, was assigned to collect together all the paraphernalia for preliminary sketches. I was then about twenty years of age and just above the bottom of the heap, a journeyman assigned to backgrounds and drapery. I was keeping my head down and putting the final touches to the dark-blue backcloth to the portrait of a local merchant when Rogier went by in a flurry of gown and sleeves, trailing the unfortunate boy who, too flustered, had not grasped the easel at its centre of gravity and consequently was struggling to keep it upright.

As he drew parallel with me he failed miserably in this task, tripped and came crashing to the floor only a few paces away from where I was working. I kept my face to the wooden panel; it was never a good idea to annoy Rogier too early in the morning, or the remainder of the day would be black for all.

The master bawled at the top of his voice, came back and, aiming a kick at the lad, told him to get up and take his miserable carcase off to mix some oils. Then I heard him say, 'Very good. Yes, that'll do. Now leave it, leave it.'

I looked round but he was already wandering away. 'Come along,' he said snappily. 'No delay now. Come with me. Bring my easel and charcoals. Someone else can do that.'

I was a little displeased to think that carrying Rogier's easel was considered more useful than finishing a painting, but I did as I was told. Rogier was the master, after all. To this day I don't know why he picked me, except perhaps that I was working nearest to the door and thus was most handily available when he realized the young boy couldn't manage all of his accoutrements. Fate touched me on the shoulder, that's all.

I wiped my hands on a piece of rag, thrust my left arm through the triangle of the easel so it rested on my shoulder, tucked the charcoal box under my right arm and followed

Rogier out into the street. He had already walked on but was easy to spot, being well above average height and with a full head of grey hair. The old man carried himself erect, and plumes of breath preceded him, flaring out as he strode away.

The sharpness of the air bit into my nostrils, and I set off after him. I did call out at one point, 'Where are we going, master?' but Rogier was oblivious to me and simply ploughed on, barging his way through the crowded streets and leaving small gaps in his wake which I was able to utilize as I struggled to keep up with him, the easel seeming to get in the way of every second person in the streets that cold morning. I barked my own shins once or twice, but after a short time I realized that we must be going to the palace, and was able to take it a little more easily, confident that I would not now lose Rogier in the crush.

Consequently I was tardier than him when we reached the steps of the palace and predictably he had used the time to work up a temper. Outraged at my inability to stick to his heels, he fetched me an almighty cuff as I came up to him and knocked the charcoal box from under my arm. It broke open and bits of the black stuff mingled with chunks of crayon and cascaded down the palace steps. 'You oaf!' Rogier took a step forward and swung at me again. Naturally I ducked, and he cracked his knuckles against the upright of the easel, taking the skin off them and thus mollifying his temper not at all.

I was now in a quandary. If I didn't stoop and collect Rogier's charcoal he would call me a seditious, insubordinate upstart and take another swing at me; if I did bend down he would kick me from the top to the bottom of the ducal steps.

My dilemma was resolved by the advent of a chamberlain, who attracted Rogier's attention by utilizing those twin strangers to my master, silence and dignity. I retreated to the bottom of the steps and began to gather the charcoal from there upwards, which would at least give me more room to evade my master's rushes, should he see fit to resume his attack.

But the proximity of the chamberlain calmed him, and by the time I had collected the last stick and replaced it in the box he was being led inside. I followed on at a safe distance.

We were not kept waiting much above three hours, which I idled away by surreptitiously sketching some of the courtiers who were hanging around waiting to be admitted. Clearly we were to see someone who was important; if Rogier knew who it was he wasn't telling me, but I was grateful for the quietness of the antechamber; even Rogier would not dare to despoil that peace.

Even in those days there was a hierarchy of waiting; anyone who was ushered into the illustrious presence immediately on arrival was a prince, a papal legate or a prisoner on the point of being executed. Other than that, the longer the wait the wider the difference in status; three hours was about middling. We began in the outer court, a high-ceilinged building with expensive tapestries hanging on the walls and a multitude of civil servants hurrying about clutching papers and edicts. Occasionally one of them would approach a waiting suppliant and conduct him away. When it was our turn we were filtered through two inner courts, smaller but similarly furnished, until eventually a courtier beckoned us through a large pair of oaken doors and I saw who it was who had issued the summons.

He stepped forward, saying, 'Mynheer van der Weyden; you are most welcome,' and was quick enough to stop Rogier dropping to his knees.

I recognized him immediately, of course – who wouldn't? The most famous soldier in Europe, Charles, Count of Charolais and heir to the dukedom of Burgundy, was then about twenty-seven years of age. He was of middle height, with short dark hair brushed forward onto his brow. He was dressed simply and plainly, in a dark gown, his only jewellery a gold necklace with what appeared to be a little dead sheep, also of gold, hanging from it. I later found that it was not a sheep but a fleece, the insignia of the Order of the Golden Fleece, of which he was grand master.

He beckoned me to rise and made us welcome, his voice low and gentle, and dismissed the servants. 'I want an undisturbed talk,' he told the chamberlain, 'for at least an hour.' He led Rogier to a chair near the fire and seated him, showing due deference to the master's age and venerability, and then sat opposite him to talk.

Even I was allowed a seat, over against the wall and out of the way, although I was just within earshot and heard most of what was said. I spent my time trying to catch the count's expression on one of my scraps of paper. It was a portrait that he wanted, of course, a secular one, to hang in the city hall and remind the burghers who was going to be in charge when, in the fullness of time, the Count of Charolais became the Duke of Burgundy.

Rogier was flattered to be chosen, naturally, and when all was agreed he called for his equipment to do some preliminary sketches there and then. I carried the easel over, depositing the charcoal box on a small table. Out of the corner of my eye I saw the count's hand reach out towards it, but I was too late to prevent him, and he picked up what he wanted. I averted my eyes and continued putting up the easel.

When all was ready I bowed and stepped back a respectful distance. Rogier selected a piece of charcoal and began to draw. I found the count looking at me, a strange expression on his face and a faint smile playing around his lips. I averted my eyes, more than a little concerned about what might be amusing him, and busied myself with my own idlings.

Rogier's memory was failing, so he needed to get down as much as he could in order to make the preliminary sketches more impressive, meaning that the sitter had to sit still longer. At an initial sitting like this, Rogier might draw the face eight or nine times, trying to catch different expressions, and adjusting his angle marginally in order to catch the best profile or disguise a cock eye. Some found it irksome.

There was an additional problem, in that increasing pain and stiffness in the joints of Rogier's hands meant that his periods of work became shorter and shorter. The greater the status of the client, the greater the care he had to take, and holding the charcoal became more and more excruciating.

The signs were very clear on this cold day, and when there was a small commotion at the door of the chamber it was clear that he welcomed the interruption. The count signalled to him to stop working, and he put down his charcoal and resumed his seat with a deep and grateful puff of air.

The count went to the door, and arrived at just the same time as a tiny girl entered, closely followed by the once-dignified chamberlain and a flustered maid.

'They say I may not see you, father,' the girl said. 'I have told them that no man may say, "You may not" to me, but they do not believe me.'

'And who has told you that no man may say, "You may not" to you?' the count asked, clearly amused.

'My grandmother,' the girl said. 'She said that I am always to remember who I am, and to remind people lest they forget.'

'When you are a little older,' the count said, his smile now including both Rogier and myself as an audience to be entertained, 'then it is very like that no man will say, "You may not" to you, and indeed it may well be that no man will wish to say, "You may not" to you, and even some of those who do wish to say, "You may not" to you may not have the heart to do so, but while you are a little girl the number of men, and women, that are allowed to say, "You may not" to you is as numberless as the grains of sand on the shore and as the blades of grass in the meadow, and when those people decide to say, "You may not" to you, then the end result is that you may not – whatever it is you wish to do, and no matter who you happen to be. Is that clear?'

Somewhat put out, the little sprite stood before him and pushed her lower lip out a considerable distance so that all might see her displeasure. When it would protrude no further, she said, 'I suppose so.'

'Good,' the count said. 'I can tell you, however, that on this particular occasion those who tell you that you may not see me happen to be in error, and you may.'

The pout turned into a grin, and the child threw her arms about her father's neck as he lifted her up.

'So, what do you want that is so urgent?'

She looked about her, somewhat suspiciously, I thought, and treated both Rogier and myself to a long, serious gaze. 'I want to see what you are doing. What is happening?'

'This is Master Rogier,' her father told her, 'and this is his assistant, whose name I do not know.'

I opened my mouth to enlighten him, but Rogier shook his head sharply, and I snapped it shut again. I suppose that nobles are sometimes polite, but it does not necessarily mean that they are interested.

'Let me see,' the mite said.

'You can probably guess that this is my badly behaved

daughter,' the count said. He looked at Rogier. 'May I show her?'

The old man inclined his head, and Charles carried his daughter behind the easel where she could examine the portrait. 'It is only a sketch at the moment,' he explained. 'The real painting comes later.'

The sketch was given the same long, serious gaze as had been inflicted on Rogier and myself. 'It does not look like you,' she decided eventually.

'It is not supposed to yet,' the count told her. 'Master Rogier is just preparing – practising, you might say.'

'Oh.' She wriggled to be put down and slid down his body. 'May I watch?'

Charles raised an enquiring eyebrow at Rogier, received a deferential nod in return and placed the girl on the ground. 'If you are quiet,' he said.

The count returned to his seat and Rogier rose to his feet again, massaging his right hand with his left, and picked up his charcoal. The child sat behind him and watched as, with infinite slowness, he began to draw the line of the count's nose for the fifth or sixth time.

It was no sport for spectators, this infinitesimally slow artistry, and she was predictably bored before he had shaded his first nostril. She clambered off her seat and wandered over to her father, but he whispered, 'I must sit still.'

'I want you to talk to me,' she said.

'I may not,' he answered with a smile. 'Master Rogier is in charge here, not I. You see, even your father has people who say to him, "You may not." '

She sauntered behind his chair and emerged on the other side. Then she wandered in my direction. I hurriedly stopped what I was doing, but it was too late. She reached up and plucked the paper from my hands. I licked my lips, anxious to take it from her, but dared not. I was sure that I was not one of those entitled to say to her, 'You may not.'

'This looks more like you,' she said, and I was too slow in stifling my groan.

Rogier stopped, apparently paralysed, but for certain his palsy had nothing to do with his joints. The unwitting insult to his technique had struck home, for he knew as well as I what the little girl was holding.

The count tried to smooth it over. 'They are not sketches for my portrait,' he said. 'They are just for practice.'

'The artist who drew these does not need as much practice as Master Rogier, then,' she said, and my fate was sealed.

'Those are mere scribblings,' Rogier said, 'not the work of an artist,' and of a sudden there was the faintest hint of a raised eyebrow about the face of the Count of Charolais.

'I would say that the scribbler had had an excellent teacher,' the count said diplomatically. 'It has taken the encouragement and example of a master to bring out the talent – I should say, the promise – that this hand shows.'

Rogier grunted and threw a look of pure rancour at me, but made no comment. He controlled himself, and then went through the rigmarole of 'making so bold as to ask his lordship to sit back' while he completed what he was doing, but the heart had gone out of him; the diminutive critic had shown him what he had long known in his soul – that the cunning had left his hands as the arthritis had attacked them. Before long the sketches were finished, or as finished as they would ever be, and Rogier laid down his charcoal just as the chamberlain arrived at the door and coughed discreetly. 'I thank your lordship for his patience,' Rogier said, 'and will send the sketches for his approval in a very short time.'

'You will need these back, then,' the child said politely, and offered him my sketches.

'They are not mine, your ladyship,' he said stiffly, and pointed at me.

She came over, all of the sketches but one held out to me. 'May I keep this one?' she asked. It was that which I had made of her while she was discussing 'You may not' with her father – her perfectly oval face framed by her long hair, reddish-brown in reality but charcoal black on the paper.

'It is not worthy, my lady ...' I began, but behind her the count forestalled me.

'Here, Marie,' he said. 'An artist should always be paid for his work. Do not ask to be given it, but ask if you may purchase it.' He placed a gold coin on the arm of his chair and she ran to collect it, returning with it held out to me. Behind her the count's lips formed the word 'Please'.

'May I?' she asked, proffering the coin.

Thus it was that I became the first of many men who discovered for certain that they had no power to say, 'You may not' to the Princess of Burgundy.

I may have been paid for my labours, but I repaid my fee back again a dozen times over as Rogier and I made our way back to the workshop from the ducal palace. My presumption at having the effrontery actually to draw sketches in the presence of the count, and that without permission, and to be drawing the count himself, and then, and then – and here Rogier became almost apoplectic – and then to dare to sketch the count's daughter, his only child, and that too without permission, and then – and this is where he went off like a faulty handgun and sprayed expletives and spittle the width of the street – and then actually to accept money for my barefaced audacity was more than he was prepared to countenance, and he began to belabour me with blows and kicks, finally toppling me and the easel head over heels into the mire and dung of the roadway. He hauled me to my feet and, still cursing, dragged me across the threshold of the workshop where, to the amusement and no doubt delight of the rest of the workshop, he railed me up and down, demanded with menaces the gold I had been given (which was legally his by right, in truth), confiscated my sketches and then told me to get out of his sight, an order with which I was glad to comply.

The next day I crept into the workshop as unobtrusively as I could and got on with painting the drapery from the day before.

'Leave that,' Rogier's voice said behind me. I looked round, ready to ward off a blow, but one of his crooked fingers was beckoning, and when I went towards him he walked off to the part of the workshop which was roped off for his own use. He kicked a stool at me and said, 'Sit down.' Then he stood, stiff and awkward, staring at me and nodding slowly.

My sketches were on the table. 'These,' he said, and coughed. 'These . . . I have to confess that they are good.' Having got that admission out of the way, he relaxed. 'You have a nice line,' he said. 'You catch the character well. Realistic, lifelike.'

I waited, and he coughed again. 'Perhaps I was too hard on you. Best not waste your time on drapery.' He pushed the sketches across to me. 'Work these up,' he said. 'Let me see you try a portrait.'

There was a pause, and then he placed a gold coin on the desk. 'I suppose you'd better have this back, too.'

Well, my memory came in handy. I sketched the count, and a couple of days later my, not Rogier's, sketches were sent around to the palace. I was not allowed to go, lest I cause more trouble. The sketches were deemed acceptable. Then began the subterfuge. Charles de Charolais wanted a Rogier van der Weyden portrait, not a Hans Memling. We would therefore, Rogier and I, go round to the palace for the sittings, where he would sketch obviously and I circumspectly, and at the end of the day I would adjust what he had done. Then we would paint it in tandem, Rogier spending his time on the fleece and the count's clothing, and I on the head and hands.

Despite his propensity for warfare and a violent temper that could explode without warning, the count was in general a gentle, kindly man, and I tried to reflect that in the softness of his gaze and the set of his mouth, which was always ready to turn into a smile. I had him with eyes unfocused, as if in thought, and with no sense of unease, a man accustomed to being looked at.

His hands too were distinctive, with the long, fine fingers which some people have come to associate with artists. I can't see it myself – my own are short and stubby, and so were Rogier's – but the count's certainly were slender. If you looked closely, though, you could see the signs of the worries that were to plague him all his life – the lack of a male heir being the most prominent, I suppose, along with the constant struggles with France and others who would try to wrest Burgundy from him – and I tried to show that in a subtle way, too. I had noticed that he had a habit, when deep in thought, of gnawing on his left thumbnail, so in the portrait I made the nail slightly irregular, as if he had not long given over nibbling on it. No one said anything. Maybe they didn't notice.

Any work that emerged from Rogier's workshop with his approval was deemed to be the master's doing, so I never got any public credit for the picture I painted, and when it was put into the world I soon forgot its existence.

Of the End of My Master

(June 1464)

Every man knows that death must one day pay him a visit. Even when expected its advent is a shock, but an unexpected death changes the lives of all connected with the victim.

I turned the corner that fine June morning to find the street in turmoil, and members of the workshop scurrying away carrying the likes of pots, lengths of dark cloth and paintings in their hands.

Joris was struggling along with, of all things, an easel. I grasped him by the shoulder. 'What is it?' I asked. 'What's happened?'

'The master is dead,' he said. 'The workshop is finished. Take what you can; there will be no more.'

I pushed my way through to the door and stepped through. The interior was all confusion, with paint and chalk, pots and charcoal strewn over the floor and trodden into it. Madam van der Weyden stood in the midst of it all, in confusion and with a look of horror on her face. One of the hired men scuttled through the door, something big and round in his hands; my mind registered 'laving bowl' and then I shut the door. He must have been the last, for the house was suddenly quiet except for the sobbing of the woman.

'Is it true?' I asked. 'The master is . . .' I didn't like to say 'dead', so I compromised with 'gone'.

She nodded, unable to speak, and I put my arms around her and led her to a stool.

'What happened?'

'In the night,' she said, 'he rose and said that there was a pain, a heavy pressure in his chest. He stood bent over, holding himself tight, and I sent the maidservant to run for the physician, but before he could come Rogier fell like a stone. He breathed for a while thereafter, but in the hour before dawn it ended. The physician said that his heart had failed within him. I came to tell everyone what had happened, and they just took everything and went. Why would they do that, Hans?'

'Without Rogier there is no workshop,' I said gently. 'It is his reputation we traded on. No other of us has such a name, so work will not come. They know there will be no more wages, so they made off with what they could. I suppose it's natural.'

'Could you start here?' she asked. 'Do your work and continue the workshop? The rent would be low.'

'You were better to sell the place,' I told her. 'You could live out your days in comfort with the money it brings.'

'Will you stay and help me?'

I looked down at her, a poor old woman, confused and bereaved. 'Of course,' I told her. 'For now, anyway.'

She gestured towards the chaos. 'Do you want something, some memento of him? Take what you like, if there is anything left.'

There was nothing there that I wanted, I knew that, but the old woman needed help. I locked and secured the workshop and then followed the master's wife up the stairs so that I could pay my respects. He was laid out in a linen nightshirt, with a cap on his head tied under his chin with string and his hands down by his sides, the thumbs tucked under his buttocks so that he would stiffen in a dignified posture. His big toes were tied together with a piece of bandage so that his feet would lie straight. He looked more peaceful in death than he ever had in life.

I told her I would sleep in the workshop that night to make sure there was no more looting, but that on the morrow I would have to start making arrangements for my future. I still had to eat.

When I got back to the workshop I hunted around, but I knew that what I was looking for was gone. One of the day men would have had it, and will have sold it on as a Rogier when the time was right, although anyone with half an eye would have known it was no Rogier. It was the portrait of a lawyer, a man reading a document, and the first my master had allowed me to do completely by myself, although it was never to be acknowledged as mine. I made sure no man could mistake it for a Rogier, though, by putting a shuttered window behind my sitter and a view through it of a castle on a hill overlooking water. Rogier had no patience with such things; his sitters were placed always before a plain dark cloth. It was good, I thought, and I had finished it only the day before my master died, so it was not quite dry. I hope the opportunist thief took care of it before taking his profit, although the purchaser got no bargain if he thought he was buying a painting by Rogier van der Weyden.

And then, in the dark hours after midnight, I thought of something. I rose up from where I was lying, wrapped in a length of curtain, lit a candle and went to Rogier's private section.

The place was a mess, of course, the drawers and cupboards having been ransacked for anything that could be sold. My hope was that none of the men had placed any value on what I was looking for, and that it might still be there.

I couldn't see, and had to light an oil lamp from the candle. During the day I had begun to tidy up, but had not yet reached Rogier's private area when I lay down to sleep. It was the biggest of the cupboards that I wanted. It lay face down, one of the doors beside it, the panels splintered and the hinge broken. I got my fingers under the edge of the cupboard and heaved it upright, ignoring the rolls of paper that cascaded around my feet.

I picked up one of the bigger cylinders and unrolled it; it was a sketch – a seated woman in the centre holding a child and flanked symmetrically by a series of figures becoming smaller as they approached the edge of the paper. I plucked another from the jumble; this turned out actually to be two smaller pieces of paper rolled together, one a sketch of a crucifixion, the other a scene where the body of Christ has been taken down from the Cross and is being enfolded in the shroud. Other rolls had sketches for diptychs and triptychs, drawings of trees and animals and various other scenes.

I had found what I was looking for – Rogier's compositional patterns. With these I could reproduce his layout, his style, the angles of his heads and torsos – much, in other words, that went to making up a successful workshop. I rolled them up, all that I could find, one inside another, and tied them with string. Then I hunted through the house until I found a large piece of canvas, and this I formed into a cylinder long enough to contain them all, and spent the rest of the night fine-stitching the edges to make it as close to waterproof as possible. It was almost dawn when I lay down to sleep again, but I knew I had the means to start my own workshop when the opportunity arose.

But not in Brussels, I told myself. Rogier was too well known, too popular. My work would be forever under his shadow, always being compared, especially if I were to take over the very house where he had worked. No, it would have to be somewhere else, somewhere where I could be known for my own work and could build my own reputation.

Even if I used Rogier's patterns.

The next morning I tightened the roll of papers until it was as rigid as a pilgrim's staff and inserted it into the canvas cylinder. I knew that I was carrying my fortune in that sack. After that I stayed at the workshop until the master was interred, saw his widow settled about what to do with it (to say true there were already enquiries from painters who wanted to rent it, hoping that Rogier's talent would rub off on them) and put her in the capable hands of the Painters' Guild. Then I said my goodbyes, although she offered me much, not excepting her dumpling of a daughter, if I would stay and run the workshop, but my journeyman years were done, and if I were to be a master it could not be in Brussels.

To tell the truth, I have little enough skill; I can draw a figure or a landscape well enough, and make a lifelike picture of a man or a woman, but I learned what I know of composition from Rogier, and if you know his pictures and then look at mine you will see which of us is the master and which the pupil easily enough.

I realized that I was never going to be as good as Rogier, and worse, that the good folk of Brussels knew that as well as I did, so I slung my packet of patterns over my shoulder and shook the dust of that town off my feet. I wanted to find somewhere that was not so fussy.

Of the Monastery
and the Camp

(June to December 1464)

It was a bad time, though, to start a new venture. It was a campaign summer (although what summer was without its war at that time?) and people had better things to do with their money than invest in new artists with neither name nor connections. The little I had saved became less and in time disappeared. For a time I even thought of selling the patterns. For the right painter they could be priceless, but I knew if I did that then there would be no way forward for me, ever, and I held on to them.

In the end there was only one section of society that was hiring, and slowly, remorselessly, relentlessly, despite everything I thought, despite it being the opposite of what I wanted, I was drawn into it. At the end of August I was in Liège, with no money, my clothes threadbare and a stomach that had not welcomed a visiting bite for three days, and I sold my soul for a hunk of bread and a stoup of wine, and became a pikeman in the ordonnance of the Count of La Roche in the interminable wars against the French. I was read the terms of the ordonnance, asked if I understood them, and told to make my mark to acknowledge this. Then I was issued with a red and white quartered jacket for warmth and identification (and more of the latter than the former, it has to be said), a breastplate, some armour for my right arm, a small shield to be attached to my left as a mockery of protection, and a twelve-foot pike for annoying the enemy, should he become so bold as to approach. The pikemen were the lowest of the low, having no particular skills to boast of. An archer or a gunner had expertise and talent for which the nobility were prepared to pay, but the pikemen were paid in buttons and left to fend for themselves if the rest of the army should take it into their heads to run away, which, my fellow pikers told me, was by no means unusual.

Not that the work was arduous. We trained in the morning, levelling the pike, presenting the pike, preparing to receive cavalry, kneeling in front of the archers and all the rest of it, and spent the rest of the daylight hours doing general repairs and preparing food.

I made my pike easily recognizable. The pole was just thin enough to slip into the top of my cylindrical canvas bag and slide down inside the roll of patterns. The canvas tube provided a secure grip for about a third the length of the weapon and I made it all the more so with short leather straps at regular intervals. As the regulation was that I had to have my pike beside me at all times, I always knew precisely where my treasure was.

I also became in due course one of the richest of the new recruits, exchanging sketches of the faces of my fellow trainees for them to take home to their sweethearts for a couple of pennies, and odd scraps of paper became precious, my comrades in arms thinking I was mad to be prepared to pay a couple of small coins for any they found.

Otherwise we got two francs as a signing on fee and four francs a month thereafter, paid quarterly in arrears, and we were garrisoned at the barracks in Liège until their lordships required us to pay for our keep with our deaths.

These debts were called in within a couple of weeks, and we marched off to the south to help the army cross a river. The French had destroyed the bridges, so it was necessary to construct one. On the first day we were hardly involved; the enemy stayed on their side of the river and we on ours and we bombarded them with serpentines and a veuglaire, or so Joos, my file leader, informed me, he having some greater knowledge of artillery than myself, which was not difficult, as my own was nil.

The next morning some of us were ordered to climb into a small boat and cross the river with a detachment of archers. First we went to a small island in midstream and sat there while the coopers finished constructing a bridge of planks and barrels, and then late in the day we were ferried to the opposite bank to form a bridgehead while the second half of the bridge was constructed. Apparently our army outnumbered the French considerably, and thus our coopers remained undisturbed as they went about their business. We were there to provide protection for the archers in case they were attacked while covering the coopers (which apparently makes sense to the military mind), but the French simply sat on the nearby hills and watched.

At dusk we were ferried back across to our island for the night, and the next morning crossed again while the coopers continued their construction. By midday they had completed their task and our work of guarding was done. The army began to move across the river and the French, having seen all that was to be seen, went off and left us in peace. According to Joos, the serpentines had kept them at bay, as the French did not dare come down to the water's edge as they would have been in range of our guns.

Late in the afternoon a party of about twenty of us was

detailed to advance and reconnoitre. There were a couple of coustilliers on horseback, with the rest of us either archers or pikemen, and we were told to go and secure a little village over the hill. The masters were pretty sure that it was empty of French soldiers, but we were their insurance.

As we were marching towards the village one of the officers pointed up a hill to our left, where there was a church. 'Take your file up there,' he said to Joos, 'and make sure it's clear,' and the four of us obediently began to climb towards it.

It was not merely a church, but in fact a small monastery, and although from the outside it had looked undisturbed, inside was chaos. The French had slept and caroused there and quartered their horses in the chancel, and the place was littered with broken pots and bottles and the bones of various animals. The rood screen had been broken up for firewood. The soldiers of France were less pious than those of Burgundy, it appeared.

'There'll be stuff left here,' Joos said. 'Good stuff. They can't have taken all of it.'

One of the others, Jan, placed his pike upright against the wall and put his bag beside it. 'Let's have a look round,' he suggested.

'Not me,' I said. 'I'm dog-tired.' I slid down the wall and sat on the floor, my pike across my knees.

The three of them went scrambling off to see what pickings they could find, and soon I heard shouts of delight as they turned up something that interested them.

After a few minutes I was rested and wandered in the opposite direction, through the empty chapel and into the building beyond. In one of the rooms I found the remains of illuminated manuscripts; a vast library – dozens of books, perhaps – had been torn from their lecterns and wantonly ripped and slashed. There was not a volume left intact. The lecterns were mostly gone – for firewood again, probably. There was a large Bible, a printed book, one of those Mainz ones, not a manuscript, but little was left of it; the pages would have been used as kindling, I suppose. The scriptorium, a place of quiet learning and industry, had been pillaged ruthlessly but inefficiently, and the things that had held both beauty and wisdom were destroyed for ever.

In the corner was a desk that must have been where one of the younger monks worked. It seemed to be in a training area, for there was charcoal scattered about and scraps of paper, some with lettering on them, some blank. I gathered up as much of this as was useable and stuck a few pieces of charcoal in my scrip. Then I went back outside to wait for the others. The monastery was on a slight hillock, and I moved down the slope slightly to where there was a large boulder. I sat on it and looked out across the fields.

A party of horsemen was moving along the headland towards me: two or three noblemen, a cleric, and a detachment of perhaps thirty men-at-arms, picking their way along the edge of the field. They reached the track eventually, and followed it a little way until they reached the main road. Then they cantered along that and turned up the approach road to the monastery.

As they drew level with me the cleric was in the lead. He reined up beside me and shouted, 'You! Were you in the monastery?'

'Yes, your honour . . .' I began, but he swivelled in his saddle and called back to those following him.

'From his own lips you hear it!' he shouted. 'Take him! Take him and bind him! He is a desecrator of the Lord's house, an abomination, a blasphemer.' Then he turned again and spurred on up the hill. I was too astonished to move, and four of the men-at-arms dismounted and grabbed me. Soon my arms were pinioned behind my back, and the rest of the party rode on.

'Now you're for it,' I was told. They were mounted crossbowmen, their various bits of machinery dangling about their persons like a tinker's stock.

'Why?' I asked.

'Sacrilege,' said the one who seemed to be the leader.

'And desperation,' added another.

'He means desecration,' the leader said. 'Keep quiet, Simon.'

We turned to look up at the monastery, and I saw Joos and the others, who had come out of the building while I was being tied up. At first they stood, looking at the party approaching them, and then suddenly they set off, running away down the other side of the hill. They disappeared from sight, but the crossbowmen set off after them, and it was clear that the chase would end quickly in either surrender or death, and so it proved. Before long they reappeared, their hands behind their backs as mine were, and being ushered along until they stood in a small group outside the chapel. The clergyman and the nobles had disappeared inside the monastery, and we stood and waited while they inspected the interior.

When they came out again any lingering hope we might have had was dispelled. The clergyman emerged from the church at a run and began to berate Joos and the other prisoners, kicking and cuffing the defenceless men. His voice came down to us on the wind, the anger apparent, although at that distance we could not make out the words.

Then as we watched my three comrades in arms had their hands untied and then tied again at the front with longer cords, each attached to a saddle, and the party set off back down the hill with my companions stumbling along trying to keep up, and their pikes and scrips divided among some of the horsemen.

As soon as they saw this my captors did the same to me, and as the rest came level with us, off we went down the hill at a slow trot that it was barely possible to keep up with on foot.

We were dragged along like this for a couple of miles or so, and then the party turned into a field where there was a camp, and we were halted outside a tent where a fire burned. The ground frost had melted around the fire and it was pleasant to feel the warmth on our faces and throats. I looked around; there were banners flying outside a number of tents, and the camp had an air of prosperity – not an ordinary soldiers' bivouac, then; the presence of finely dressed servants betokened some nobility. When I saw the red and white standard flying above the tent in front of me I realized that we had been brought to see the Count of La Roche himself, our commander.

The cleric got down off his palfrey and after a brief parley with a servant went into one of the tents behind us. Our hands were untied long enough for the briefest of rubs and then tied again behind our backs.

'Sit,' someone said behind me, and we were pushed down. The ground was cold but still rock-hard, so there was no mud.

'This yours?' someone else asked, and I looked up to see my bag and pike being held in front of me.

'Yes,' I said, and they were thrown to the ground between me and the fire; the rest of the prisoners had their stuff thrown in front of them, too.

It was a relief not to have to run behind a horse, even if there were new problems in the place of the exercise. We did not have to wait long: a bad sign. Before many minutes had passed the cleric crossed in front of us escorted by a soldier and entered the count's tent. When they reappeared there was a third man with them wearing a surcoat of red and white; this had to be the Count of La Roche.

The cleric took charge. He advanced and stood in front of us, glaring at each of us in turn. 'Desecrators!' he said. 'You have vandalized the house of God and destroyed His property, and made off with that which belongs to the Church.'

'We didn't do no vandalizing,' Joos said. 'It was already destroyed when we got there. The French did all that.'

The man walked over and kicked at Joos's scrip, which rose in the air and then fell, mouth side uppermost. Out of it rolled a small silver cup, the sort of thing they use at communion. 'The property of the Church,' he said, and then went close to Joos and screamed in his face, 'You have looted the house of God.'

'It was just lying round,' Joos said. 'The French must have left it.'

'And you offer me that as an excuse for looting and pillaging?' The priest was beside himself with anger. The nobleman stepped in to take charge. He went to the end of the line and picked up the scrip belonging to the fourth member of our group – Piet, I think his name was – and emptied it on the ground. A small crucifix of silver fell to the ground, and the nobleman took it and held it before Piet's face. 'Is this the property of the monastery?' he asked.

'Yes, sir.'

'Taken by you as pillage?'

'Yes.'

'Then by your own mouth you stand condemned.'

He moved on to Jan. Again he turned the bag upside down, and this time it was a pyx which fell to the ground. The nobleman's hand held it out to Jan and the same questions were asked, the same answers given and the same sentence pronounced.

He moved on to Joos, and the small silver cup and another,

a little smaller, that was still in the bag were held up in front of him, with the same questions, answers and sentence.

Then it was my turn. My bag too was picked up and emptied. There was nothing metallic in it, of course.

'This bag has nothing in it of the monastery's, I think . . .' the nobleman began, but the priest darted past him.

'This,' he said, pointing. 'This is the property of the monastery.'

'What is it?'

The priest bent down and snatched a handful of fragments from the ground. 'Paper,' he said triumphantly. 'He has stolen paper that belongs to God.'

'Paper?' the nobleman said. 'You surely cannot hang a man for a scrap of paper.'

'You can if he is guilty, my lord,' the abbot said.

The count paused, waiting as long as it takes for a man to count to ten, and then made up his mind and looked at me. 'The paper belongs to the monastery?' he asked tonelessly.

'Yes, sir.'

'Taken by you as pillage?'

'Yes.'

'Then by your own mouth you stand condemned.'

'They must hang,' the abbot said. 'Such sacrilege against the Church cannot be countenanced. They must hang.'

'My lord abbot,' another voice interrupted, quiet and calm in contrast to the anger of the cleric. 'These men, if guilty, will pay the full penalty, but we must first ascertain that they are truly so.' The voice came from behind me, but I did not dare swivel to see who it was. It was obviously someone important, though, because everyone I could see, including the cleric and the count, had dropped to one knee.

'Yes, my lord,' the priest said, suddenly subdued. 'Of course.'

The lord stepped between Joos and me, his back towards me, and spoke in the same calm voice. 'Tell me what happened,' he said.

Joos told him how we had come across the monastery and gone inside to investigate and make sure that it was clear of the enemy.

'And was it?'

'Yes, sir.'

'And did you then come out?'

'Yes, sir.'

'With their arms laden with ecclesiastical treasures,' the abbot said.

The nobleman quietened him with a gesture. 'Did you take from the monastery that which was not yours, the property of the Church?' he asked, almost gently, bending forward to speak to Joos.

Joos waited, trying to find a way out of it, and then bowed to the inevitable. 'I did, my lord.'

There was a long pause, and then the nobleman asked, 'Are you not aware of the ordinance regarding pillaging?'

'Yes, sir.'

'And these men of yours, are they also aware of it?'

'Yes, sir.'

The nobleman straightened up and stepped a little way off, turning to address us all. 'Can any man of you tell me that he is not aware of the ordinance regarding pillage?'

None of us spoke.

'Or of the penalty?'

Still silence.

'Silence implies consent,' he said, and walked to the end of the line, down to my left.

'Let me see what was taken,' he said, and the cleric hurried forward to display the spoils and identify them as belonging to the abbey. The nobleman glanced cursorily at the booty and turned to the Count of La Roche. 'It would seem that my lord abbot has proven his case,' he said. 'Do you wish to proceed, my lord?'

The count nodded and stepped forward. 'On your feet,' he said, and we all struggled to get up, more or less helped by the guards behind us, who were suddenly less rough. In their eyes we were no longer prisoners, but condemned men, and no man wished to do us any more harm than we were already going to suffer.

'Four items,' he continued, 'and four men. The theft of even so small a thing condemns each of you.'

'Hang on,' Joos said, 'you got that wrong, sir. I took two of them cup things, and these other two had one each, but Hans there never took nothing.'

The count stopped, but the cleric stepped in. 'The paper, my lord,' he said. Then he turned to the other lord, the senior one, and said, 'He stole paper from God's house, my lord.'

'Paper?' the senior lord said. 'What kind of soldier steals paper?' He walked down the line and looked me full in the face, and for the first time I realized who he was. 'My lord of Charolais,' I said.

Taken aback, he said, 'Do I know you?'

'I am beneath your notice, my lord, but I have been in your presence more than once before.'

'When? On trial?'

'No, my lord. It was in Brussels, perhaps four years ago. I was then a journeyman painter with Mynheer Rogier van der Weyden.'

'What?' He reached out and took my chin in his hand and turned my face to the firelight. He looked for a long time, and then I saw the light of recognition come into his eyes. 'Ah,' he said. 'The painter of faces, is it not?'

'Yes, my lord.'

'He that sketched my Marie?'

'Yes, my lord.'

'Why did you steal the paper?'

'To draw on, my lord, for practice. That is God's charcoal, too,' I added, 'although my lord abbot does not recognize it, I think.'

'Have a care, boy,' he said calmly. 'You stand on the brink of death, and do not need to give my lord abbot any more encouragement than he needs to push you into hellfire.'

He stepped back. 'Why are you soldiering?' he asked. 'Is the painting of portraits not exciting enough for you?'

I told him of Rogier's death, and how getting started was too expensive, and how no one was hiring or commissioning because of the war. He listened carefully, and then turned to the abbot and the count. 'Anthony, a word,' he said, 'and you too, my lord abbot.' He drew them aside and spoke softly. The rest of us waited in the light of the flames. There seemed to be a difference of opinion; the Count of La Roche appeared to be agreeing to what he wanted, but I heard the abbot say 'No, no' once or twice, and then 'Out of the question', but he calmed down as the lord went on, quietly talking and persuading and eventually, it seemed, getting his way, as the abbot began to nod, at first dubiously and then with more enthusiasm. Finally Count Charles clapped the abbot on the back and turned to face his prisoners.

'You men are condemned out of your own mouths,' he said. 'Each of you will have his nose slit as the sign of a thief. Then you will be hanged. The sentences will be carried out immediately. Take them away.'

I did not at first realize that he was not talking to me, and that I was not one of those he was referring to; it was only when the guards dragged the others away and left me standing there that a faint, breathless hope began to grow in me that I was not to die. The lord beckoned to one of his entourage. 'Take this man to my tent,' he said. 'I shall sentence him there.'

Once again my hands were tied in front of me. My escort gestured to one of the soldiers who had brought us in and my pike and scrip were handed up to him. Then we set off, with me once again running behind the horse for a mile or two until we reached another camp, this one bigger and with larger banners fluttering above the tents. Again I was told to sit myself before the fire, and I waited in the cold December air until the sun had set and the sky grown dark. Then suddenly there was a hustle and bustle behind me, and the Count of Charolais and his entourage arrived and dismounted. Charles stopped to look at me as he went in. 'I have some business to attend to, face painter,' he said, 'and then I will deal with your case. Do you intend to run away?'

'No, sire.'

'In that case, you need not be tied,' he said, and pointed to my wrists. Immediately one of his men stepped forward and cut my bonds, and my frozen fingers started to tingle with the flow of blood which they thought had forgotten them.

Eventually his military matters were dealt with, and I was called in to the tent to hear my fate.

'The sentence for looting is death,' the count told me, 'and technically you are a looter. However, your crime is less serious than that of a man who steals church silver for personal gain, and after a little persuasion both my lord abbot and the Count of La Roche have agreed that death is too severe a punishment for the theft of a little paper. It is the Abbey of St John; you will remember that, and be appropriately grateful to the saint. Can you remember John?'

'It is my own name, my lord,' I said.

'There is too little talent in the world for we soldiers to be killing those who have it,' he said. 'I am prepared to release you on condition that you go to my city of Bruges. There will be plenty of work for you there. My officer will guide you as to where to go; you will be given letters of introduction. This is my gift to you at the time of Our Saviour's birth, in memory of your kindness to my little one.' He held up a hand to stifle my thanks. 'There are two further conditions. The Count of La Roche, as you may know, is my half-brother ...' – I did know, but had forgotten it in the events of the day, my mind being occupied with other matters – '... and some years ago he sat for a painting in Brussels executed by Rogier van der Weyden. He has long admired a certain portrait of me, also executed some years ago in Brussels, and also ascribed to the same Rogier van der Weyden.' He allowed himself to smile. 'In recompense for his compliance with my recommendation for mercy, I have told my brother that you (or Rogier, perhaps?) will paint him a similar portrait, free of financial consideration, at some date to be arranged in the future. Are you agreeable?'

I could not believe this turn in my fortune. 'Of course, my lord.'

'Good. My lord abbot was less easy to convince, but eventually he came round to our way of thinking. Apparently it is now his view that the Good Lord may have inspired you to take the paper, the better to reveal to the abbot His intentions regarding you. Hence the abbot too will drop all charges, and he offers this to you as a Christmas gift.' He paused, the gentle smile becoming more obvious. 'However, he drives a harder bargain than my brother. In return for his generosity you will paint him a diptych, also without charge. Are you agreeable?'

'Yes, my lord.'

'No doubt these two commissions, if well executed, will lead to further, more lucrative ones.'

The turning around of the day was complete.

'And you are never to enlist again. Do you understand?'

'Yes, my lord.'

'And never to steal again – not even paper.' He turned to a man seated at a portable desk who was himself surrounded by pieces of paper. 'Take this man and find him some food,' he said, 'and then come back so I can dictate a letter. You, Memling, will return here in one hour, but for now you may go.'

Anxious as I was to get out before he changed his mind, I was forced to linger on a matter of much moment to me.

He looked at me. 'You may go,' he repeated.

'Beg pardon, my lord,' I said, 'but I need my pike.'

He looked at me and pursed his lips. 'You will not need a pike,' he said. 'I thought I had made that most clear.'

'It's not the pike, my lord,' I told him, 'but the handle.'

He looked puzzled, so I tried to explain.

'Well, not the handle, either, but what is around it.'

'What is around it?'

Given all that had happened, I thought it best to tell the truth. 'Paper, my lord,' I said.

Of Bruges

(December 1464 to January 1465)

Thus it was that I entered the city that was to become my home for the rest of my life – not quite thirty years yet, but more to come, if God should spare me. It was a bitterly cold day – the eve of the feast of the Circumcision of Our Saviour, I think, although I cannot be absolutely sure of the exact date. The gateway of the year is a suitable day, however, symbolically speaking, and the Feast of the Circumcision it shall be, for the record – the day of my resurrection as an artist.

I might have frozen to death that first night had it not been for the foresight of Count Charles. He had given me a letter to be taken to the palace, and there I presented it to a chamberlain who bade me wait, and then showed me into a large room well hung with warm cloth and with a great fire blazing and a warmly clad and no doubt well-fed official sitting in front of said fire.

'You know what's in this?' he asked casually, waving the letter at me.

'Not in detail,' I said. All I had been told was that I would be 'provided for'.

'It is too late for you to wander the streets tonight,' he said. 'You can sleep in the great hall.' He noticed my glance. 'Fear not,' he said. 'There is a fire in there too. Then tomorrow you must find yourself a place to stay. I know, I know; you have no money. No matter: the count will pay your rent, if it is reasonable, for three months in advance. Then you are to be given a daily stipend, enough to buy you a hot meal and some wine, for six months. There is also your back pay from your military service, which it says here you will use to buy . . .' He hesitated, finding some difficulty in reading the words, and then ended, '. . . items pertaining to the work of a master painter.' He paused. 'Does this all make sense to you?'

'Yes,' I said, my head nodding frantically. 'Perfect sense.'

He carried on perusing the letter. 'Further, you are authorized, should you wish to do so, to inform anyone of your choosing that you are a portrait painter to the Count of Charolais and the Count of La Roche, and to the Abbey Church of St John, and I am to issue you with letters of introduction to that effect, if you so wish.' He looked up and cocked his head at me. 'Do you so wish?' he asked.

I indicated that I did.

'Finally, the count has directed me to write to the city authorities to the effect that he intends to sponsor you for citizenship, should you wish to take up the privilege. I presume that you find this acceptable?'

Again, I made my acceptance clear.

He drew a piece of paper towards him and scribbled a note on it. 'You can collect the letters after the noon angelus tomorrow,' he said; and then asked, unnecessarily, I thought, 'Painter, are you?'

'Yes,' I told him, quite truthfully. I was certainly not a soldier any longer, and there were no other skills I could lay claim to.

'You must have impressed him. Did you save his life in battle or something?'

'No,' I said. 'I painted his face once, in Brussels some years ago, and I did a small charcoal sketch of his daughter.'

'A tiny thing?' he asked.

'She was then, but now . . .'

'No, I mean the sketch.'

'Oh. Yes. About the size of my palm.'

'That explains all,' he said. 'I have seen the sketch; he takes it with him everywhere he goes. The Lady Marie is the apple of his eye, you know – his only child. Maybe he wants more of them; she's a pretty child.'

I remembered a perfectly oval face and the reddish-brown long hair, and was forced to agree.

I spent the night rolled in my cloak on the floor of the great hall, and the next day I went and found a room in a house in Monachenstraat, one with large windows and an outlook to the north for the light. I put Rogier's patterns in the back of the garde-robe and then took the rent demand to the count's man.

He gave me chits to take to various officers, and I duly picked up my eight duits for the day's food and a small amount for the army back pay, and went along to the count's secretary for the letters sealed with Charles and Anthony's seals. These he handed to me, and then gave me a small bag. 'What's this?' I asked.

'There are three routes to citizenship in Bruges,' he told me. 'You can reside here for a year and a day, you can marry a citizen, or you can pay a fee of twenty-four shillings.' He grinned. 'My lord suggests that the first is too long to wait and the second too rash at this early stage, and has offered to pay the fee on your behalf.'

'I am most grateful to his lordship,' I said, and picked up the bag.

'Lest you feel the temptation to spend the fee on other things and wait out the year,' he said, 'I would point out that no foreigner can engage in his business or profession until he has become a citizen.'

'I see,' I said. 'Thank you.'

I turned to go, and he shuffled the papers on his desk before adding, in an amused low tone, 'Of course, there is always the possibility of love at first sight.'

I grinned and went out to look for commissions. I say 'I', but truth to tell at first it was Rogier van der Weyden's name that did the business after I started dropping it all over the town. People who mattered thought that if I had worked with him then I couldn't be totally hopeless, and the natural inclination that many people have to be in some way associated with the great and the good also worked in my favour. My letters from Charles opened doors that would have remained shut even to Rogier's name, and the small number of charcoal sketches that I had with me and a couple of others that I improvised on the spot convinced people that I could do a reasonable job. Whether it was bonhomie or just the hope and good spirits that go with a new year I know not, but before the day was out I had two confirmed commissions and two further tentative ones.

Both my first commissions were triptychs, the first from Francisco de Rojas, the ambassador to the court of Burgundy of his Most Catholic Majesty, the King of Spain, and the other from the Count of Charolais's former banker, Signor Angelo Tani of the Medici bank in Bruges. The ambassador wanted his painting as soon as possible, while the banker, who was planning his wedding, was prepared to wait until his prospective bride arrived later in the year before I made a start. Things could not have fallen out better if I had planned them.

The Master of Bruges

With a guaranteed income, for a few months at least, a place to stay with the rent and food paid and at least two commissions from people of quality I was about as secure as a painter could possibly get. Despite the January cold, I felt a pleasant warmth sweep over me as I traversed the Bruges streets that day.

Of the Composition
of a Portrait

Remember always that the patron pays your bill. He it is who puts bread into the mouths of you and your family, and who provides the roof under which you sleep, and thus he is not to be taken lightly. In a word, he gets what he wants; he is always right. You may suggest improvements and show him sketches of how things will look if done your way, but in the end it is his portrait, and he must be allowed to see himself as he wishes – truth is secondary. You can hint at it subtly if you like, but be careful; rich and important men do not generally become rich and important by being stupid, and there is an astuteness that you ignore at your peril.

Some are aware that they are not perfect, and will pay you to include some (if perhaps not all) of their bodily defects so that they can appear more realistic, more a man of the world. Their wives and children, on the other hand, do not have imperfections, at least in portraiture, and these must appear immaculate, impeccable, steady of gaze and sound in wind and limb and so on. Paint them with their eyes and mouth closed if you must, to hide the squint and the rotten teeth – well for you if you do, as they will appear the epitome of sobriety, piety and religious observation, to the delight of your patron and the enhancement of your reputation, not to mention your fee.

It goes without saying that your subject must appear in only the best of circles. Surround him with saints (or, if he prefers, Caesars), clothe him in glorious raiment, put him in the company of the glorified servants of God, among the angels of Heaven or leading the procession of the saved of the earth and he will love you for it. More to the point, if you can, put the faces of his enemies and his business rivals among the suffering damned in Hell, and you will be well rewarded.

As long as the patron sees what he wishes to see, all other matters – truth, art, reality, all the rest – are of secondary consideration. If you wish to eat, remember that. If you wish to eat well and often, engrave it on your soul.

Of the Visit of My Lord
to My House

(1465)

He was completely unannounced. One moment I was alone in the workshop, towelling myself down after my morning swim in the canal and ready to start painting the background to the Tani triptych, and the next there was a commotion on the stairs and I was surrounded by courtiers in huge numbers. The line spilled out of my door and down the staircase, and for all I know out into the street and back in a long trail as far as the Burg. Count Charles led them, of course, striding into the room resplendent in a curious outfit of cloth of gold lined with sable and stitched with silver thread, the whole topped off with a black velvet hat studded with numerous precious stones. 'I have come to see that you are using my money well,' he said, ignoring my near-naked state, although he had the grace to push the door to while I put some clothes on.

In the meantime he advanced to the panel and peered at it. 'Ah! The Last Judgement,' he said. 'This will be Tani's, I suppose?'

From my knees, I answered, 'It is, my lord.'

'And no doubt you will have put him among the saved, will you?' He bent down and peered. 'None of them have faces yet, I see. Get up, man.'

'No, my lord.'

'I beg your pardon?'

'I mean no, there are no faces,' I said, hurriedly complying with his instruction.

'Ah, I see.' He returned to his perusal of the painting. The faint flush of anger that had risen to his face faded quickly enough. 'Who will be there? Apart from Tani, I mean, who has paid for his place in Heaven?'

'My lord, it is not the place of a mere painter to decide the eternal destination of another man.'

'Not of a painter, perhaps, but a prince could decide, could he not?'

'If my lord thinks so . . .' I began unsurely, but he burst into laughter.

'If I may command,' he said, 'and as your sponsor for citizenship I feel you owe me something, then put me among the saved. Find a place for me in the legion of the blessed.'

'Yes, my lord,' I told him. What else could I say, especially after having seen the sort of anger that even a hint of minor disobedience had produced?

But he wasn't finished yet. He turned and threw open my door. 'Who among you would like to be of the elect?' he called out, turning to what could be seen of his entourage at the top of the stairwell. 'Don't be shy, now. Mynheer Memling here will give you eternal life, as he has with me, even if you are not able to qualify through your own efforts.'

Fortunately, none of the courtiers were bold enough to put themselves forward, and I was saved the difficulty of having to try to sketch dozens of faces in an afternoon. Charles was not prepared to take 'no' for an answer, however, and had one last try. 'You, Tommaso,' he called jovially to a sober-looking man just beyond the threshold, 'you will have no objection to joining me in Heaven, surely?'

'Your Highness is too kind,' the man so addressed said quietly. 'I would not presume that my good qualities so far outweigh my faults as yet to merit a place in Heaven.'

'Spoken like a true banker,' Charles said, 'with extreme caution, after having weighed all the pros and cons, and reaching no decision at all.' He turned back, away from the panel, and faced what was to be the central part of the painting, which was leaning against the further wall. He stepped closer to the panel, peered at it for a second, and said, 'Yes, here,' and indicated a soul that I had sketched kneeling in the pan waiting to be weighed by Michael the Archangel. 'This, I think, is our Portinari. And that, of course, is where you must place him, Mynheer Memling – being weighed in the balance.'

I glanced across at the hapless banker, who replied with a resigned smile and a shrug of acceptance.

'Where are your damned, Mynheer?' Charles went on. I indicated the right-hand panel, propped behind the door. The count expressed his disappointment. 'Even fewer faces in evidence here, master painter,' he said. 'The damned seem to consist entirely of arses and backs of heads. Who will you be placing in Hell?'

'If I am not qualified to grant a man perpetual happiness in Heaven, my lord, how much less am I qualified to condemn anyone to eternal fire?'

'I could think of a few who might qualify,' the count said. He pointed at one of the writhing damned. 'Make that one Louis of France.' Then he saw the look on my face and burst out laughing again. 'If only all my wishes could so easily be granted, eh?' He clapped me on the shoulder and said, 'Glad to see you doing so well.' Then, without another word, he turned and set off down the stairs, the crowd parting in front of him and then foaming down in his wake. One of the courtiers paused for a second, handed me a heavy little bag and then, with the slightest of smiles, joined those surging after his master. From the bottom of the stairs I heard his voice echoing back: 'Louis of France, I say, Hans. Do not forget.'

The bag was gold, of course, and of course I did as I was told. Despite his obvious embarrassment, Tommaso Portinari duly found himself being weighed in my balance, and in the fullness of time one or two courtiers found their way onto the steps of Heaven, having reconsidered their positions and come to my house later, pressing more little bags upon me. I put the Princess Marie there too, but only a modest view from the rear; she is recognizable only by her hair, as her lower half is covered by two saints on the next lowest step. They are taller than she, so she looks to be the same height as them. Given the subsequent fate of the painting I doubt that Louis XI ever saw it, which is perhaps just as well.

I did put Count Charles in the painting, but not on the steps of Heaven as he asked; I exalted him a little higher. He appears in the semicircle of the elect behind Christ, the third of the saints to the right of the Saviour. I thought it fitting that the count's likeness should represent St Andrew, the patron saint of Burgundy, but in order to make his appearance more fitting for a mortal in this divine company I directed his gaze downwards towards earth, although why I should mention this I know not, as no civilized man is ever likely to lay eyes on Tani's painting again. Anyway, the count was satisfied – at least, he offered no complaints.

I had Rogier to thank for the layout of the picture. It was taken directly from his own pattern, which I still had, and which he had first used twenty-five or thirty years before, even down to the rainbow.

Of the Portinari Commission

(June 1467)

Tommaso Portinari was by no means pleased that he had featured in my painting of the Last Judgement. He had come to my workshop with it in his mind to commission a painting, and there stood the reminder that he was already in one, his hands clasped before him as the Archangel Michael weighed him in the scales, his tiny paltry penis barely visible to the eye.

'Does it have to be so?' he asked mournfully.

'It is by order of the count,' I pointed out, 'and you yourself raised no objection.'

'It is difficult to raise objections to a man who is already one of the most influential princes in the world,' he said, 'and will be even greater in the course of time. I suppose you had better leave it where it is. I don't want to offend him.' He crossed the room and looked down on the street. 'Are you taking commissions at the moment, Signor Memling?'

'Not at this immediate time,' I said. 'There are numerous paintings which are waiting to be executed.'

'Ah.'

He looked disappointed, so I added, 'The accumulated work should be cleared by the end of the summer, sir. I should be able to make plans for the coming months then if you had something in mind.'

He took another turn round the room, and said, 'Well, I was thinking of something like this,' he said, pointing at the Last Judgement, 'but with the donors featured a little more prominently. Some event in the life of Our Saviour, perhaps.'

'Who would the donors be, sir?' I asked.

'Ah, yes, of course.' He drew in his breath and stood more erect. 'I am to be married. A lady I met in the summer while in Italy. She and I will be the donors, of course. The painting would be to commemorate our marriage.'

'Would it be for your own use, sir, or for display in a public place?'

Since he had replaced Angelo Tani a couple of years before, Portinari had striven to appear at the forefront of Bruges society as a patron of the arts and an intimate of the great, and any ostentatious display of wealth was irresistible to him. I was well aware of this trait. 'Well, it would be nice to have it shown somewhere public, in Sint Jacob's, perhaps.'

I kept silent, allowing this to stew in his mind, and then he convinced himself, and went on, 'On the other hand, it would be fitting that my wife and I should have some private devotional object, too, would it not?' He had another good look at the Last Judgement, which was by now in its final stages. 'What might the cost be of a painting such as this?' he asked.

I named the figure.

'What if I were to order something on a lesser scale than this, for public display, but with an additional triptych for private devotions?'

'That would depend very much on what you had in mind,' I told him, and added, for the sake of the flattery and to set his banker's brain a-calculating, 'although for such a large order and such a distinguished friend of His Grace's I could arrange for a substantial discount.' I wondered if he might turn out to be the patron I had been waiting for, and decided that he was indeed the very man. 'I have an idea for a new type of painting, sir, if you would be interested, a devotional painting, but one like no other ever seen.'

'Nothing scandalous, I hope?'

'Oh no, sir, quite the opposite, but in its own way revolutionary.' I saw the flicker of interest in his eyes, and went to the cupboard to fetch the pattern I had prepared against a moment like this. I spread it out on the table. 'Call to mind, signor, the events of the Passion of Our Saviour.'

He leaned over to look at my sketches, and before I had finished my second sentence he was rubbing his chin, his interest captured by the originality of what I had in mind.

Of the Accession of Duke Charles

(June to August 1467)

The bell began to toll just before the end of the working day, and for that reason most took it to be the angelus and downed their tools. It was not until the bell continued to chime long after the angelus would have stopped that we realized that something else was afoot, and I sent the boy Nicholas down to the square to find out what the matter was. He was gone only a few minutes, and burst back into the workshop hot and sweaty, having run all the way. 'Master, master,' he blurted out, 'His Grace the Duke is dead.'

I dismissed the three journeymen for the day, ordered Nicholas to tidy the workshop and went up to my living quarters to wash my face and don a fresh shirt. Then we all walked together to the ducal palace. A queue had formed outside and we joined it, anxious, like most of the people of the city, to pay our respects to Duke Philip – not for nothing had he been called 'the Good'. We were allowed in a dozen or so at a time, and filed through to the duke's private apartments, where Philip was laid out on his bed, a black cap on his head. The press of the crowd without was so great that there was no time to do more than stand at the foot of the bed and say a brief prayer for the repose of His Grace's soul, and then we were ushered out. The new duke, Count Charles, had arrived earlier that afternoon from Ghent, and was praying alone, we were told, in the family chapel, where the old duke's body would be taken after embalming later that night.

There was a solemn air to the city; even the taverns were quiet. That night a servant of the new duke called at my house and left eight ells of black cloth to make a mourning robe – as a protégé of the new count's I was to attend the funeral, which we heard was to take place at St Donatian's in due course.

I spent the next few days having the mourning robe made, and then on the day of the funeral I reported to the marshal of the funeral procession at the ducal palace, being one of the many who were to precede the old duke to the church. The streets were crowded but silent, with only the tolling of a single bell and the occasional cry of a child disturbing the stillness as we paced slowly and the evening darkness began to gather.

The procession reached the church some time before the coffin, and we were allocated places to stand for the service. Mine happened to be near the central aisle, down which the coffin was to be processed, and gave me a good view of the dignitaries as they filed along behind the body of the old duke. Count Charles was the main mourner, of course, and behind him his daughter. I had seen the princess from time to time over the last two years, whenever she had been in Bruges, but had not paid much attention to her. Now, as she came down the aisle, I was struck by her comportment and her composure. Just over ten years old, she bore herself with the gravity of a woman of three times her age. Dressed simply in a long black dress, she walked with her eyes modestly on the ground, her face an impassive mask and her long hair gathered up beneath her cap of mourning.

It struck me at that moment that it was not only Count Charles's status that had been elevated with the death of Philip the Good. The princess was now in reality what she had threatened to be since her birth, a role that neither she nor her father could have desired for her – the heiress to the Duchy of Burgundy, and the most sought-after virgin in Europe. Little wonder, then, that she looked so solemn.

The new duke did not stay in his city long. There was unrest at Ghent, at Liège and at Malines, and no sooner were the old duke's bones interred than Duke Charles mounted his horse and, still in his robes of mourning and trailing his daughter and his father's treasure, rode off to quell the rebellion that was threatening to break out.

Our lives returned to normal, but the black mantle remained in my garde-robe in the new house in Sintjorisstraat, a reminder of the improvement in my status – a follower now of Duke Charles, no longer merely Count of Charolais, but Duke of Burgundy and one of the foremost princes of Europe.

Of the English Commission
and the Wedding of His Grace
(July 1468)

Where there is a royal wedding, there is always a nobleman or two with spare money, and some wedding guests do like to commemorate the occasion with a picture or two. I was offered more commissions than I thought possible in such a short space of time.

Half the nobility of Europe attended Bruges for the wedding of Charles, who had now been Duke of Burgundy for a year, to Margaret of York, the sister of the English king. The royal houses were there in force, of course, and there was a smattering of princelings and ambassadors from every nation in Europe, and not a few from elsewhere – even Muscovy sent an envoy with a wedding present. The French did not turn up, of course, and I never heard tell that even good wishes were expressed by Louis, but that was not unexpected. Nor was it unexpected that Edward of England was unable to attend; the chronic instability of his realm meant that it could not be left even for as short a time as a day.

With more nobility in the city than is buried in Nôtre Dame de Paris I soon found myself entertaining members of the quality in the house in Sintjorisstraat. Three or four commissions came from the celebrations, but one of them was to lead me further afield than I had expected.

A good English diplomat commissioned a triptych from me. John Donne his name was, a minor official in the service of Edward IV of England and in Bruges as part of the bride's entourage. I demanded a huge fee, as befitted my burgeoning status, and he agreed without a quibble. Even there I was clever; I offered him a big reduction if, when he had the work in front of him and was satisfied with it, he would tell his friends and acquaintances at the English court where it came from and who had done it, and of course he jumped at the chance to pay less; I think the celebrations cost him more than he thought, so a saving afterwards was most welcome.

I went to Donne's lodgings to show him what I had in mind, and we agreed on a pattern. He had seen Rogier's *Adoration of the Magi* and wanted something similar in size and scope, except that instead of wise men I would put in saints and members of his family – himself, his wife and enough space for the sons and daughters to come. He asked for two different St Johns, and I quickly sketched him an impression, and incorporated them all, saints and family, into the overall balance of the work.

'Fine,' he said. 'This is most excellent.' He gave me a small sum of money on account.

And that was the last I saw of him for three years.

The duke had had remarkably bad luck with his women. His first wife had died very young – no more than a child – and his second, Isabella of Bourbon, of a fever in the September after I arrived in Bruges. Soon after that he had begun negotiations with Edward IV of England for the hand of his sister, Margaret of York. Edward had at first insisted that any contract should be conditional on the betrothal of his brother George of Clarence to the Princess Marie, but Charles had reacted so negatively to this grossness that the idea withered away. Eventually, Edward came round to seeing that alliance with Burgundy was a good idea, and the condition was dropped. Parallel with the marriage treaty was a commercial treaty, and Edward saw that Charles would be a useful ally in his grand scheme to invade France and recover Normandy and Gascony for England.

The duke and his bride were united on the third day of July, 1468, in the church of Nôtre-Dame at Damme, a little way outside the walls of Bruges, at five o'clock in the morning. They rode back to Bruges together, and pageants were played along the roads as they rode. When they came to the city they were to ride through streets as decorated as they were crowded, to a wealth of cheering and shouting.

My own contribution to the festivities was relatively small, if time-consuming, but was all over long before the day itself. Some months before I had been asked to design a tapestry to be displayed at the convocation of the Order of the Golden Fleece in May, and in the spirit of parsimony which occasionally affected him, the duke decided to display it again for his nuptials. He also commissioned a design for a tapestry of the Passion of Our Lord. These took no time at all to prepare, as they were simply charcoal sketches with some indication of colour, and once that was done the tapestry weavers set about their work. I was, however, well rewarded for my efforts.

On the great day itself I was not involved, being extremely low in the social rankings, but was able to see the great and the powerful as the wedding procession wended a circuitous route through the town in order to give all the citizens a chance to view their new lady. It happened to pass along Sintjorisstraat outside my house, and I was thus able to rent out one of my windows for a couple of crowns to a desperate burgher named

Mathieu Bay, who wanted to pacify his wife by supplying her with a close view of the duke and his new bride. He was French, not from Bruges, and was chagrined that the house he kept here was not on the wedding route.

The duke went beneath our casement with his full attention on his bride, but his daughter, who rode some way behind in the parade, knew my house, having visited once in the company of her father, and she waved and smiled at me. As it happened she also favoured Mistress Bay with a momentary eye contact, which sent the good dame into raptures.

The festivities continued for a week; there was jousting in the marketplace during the day where my lord Anthony the Bastard of Burgundy took on all comers – at least he did until a horse kicked him and broke his leg – and feasting and dancing at night. We were told stories of miniature castles which contained donkeys able to play upon the reed pipes and boars blowing trumpets as well as other musical animals. It was difficult to know what to believe.

Mynheer Bay confessed himself well satisfied with his view of the proceedings, and confirmed his good opinion of me, my home and (especially, I suspect) my ducal contacts by commissioning a diptych of himself and his wife, which went some way towards making up for having him sitting at the window all day.

At the end of the festivities the English went home and the duke went off to fight the French, and so life returned to normal.

Of the Ter Duinen Triptych

(March 1470)

'Time for a portrait, do you think, Hans?' the duke said to me.

I looked around to see to whom he was referring. I was at the ducal palace, having had permission to sketch an interesting geometrical pattern on a new tile floor that I wanted to use in a painting, and the duke was wandering about in that hour just before dinner when men's minds trail off on adventures of their own. It was the Princess Marie he was referring to, returning from her daily devotional visit to the Chapel of the Holy Blood.

'She is a most beauteous maiden, Your Grace,' I told him. It was the truth, too. The early promise of her beauty had begun to blossom.

'Time for a portrait, then?' he repeated.

It was by no means unusual for girls to be painted so young, with parents anxious to preserve their daughter's little girlhood against the day she became a woman and left home. Fathers, indeed, were particularly fond of such sentimental commissions, and fathers of only daughters more than most.

'Is Your Grace contemplating a commission?' I murmured. I had heard from Portinari about the duke's money problems, which had arisen from his perpetual need to wage war against his enemies and to entertain his friends. Which was the greater drain on the economy was difficult to say. One thing I was certain of was that patronage of an artist would presently come low in his order of priorities.

'It is perhaps a little early for that,' he conceded. 'We might wait a year or so, until the full bloom of young womanhood is upon her. What commission are you working on at the moment?'

'An altarpiece for the monastery at Ter Duinen,' I said. 'A crucifixion with donors.'

'For Jan Crabbe?'

'Yes, sire.'

'Is there any room in it for a portrait of a beautiful young girl?'

'If you search the scriptures, sire, you may perhaps find mention of such a young lady at the foot of the Cross, but I do not myself recall her to mind.'

'Jan Crabbe wasn't at Calvary either,' he pointed out.

'Well, he's paying, sire,' I said, 'so he can stand at the right hand of God if he wants.'

He gazed at me for a moment as if contemplating a charge of lese-majeste, but then grunted and wandered off.

It was a few days later that a note was delivered to my house. 'Crabbe tells me that the outer wings of his triptych will feature an Annunciation. He has agreed to my suggestion for a model for the Virgin Mary.' It was signed with a large 'C' and the ducal seal.

I could not, of course, raise any objection, and thus it was that I painted the princess for the first time. She was just thirteen. I placed her on a pedestal in a niche, reading a book, with a lily to her right for purity and dressed in virginal white. I was never entirely happy with the painting, though. The princess was away so much from Bruges that summer I was never able to sketch her likeness from life, and as a result the portrait caused difficulties and delays. Her eyes in particular were hard to capture exactly, and eventually Abbot Crabbe was able to delay the dedication of his altarpiece no longer. It displeased me that I had to hand the princess over in a less than perfect state; it is by far the least successful of my attempts to catch her character.

Of the English Merchant

(April 1470)

'It is as remarkable a painting as I have seen,' the foreigner said, 'a real tour de force. And executed here in Bruges, you say?'

'I believe the painter is a local man,' his companion replied. 'Certainly a great deal of his work is exhibited here. You must have seen examples of it in the past.'

'I have not paid as much attention as I should have done to the art of painting.' He waved something that was in his hand. 'This has taken up too much of my time.'

'Well, this one was painted for the banker Portinari. That is he.' He pointed to my tiny portrait of the donor.

The foreigner leaned forward for a closer look and said, 'So it is. So we must presume that this is Signora Portinari on the right here, opposite her Tommaso.'

'Indeed,' said the other. 'That is the lovely Maria. You do not know the lady?'

'No, I have not yet had the pleasure.'

I had wandered into the side chapel of Sintjacobskerk, Signor Portinari's parish church, where he had caused his new triptych to be displayed until such time as he decided to have it removed to Italy. (The truth is that it is still there, as he is still here in Bruges, and showing no sign of retiring after all these years, although he no longer represents the Medici bank, of course.) Naturally, I was listening with some interest to the comments of the two gentlemen, as the painting they were so enthusiastic about was my own.

It happens to be a work that I am particularly proud of, a type of painting difficult to do but well worth the effort. It asks the viewer to empathize with the suffering Christ and to follow His footsteps through His final days and hours in Jerusalem. I am not, I think, saying anything other than the truth when I tell you that I think there is no other like it in the world.

The two gentlemen had obviously been contemplating my work for some time when I arrived, and I merely stood behind them and listened to their comments, for who can resist the temptation to eavesdrop when his name is mentioned, be it in a complimentary way or otherwise?

The older of the two men was perhaps fifty years of age, a solid, square man with a full beard that was in the last stages of turning from brown to grey. He was by far the more animated of the two, moving hither and thither to get a better look at one event in the painting or to compare one part with another, maintaining a running commentary as he did so. 'See how the events are linked by pathways,' he exclaimed, 'so that our eye can follow the people as they move through the day, and the painter leads our eye from event to event. And the people of the scenes, see how they also direct us from event to event. Look at this yellow-jacketed one here.'

'It is very like the Stations of the Cross, then,' drawled the other, who was much less enthusiastic in his response, 'or like our religious processions on feast days.'

The other nodded. 'It is,' he said, and then he went off again, his plain, honest face having noticed something else. 'Do you see here,' he said, 'how Christ looks directly out at the viewer, and invites our sympathy? Again and again we are drawn in to the events of the day.'

'You at least certainly are, William,' said the unenthusiastic one. 'If you place your nose any closer to the panel it will be necessary to call the painter in to repair his work. Either your nose will be smeared with his paint or his painting with your snot.'

The other man's response was to lean closer.

'I must return to business, William. Do you come?'

'No, Colard, you go. I must contemplate this work some more. I shall not be long in returning.'

'Very well,' said his companion, and took his indifference away with him.

This was sad for me, for of course without an audience the gentleman's stream of comments slowed to a trickle, with only the occasional 'Remarkable!' or 'Ah!' being dropped into the church's sea of silence as he found more to admire or recognized a character. I sat there behind him for a full hour while he contemplated my work, moving from scene to scene with little appreciative grunts. In my turn I was, I suppose, like a man who tells a story in a tavern – glad to have the attention of an appreciative audience.

Eventually he turned away from his scrutiny of the panel for the last time, noticed me for the first time, started, composed himself, nodded a surprised greeting and walked off out of the side chapel. As he went, though, there was a soft sound as something small slipped from beneath his gown and was left behind on the floor.

'Sir,' I called, and picked it up for him as he turned in response. 'You have dropped something, sir,' I told him, and held it up before recognizing it for what it was. 'Oh, it is a book,' I said.

'Thank you,' he said.

I must have turned it over in my hand, for he saw, or sensed, my curiosity, and said, 'Please, sir, examine it.'

'It is a very small manuscript,' I said, and then I opened it and saw that it was not a manuscript at all. 'This is one of those made in Mainz,' I said, recognizing the neat rows inside, 'one of Herr Gutenberg's.'

'It is indeed,' he said, as delighted by my recognition of it as he had been by the contemplation of my painting. 'Are you familiar with his work?'

'No, sir,' I said, 'although I have seen examples before.'

'It will change the world,' he said.

I looked up at him. He was deadly serious. 'This?' I asked, incredulous, still holding the volume.

'This,' he said.

'How so?'

'Because it will render books affordable to all,' he said. 'Herr Gutenberg's invention means that the preparation of books is being removed from the skilled hands of monks who spend years on emblazoning beautiful manuscripts for the powerful and wealthy. Now it will be placed into the ink-stained fingers of workmen who will make books by the thousand that can be read by the many. In a few years' time books will be so cheap that anyone will be able to afford one.'

'But, sir,' I said, 'most people cannot read.'

'They can learn,' he said. 'A child can be taught to read, and once he has learned it is a skill which will never leave him. No man ever forgets how to read – it would be like forgetting how to breathe. No, mark my words, soon the common man will be able to read a book as easily as, as . . .' He looked around for inspiration and lit upon my work, '. . . as easily as he can read that painting over there.'

'Surely not,' I objected. 'To read that painting a man needs only to have eyes to see with; to read a book he needs to master the skill, which may take years, and even having mastered it his work is not over. He must be able to imagine that the words he reads are concrete objects, and that the names he reads are veritable people that move through the streets of the town that yet exists only in his mind. The painting, on the other hand, gives him the subjective experience and provides him with a visual stimulus. It takes, surely, much less effort to read a painting than it does to read a book.'

'It does, I admit,' he says, 'but it is not so difficult as all that.'

'Gentlemen,' a voice said behind him, 'do you forget that this is the house of God? I pray you moderate your tone.'

Chastened, we nodded dumbly. 'Perhaps we could continue this discussion over a cup of something,' my companion said. 'I need not return to my work just yet; I have able assistants.'

'Gladly,' I told him, and we left the church and proceeded the few paces to the sign of the Gouden Cop. I was known to Roos the landlord, and at my signal he brought the flagon over to where we sat. 'Mynheer Memling,' he said as he set the wine down.

'Memling?' my companion said. 'Is that your name? I have heard it somewhere, I think. But I have the advantage of you now. My name is Cakkeston, and I am the governor of the English Merchant Adventurers here in Bruges. Cloth is my trade, but this is my passion.' He picked up the book from the table. 'When next I am due some leave, perhaps late next year or the following spring, I will spend it in learning the printing trade in Mainz. I had intended to learn from Johannes Gutenberg himself, but he died, of course, a year or so ago. Still, there are others there who will educate me.' Without pausing for either breath or reaction, he went on, 'And you, Mynheer Memling, what do you do for a living?'

'I am a painter,' I told him.

'Of what? Portraits?'

'I do paint portraits,' I said, 'but not exclusively.'

'In that church we were in,' he said, twisting in his seat to look back at it, 'Sintjacobskerk, there is a painting that you would do well to study and learn from. It is a most intricate work, most interesting and powerful. I cannot at present call to mind the name of the painter . . .'

'Memling,' I said.

'Yes, I know, I heard you. No, not you, but the painter of this work in the church, this Passion of Our Lord.'

'Memling,' I said.

'No, you misunderstand me, sir. I speak not of you, but of the painter who . . .' Then he saw the smile on my face. 'It is yours?' he said.

I smiled and lowered my head in what I hoped was a gesture of modesty.

'Truly?'

Again the silent nod.

'It is a most magnificent work, Mynheer,' he said, and he expatiated on its virtues at some length. I learned that day that it is well to beware talking to an Englishman in a tavern, for you will not escape sober.

It was all for the good, though, as you shall hear. I arrived home with the first cockcrow, and very drunk, and with a new friend whose amity and goodwill I thank God I have been able to retain from that day to this.

Of the Depiction of the
Saints of Heaven

One saint looks much like another, they will tell you, and they're right – there's no question of that. Holiness, like evil, has its own aura, but you can't always recognize it, much less paint it, and in their earthly form the host of the saints of Heaven look much like the hosts of sinners of earth. You can play about with halos, if you like, but they only distinguish the saint from the rest of us; they can't tell you which saint is which.

For that, thank Heaven, art and the Church have provided each saint with a characteristic, something that symbolizes each holy person – usually an object with some significance in the life (or death) of the exalted one concerned. St Catherine, for example, always has a wheel somewhere about her person, because of course she was broken on a wheel by the man that killed her, St Barbara always has the tower that she was enclosed in, St Peter has his sheep and so on.

Some are a bit more obscure, of course, although none the less easily recognizable for that – I speak of the bearded female saint, Wilgefortis, for example, or Ursula, who always bears a cluster of arrows, or Martin, with his half-cloak. There are lists of them available – any abbot worth his salt can reel them off in their hundreds.

Learning at least some of the names of the saints and the

attributes that each has will save much time and impress your patrons. It will also give you an instant starting point for any family portrait, with your suggestions of suitable saints to be included – a name saint, perhaps, or a particular patron saint – in any case a place from which to begin your discussions of style, composition, form and, eventually, of course, your fee.

Of the Displeasure of My Lady

(June 1470)

'Donors can include anyone they like in their pictures, can they not, Hans?'

'Of course, my lord.'

I had been invited to the ducal palace to 'discuss a matter of interest to His Grace', as Commynes, the duke's chamberlain, so discreetly put it.

'No restrictions at all?'

'None, my lord.'

'Tell me, Hans, how many commissions do you have in progress at the moment?'

'Seven or eight, my lord,' I told him. 'All in different stages of production, of course, and three or four others that are still in the negotiation stage.'

'Mainly religious or devotional diptychs and triptychs?'

'Your Grace seems to know my business as well as I do myself.' I had no idea where this was leading.

'Would you mind letting Commynes have a list?' he asked, all politeness and solicitude, as if I had the option to refuse. 'In each case, the subject and the donor – and of course a brief idea of what the painting is going to show.'

'Of course, my lord,' I told him, and then found myself being unexpectedly but insistently steered towards the door. 'If I might, ask, my lord, why . . .' I got no further, and so ended the shortest audience I was ever to have with Duke Charles.

'What was all that about?' I asked Commynes when we got outside.

'I can't say anything yet,' he said. 'Let me have the list, though, and I will inform you as soon as His Grace has decided.'

'Decided what?' I asked, but for answer received only a raised eyebrow and the briefest of smiles.

I soon discovered what he was up to when within the week my donors began to appear at my door. All those who had devotional or religious pictures on order either demanded a say in the arrangement of the painting or insisted on the inclusion of the Virgin. Then, without exception, they decided that they would like the figure of the virgin to be modelled on the Princess Marie, who had but recently celebrated her thirteenth birthday. In vain did I object, pointing out that in some cases the portrait of the virgin was already complete and that in others their original plan had included no vestige of any virgin, but they were adamant. One by one, politely but firmly, each of them insisted, and in due course it came out that this was because they had been placed under pressure by the duke, who had been equally insistent.

Through the good offices of Commynes, I betook myself to the palace to confirm that this was indeed in accord with the wishes of the duke.

An appointment was made for some days thereafter, and the duke greeted me cheerfully and with the revelation that he had had such an idea in mind for some time, but had only recently worked out how his object might be achieved.

'If I may be forgiven, sire,' I said, 'I have no doubt that you are unlikely to charge me with the lese-majeste and treason that such paintings could leave me open to charges of . . .'

'No fears on that score, Hans,' he boomed, and laughed aloud.

'. . . but could you protect me from the wrath of Holy Mother Church?'

'What could the Church charge you with?' he asked.

'Blasphemy, sir.'

He considered this very real possibility for a moment, and then looked up at me. 'Perhaps I ought to speak to the bishop,' he said. 'It would perhaps be unfair if my request were to result in your being burned at the stake in the Markt.'

'Your Grace is too kind,' I murmured.

In due course the matter received the imprimatur of the ecclesiastical authorities and I was free to go ahead with the model of the duke's choice. The duke's household summoned me to attend upon the Princess Marie so that preliminary drawings might be essayed, and I found myself ushered into the presence of the heir herself.

As soon as the door was closed she said, 'I must have you know, Mynheer Memling, that I do not approve of this.'

'Of portraiture, madam?'

'You know perfectly well what I mean,' she said, and flounced across the room. 'What am I to do?' She waited, and saw after a moment that I did not understand. 'I mean where do you want me to sit, or stand, or look, or whatever it is you want me to do. Are you always this obtuse?'

I indicated a chair. She sat; her two ladies perched themselves discreetly against the wall, and I hesitantly began sketching.

I soon discovered that she was not used to sitting still. She had so much energy that she wanted to be constantly on the move – in that at least she resembled her father, and the fact that she was annoyed made matters worse. My sketches were not as I wanted them, and she came out all pouts and flashing eyes, something only exacerbated by the redness of her hair. All was most unsatisfactory, and the afternoon did not go well.

Then the duke himself came in, and we all leapt to attention. 'How goes it, Hans?' he asked, and noticed my hesitation in responding. He looked over my shoulder. 'Ah, I see you are making an experiment in your art form,' he said. 'I have seen your Standing Madonna, and your Seated Madonna, but the Scowling Madonna is a novelty indeed.'

There was a muted 'Oh!' from his daughter, and she shifted her position so that her face could not be seen. From her came a muttered 'More blasphemy.'

'I fear I have displeased Her Highness,' I told him. This is a useful rule – always blame yourself, as princes and their families are never in the wrong. I knew why she was upset, of course. I considered whether or not to go further, and threw the die. 'If Your Highnesses would permit me to comment on this matter?'

They both looked interested, so I continued. 'I was not aware until this moment what had caused my lady's displeasure towards me, but now that I know, I think I can assuage her doubts.' I paused to make sure that I was not treading on ice left too thin.

'Go on,' the duke told me.

'As Your Grace knows, I too was once of the opinion that to give our Blessed Mother the appearance of Her Highness might be construed as blasphemy, or at the least in some way disrespectful to the Virgin. The Church in its wisdom ruled that it was not, which alone was enough to convince someone as unlearned as I am. However, I also thought about the matter independently of the ecclesiastics, and reasoned thus: our representation of Christ and all his saints is that and only that, a representation. It in no way reflects the reality of those in Heaven; to attempt to do so would be futile, for the sight of Christ in all his glory would surely blind us. The most accurate representation would undoubdetdly be a blank, for each man could thereon project his own image of the Almighty. However, a blank will not suffice, because the ignorant and unlearned looking at it would feel nothing. Such people stand in need of an object on which to fix their limited imaginations in order to contemplate the mysteries. This is why the Church in her wisdom has long permitted the use of pictures and sculpture in church, that in observing the imperfect image, the mind may strive towards the perfection that is the Lord.'

Well, if nothing else I had their undivided attention now. They waited while I gathered my thoughts again.

'The image, however, must not be too imperfect, because then we begin to contemplate its own imperfections rather than the perfection it is meant to represent, and the objective is destroyed – we think on ugliness instead of beauty. Therefore although the model which we choose to represent the Lord or the saint must, because it is human, be an imperfect model, nonetheless it must of necessity be the best model that we can provide.'

It was apparent that the duke at least could see where I was heading, but I was not so sure that the princess yet understood, so I continued. 'In choosing my lady as a model, therefore, we extol her beauty above the beauty of all other mortal women, but we do not presume to compare her beauty with that of the Queen of Heaven. We merely use it to remind us of that beauty. Therefore it is permissible and by no means blasphemous to use my lady's image in paintings of this type.'

I felt myself extremely satisfied with this cogent and logical explanation of the position. A raising of the eyebrows and a slightly amused movement of his lips suggested that the duke had not only followed the argument to its conclusion, but was also in full agreement with it. The princess, however, was goggling at me.

'Perhaps if I explained again,' I began, 'using less complex terms . . .'

'I am astonished,' the child said.

I smiled, fool that I was.

'I am astonished,' she said, 'that you can take so long a route to such an obvious conclusion. What you have said I was able to work out for myself within moments of hearing my father's plan, as indeed the meanest of his subjects could have done. Do you presume to lecture me, Mynheer Memling, on the orders and customs of Holy Mother Church, her practices and philosophy? I can accept your long-winded treatise on the nature of religious art, in which matter it is conceivable that you may be considered to have some expertise, but farther than that you should not go.'

Her father was as taken aback as I was. 'It is not the question of blasphemy that upsets you, then?'

'Of course not. The painting itself is not blasphemous.'

He nodded his agreement. 'The Church does not think so,' he said. 'It is clear that the Virgin will not be offended.'

'Well, this virgin is,' she said, glaring at him and emphasizing each word separately. I took a step back, as if her anger were a physical blow.

'So the offence is to you, then, not to Our Holy Mother?' her father murmured.

'Yes.'

'But if she does not take offence . . .'

'She may not do so for herself, but I most assuredly do.'

'So the true offence is to you?' he insisted.

74

'It is. Am I a piece of meat, to be hawked around the market-places of Europe?'

'You are not, and you know you are not,' he said tenderly, 'but we must face the realities of life. Your hand will be much sought after.'

'Is it not sought after enough, without this unseemly advertising?'

And of course immediately I knew the real reason why she was so annoyed. The duke was using all these paintings to display his desirable daughter's beauty to the world. The more paintings I completed, the more she would be seen; those suitors who could not see her in the flesh could look at the pictures. Even if she were away from the city where they were displayed, interested princes could gaze upon her and make their calculations. In addition, her beauty would be immortalized, and all without a penny cost to the Duchy of Burgundy. I could not suppress a grin at thinking how much this latter fact would please Portinari and the duke's other creditors.

'Do you amuse yourself at my expense, sir?' the princess asked coldly. I came back from my reverie to find her gaze, as well as that of her father, fixed accusingly on me.

'Why no, my lady. It was an inner thought, that's all.'

The duke sighed. 'Perhaps you had better leave us for today, Hans. I must regain control of my unruly child. I shall send for you when I need you again.'

'The word is "if", not "when",' Marie said, and smiled icily. I remembered an earlier interview, and decided that it might be a dangerous task to have to say 'You may not' to the Princess of Burgundy.

I packed my chalks, made my bows and left. The years had added to Marie's store of beauty, but she had grown too in wisdom and intellect, and her anger was as fiery as her hair. If she did not resemble her father in all things, at least she resembled him in that. And, of course, in at least one other trait she was her father's daughter – never had I seen anyone as Lucifer-proud as she was that day.

Of the Advent of the Strangers

(October 1470)

It had been one of those fierce October days that lay siege to us occasionally, with the wind hurtling down from the north, blustering its way through the cracks in the doorways and upsetting the household. On this occasion it brought with it rain of an intensity I have never seen before or since, the water coming down in a solid, unrelenting cascade that drenched a man to the bone in seconds. I was glad to be inside, snug in my warmest robe with a flask of warm wine within reach and the fire built up to last.

At first, in my drowsiness, I thought it was the wind buffeting the chimney, but when it developed a rhythm I came out of my drowsy state and sat up. Simonelle, more sober than I, had heard and interpreted the noise correctly. 'Shall I answer it, master?' she asked.

'Yes, yes,' I said tetchily. She could be the stupidest of girls when she put her mind to it. The last thing I had expected on that God-forsaken night was a visitor, so it was obvious that whoever was outside in the rain was bearing news that was either extremely bad or extremely urgent.

There was a large heavy curtain drawn over the doorway, so I was spared the worst of the blast, but by the same token I was given no clue as to what was afoot until the wood was put back in its hole and Simonelle came back in, followed by a figure dripping water like a piece of faulty guttering. When she took his cloak and he stepped forward into the firelight I saw who it was.

'Mynheer Cakkeston,' I said. 'What brings you here on such a night?'

I handed him a cup and poured some of my wine into it. He swigged it off gratefully, but refused a second. 'It is a matter of some urgency, Mynheer Memling,' he said, 'and not a little delicacy. To put it bluntly, I need your help, and I must warn you that if you are kind enough to offer it you may place yourself and your livelihood at some risk.'

This was unwelcome news. I have always been a man averse to risk. I like to calculate my chances and know what I am taking on. 'On the other hand,' Cakkeston went on, 'it is not impossible that you could gain some benefit, in the long term. Not probable, by any means, but not impossible.'

I had left him standing, and suddenly remembered my manners. I indicated the stool opposite my chair, to draw him closer to the fire, but he shook his head. 'As I said,' he went on, 'it is a matter of some urgency. I need to know your decision immediately.'

I felt uncomfortable sitting in my warmth while he stood, and rose to stand before the fire and warm my back. 'Then you had better tell me,' I said, 'and be brief.'

'I am in need of accommodation,' he said, and then, seeing my look of surprise, laughed. 'Not for me, Mynheer – at least not yet. There is a party of some gentlemen newly arrived from England who have no place to lay their heads this night, and . . .'

'Is that all?' I asked incredulously. 'A bed for the night?'

'No, Mynheer, that is not all.' His mien sobered me immediately. 'If you accommodate some of these gentlemen you shall have my eternal gratitude, for what little that is worth, and theirs too, although the value of that is perhaps less than mine at the moment. But I must warn you that you might draw upon yourself the enmity of powerful men, both here and in England.' He must have seen the look on my face, for he hastened to set my mind at comparative rest. 'There is no danger to your life, I think, but these gentlemen have enemies who may be able to influence others against you in matters of finance and commissions and so on.'

'You have a fine and large hall for your Merchant Adventurers in the city,' I said slowly. 'Could not your gentlemen have been accommodated there?'

'Some of them are there,' he told me, 'although the company is too large for all to remain there. And you know that my own lodging in the hall is but a poor place, fit only for a single man, although I have put four gentlemen there for this night . . .' He faltered for a second, and then recovered himself. 'And it is not meet that gentlemen of this quality should be forced to sleep in such places. I . . . I . . .' Again he faltered, and I took his elbow. I realized that the man was bone-weary.

'William,' I said, thinking that the familiar use of his given name might help settle his troubled mind, 'say in plain words, without artifice or allegory or hidden symbols, what the problem is. This is two men speaking here, not one trying to divine the meaning of a painting from the clues strewn around by the other.'

I could see in his face the decision being made. 'I cannot tell you all,' he said, 'but to tell you what you already know, that my England is a troubled land. The party of Lancaster is in the ascendant, and the king is overthrown. The men I speak of are of his party, the Yorkist faction. The powers in London support their enemies, and the merchants here are uneasy about helping the wrong party lest it cost them their livelihoods. I have put some of the men into the mercers' hall and other friendly houses in the city. These men I speak of have arrived friendless and penniless. Will you take them in, Hans?'

I would like to think that I made my decision on the basis of humanity – one man stretching out a hand to another in need – but realistically I think I did my calculations, too. I saw the risks, of course – the Merchant Adventurers were a powerful group, and the cost could be enormous if they went against me. On the other hand the men he spoke of were friends of Cakkeston's. Business has a way of settling these things to the advantage of all in due course. All in all, I thought, it was worth the risk, and in an instant I became a merchant adventurer in men's souls. 'I will take them,' I said.

Cakkeston smiled and grasped my hand.

'When will they be here?' I asked.

'They are standing outside your door,' he said, 'awaiting your decision.' He strode to the door and flung it open. 'Come, gentlemen,' he cried against the gale, 'Mynheer Memling, at least, is willing to admit you to his house in friendship.'

A flurry of rain came in first, followed by five men, each drenched to the bone. 'Simonelle, hot wine,' I called, and with the help of Cakkeston I drew a chair and a couple of benches up to the fire. Four of the men slung off their cloaks; the fifth, I saw, had not even that much covering to protect him from the weather. 'Come, sir,' I said to him, 'you must be starving cold in doublet and hose. Come to the fire and warm yourself. Simonelle,' I called again, 'where is that wine?'

She eventually brought it, and we put the jugs on the hearth to keep warm while she heated up some more. The travellers were fair in need of it, and the first cups were soon drained and refilled.

The men began to towel their heads, some stripping their shirts off. The youngest, a lad of no more than eighteen or nineteen, had a livid scar, perhaps a hand span long, at the back of his right arm just above the elbow. The coatless one, still seated, stripped off his shirt, which was drenched through, towelled his upper body briefly and slipped on one of my gowns. He was no older than me, but far outstripped me in size, and I had no shirt in the house big enough for him. 'I thank you, sir,' he said, 'for your Christian charity. My name is Ned, Ned Plant. I am ... or should say, was ... a substantial landowner in England, but have been driven out by the rise of the Lancastrians.' He rose to introduce the others, and a fine figure of a man he was, well over six feet in height and well proportioned, with that golden hair that we often see in Englishmen. 'These men are some of my tenants,' he said, 'driven into exile with me.'

The English seem to have but three names among the entire nation. Any not called Ned are either Will or Dick, and the parents of these had made no attempt to make their children stand out from the crowd. Two of them were Wills, one of them surnamed Hastings and the other a name I did not catch, and the others were Dicks. One, he of the arm wound, was Ned's own brother, who looked a good ten or twelve years younger. The two were as unlike brothers as it was possible to be, with the one being so tall and golden and the other shorter and dark. Ned had full and fair lips, with bright eyes and a broad chin, while his brother's lips were thinner, his eyes dark and deep-set and his chin narrow and pointed.

'You are all welcome, gentlemen,' I told them. 'I am not a man of politics, save that I owe my life to my lord the Duke of Burgundy and will hear no ill of him in my house.'

'And shall hear none from the men of my company,' Ned

said, and conviviality reigned. They had crossed over from England, some seven or eight hundred of them, they told me, all that was left of the Yorkist faction, and between them they had not enough coin to fill a wine cup. Pursued to the very beaches of Alkmaar by the fleet of the Easterlings, they had barely escaped with their lives, and had nothing to pay their passage. 'It was fortunate,' Ned said, 'that the captain of our ship was a match for me in size, for I had a fine fur-lined coat that he took for passage money.'

The Will that was called Hastings spoke to me. 'I know of you, sir,' he said, 'although you know not me. I do believe you know my brother-in-law, who is one of the king's officials at Calais.'

I shook my head, puzzled.

'He commissioned a painting from you, though has not yet taken delivery.'

'John Donne?'

'The same. When the king comes into his own again, no doubt the painting can be paid for . . .'

'Such things are not to be spoken of, Will,' said Dick Plant. 'Be careful what you say.'

Hastings looked at him, and mumbled, 'Of course, Dick, of course.'

We made beds for them all, for there were straw palliasses aplenty, and I gave my own bed to the two brothers. There was a fire in the bedchamber. Cakkeston was worn out, and there was no question of him going back to his own lodgings in that weather. I helped him into the chamber and stretched him out exhausted on a palliasse. The four other men were accommodated where they were, and I led the brothers to bed. 'I am not going to refuse your bed, Mynheer Memling,' Ned said, 'but where will you lay your head this night?'

I had not yet considered the matter, and was nonplussed. I looked around; fortunately Simonelle, unsure of how many would be staying, had thrown an extra mattress on the floor. 'If you have no objection to my sharing the room?' I said, and pointed to it. They had none, and I threw off my outer garments and lay down in my shift, with a couple of rough blankets thrown across the top of me.

Sleep would not come, though, and I lay there staring at the ceiling and listening to the wind and rain and the cracking and shifting of the logs in the hearth.

I was just dozing off when a voice spoke softly. 'Dick, are you asleep?'

There was the sound of someone rolling over and then Dick's voice said, 'No.'

'We will take it back one day,' Ned said. 'My people will want me back when they see what happens.'

'They will,' Dick agreed. 'You will live to a good old age holding the lands that are yours.'

'That's what I need to talk about,' Ned said. 'I have a son now. What if anything were to happen to me? Who would look after the land and see that he came into possession of it?'

'Ned, you are the picture of health. You will outlive all of us, and your son will inherit.'

'We need to have a plan,' Ned said. 'We need to think the unthinkable and plan for the worst.' I heard him heave himself up in the bed. 'Listen, Dick. What if I am killed or die of plague while my son is just a child?'

'Worry about it when we have reclaimed the land,' Dick said. 'It means nothing until we do that.'

'No, listen to me,' Ned said. 'Just in case – we have to decide what to do.'

'For God's sake, Ned, won't tomorrow do?'

'Dick, we require your advice now.'

'Oh, well, if you're going to "we" at me,' Dick said, and I heard him too sit up in the bed.

I could make no sense of this comment, but the matter was not mentioned again.

'Even if we win,' Ned said, 'our enemies will not lie dormant. If I die young, Dick, you must become his protector.'

'That will not protect him from danger,' Dick said. 'It would just place one body between him and his enemies. He would be safe only as long as I lived, and not a second longer.'

'True, I suppose,' Ned said, and then, after a pause, added, 'unless he was seen as no danger to anyone, of course.'

'How?'

'I don't know.'

The two fell silent, and I thought they had fallen asleep, but a few minutes later Ned spoke again. 'Dick?'

'Yes?'

'I think that if I were to die early, the best protection for my baby might be that you should declare him illegitimate and claim the land for yourself.'

'Ridiculous,' Dick said. 'What do you think George will make of that?'

'No, it's the only way. George will have to be dealt with, that's all. He, at least, can never have the land under any circumstances. Listen – you know what was said at my birth, about me?'

'Yes, but it was nonsense.'

'I know, but use it; if you won't declare my boy illegitimate, then declare me illegitimate instead if it has to come to that.'

'Defame our father and our mother, too?'

'If it is the only way, yes. We can let mother into the secret. You are the best of us, Dick, the only one that could see it through – and also the only man I could trust to do it right.'

'And then what? Am I to spend the rest of my life fighting George for his inheritance?' Dick asked. 'No, I don't want the job. I have my estates to look after.'

'Think of it as a temporary job,' Ned said. 'When the boy reaches his majority, stand aside, reveal that the illegitimacy is false, and let him inherit his estate.'

'It's a stupid plan,' Dick said. 'You talk as if George did not exist. He is our brother, Ned.'

Ned ignored this point. 'If all goes well it will save my boy's land, and even if it goes badly then it may save his life.'

Dick grunted.

'Will you think about it?'

'I'll sleep on it, if that will satisfy you, as long as you think about George.'

'All right,' Ned said. 'George is not going to get in my lad's way, and that's an end to it. Good night.'

Dick muttered something and they fell silent. Soon afterwards, I too went to sleep.

Since my childhood, I have tried to begin the day when possible with an early morning swim. I find the exercise invigorating, something that sharpens and strengthens both mind and body. My house in Sintjorisstraat is close enough to the canal to allow me to make this a daily ritual, at least at the age I was then, and the next morning I rose from my mattress and moved quietly to the door so as not to waken my guests. One of them, Ned's brother Dick, was up betimes, however, and was breakfasting on watered wine and warm fresh bread.

'Whither away so early?' he asked, and when I told him he was eager to accompany me.

'You did not get wet enough last night then, master Dick?' I asked.

'I did,' he said, 'but I enjoy exercise for its own sake.'

'And your brother – would he like to join us?'

Dick grinned broadly. 'I think not,' he said. 'Ned is energetic enough when he wants to be, but in general he is one of the great slug-a-beds of Christendom.'

We walked down to the canalside, and Dick looked down into the water. 'It's clear!' he said in some surprise.

'Yes,' I said. 'We have town ordinances regarding the fouling of the canals.'

'So do we in London,' Dick replied, stripping down to a linen undergarment, 'but they are more honoured in the breach than in the observance. The Thames is foul, full of sewage and dead vermin.'

'Not here,' I told him, and hurled myself in. The water was freezing, and we swam to and fro for no more than the fourth part of an hour before climbing out. I handed Dick one of the towels I had taken with us, and caught sight again of the ugly wound I had noticed the previous night. He noticed my gaze, and unabashed held his arm up so that I could have a better look. Above the scar there was a curious hollow in his arm, and above that a swelling just below the shoulder.

'Battle scar,' he said. 'A spearhead got beneath my armour and tore under the skin. The physician said that there is a muscle just there that was severed, along with the tendons that bind it to the bone.'

'So that is the muscle, bunched at the top of your arm?' I asked.

'Yes. It sprang back like a cut bowstring, and is all gathered at the top. It cannot be repaired.'

'Does it hurt?'

He shook his head. 'I don't even notice it now. For a time my arm was weak on the downward stroke, but the physician said that in the end the other muscles would compensate, and so it proved. The only change I made was that I now use an axe or a mace in battle instead of a sword – the extra weight at the end gives the downstroke more force.'

We strolled back to the house, where Cakkeston had an expedition on the go, apparently to find out what help these men and their faction could expect from the good burghers of Bruges. I agreed that they could stay for a few more nights if they wished, and took myself off to the studio to prepare for the day ahead, but before the day was out they had returned, apparently with no help in the offing, packed up their meagre belongings and set off, full of thanks, to try their luck in Brussels.

Of the First Sitting of My Lady

(November to December 1470)

Later in Advent I was summoned once again to the palace. Whatever struggle the duke had had with his wayward daughter, it appeared that he had won at least a temporary victory, for the fiery tempest of the last meeting was no more, and in its place was a girl who was docility personified when I was shown into the chamber.

She was still chronically unable to keep still, though, and I spent quite a time tutting at her and muttering under my breath.

'If you have something to say to me, Mynheer, I should prefer you to say it aloud,' she said.

'My apologies, madam.' I turned away from the sketching and approached her. 'I am discontented with the drawing. I am unable to capture Your Highness's beauty as well as I might wish.'

She smiled. 'I imagine that this is my fault,' she said.

I closed my mouth and looked at the floor, not at all sure of how to reply. 'You have been a friend of my father's for a long time?' she asked.

'I am not intimate enough to call His Grace a friend,' I said, 'but it is true that he has been a patron of mine for some years now, since I first came to Bruges.'

'Before then, surely?' she said. 'I am sure that my father told me that the portrait of me that he has is one of yours.'

'Ah, that,' I said. 'Hardly a portrait, madam. It is but a sketch, an apprentice piece that I did unasked many years ago.'

'Many?' she asked quizzically. 'Do you add years to my age, ungallant sir?'

I was charmed by her sudden coquettishness, and amended my estimate. 'Some years ago, then,' I told her. 'But in passing, those years have enhanced Your Highness's beauty considerably.'

She smiled at the compliment.

'My father loves that portrait,' she said. 'He carries it everywhere with him.' Her eyes clouded. 'If truth be told, he loves the image of his daughter more than the reality.'

'I am sure that is not true, my lady.'

'It is. That little girl was the product of happier days, you see, and represented merely the first fruit of his loins, rather than the whole harvest. She was a promise, and this princess you see before you is the unfulfilled husk of that promise.' She bowed her head, and I was surprised to see a teardrop slip down to fall upon the top of her dress.

'Madam,' I said gently.

'I am sorry,' she said, and stole a quick glance at the other end of the room, where her two ladies, well out of earshot, were engaged in playing a game of dice. 'I should not be talking to you like this, but there is no one here to whom I may speak in such a way.'

'Surely the duchess, your stepmother . . .'

'No. She is not much older than I am, and is a good friend, but she is too close to my father to be a confidante. I know my father trusts you, so I hope that I may do so too, and may speak to you and know that you will think nothing amiss of it.'

'Indeed, my lady.'

'Or repeat it?'

'Or repeat it, my lady,' I agreed.

'What is your given name, Mynheer?'

'Hans, my lady.'

'May I call you that? It would make me feel I had a friend here.'

'Of course,' I told her.

She smiled again, with a true warmth that I was to see more and more in the coming months. She was, I reflected, a most unhappy young girl.

'Now, Hans,' she said. 'What must I do to make your drawings acceptable?'

Once I had demonstrated to her the necessity of remaining quite still she became all gravity and serenity. I was able to take likenesses extremely quickly, and thus completed a number of sketches before the two ladies finished their game and decided that my session was at an end.

'Show me what you have done,' the princess demanded, and I handed her the small sheaf of paper. She examined each of the sketches critically while the two ladies danced attendance, and then handed them back to me. 'Will they have the desired effect?' she asked.

'My lady,' I said, 'I am all unaware of the precise effect that is required.'

'You are unaware of the nature of my father's enterprise?' Of course I was aware of it, as she well knew, but sometimes it is more diplomatic to feign ignorance. 'Answer me directly, then – will the princes of Europe fall in love with this image?'

'I will endeavour to ensure that they do, my lady.'

'You are a man, Hans. Would you fall in love with this image?'

I chose my words carefully. 'Having the reality before me, I have no need of an image, my lady,' I said.

Her eyes became very large and round, and she coloured prettily. 'I take my leave, Hans,' she said, and swept away, but I did not think that I had caused her any displeasure.

Of Mutability

There was, or perhaps still is – I am no expert – a school of philosophers who believe that all things are transformed by the mere fact of our observing them. I don't know about things – I cannot see, for example, that a loaf of bread is much bothered whether I glance at it, look at it for a few moments or subject it to an exhaustive scrutiny. As far as I can see, it will be transformed only by time, as it decomposes, or by serving its true purpose and sustaining my body after I eat it.

For people, on the other hand, I have little doubt but that the theory holds true. The merest looking at someone, the slightest glance, can change them both inwardly and outwardly, sometimes for a mere moment, and sometimes for ever.

Think about it. You are seated in church, bored by the sermon on some obscure matter of faith and morals with which the celebrant is permitted to interrupt the mass. Your eye wanders idly about, and lights upon a beautiful maidservant in a nearby pew. You catch her eye; she tries to avoid your gaze, but of course cannot do so, for her eye is inexorably drawn to yours. Your interest has provoked a reciprocal interest in her, if only to see how far your interest goes. She returns your glance, and you smile. She blushes. Your glance has changed her. *Quod erat demonstrandum.*

What if she returns your stare boldly, you may ask. QED still; you have aroused an interest in her that was not there before, piqued a curiosity that may or may not lead to some future liaison. All this is mere conjecture, you understand; I am not one to stray from my wife's bed – at least, not while at home in Bruges. Were I to do so she too has a look which she uses to produce an unwanted effect – that of striking fear into my soul. QED again, you see.

These to which I refer are temporary and outward changes, the effects of which may be seen by anyone, even those completely unversed in philosophy, such as my neighbour van der Saar, whose pretty daughter blushed at me this morning and gave rise to this rumination. Perhaps there is another philosophical thought here; she did not observe the effect of her glance, but it was real enough. Perhaps I ought to found a school which holds that matters are transformed even when they are not observed. In this case, however, the proof was not something which would admit of being demonstrated – at least, not in church, and certainly not with van der Saar sitting next to her.

Entertaining as these matters are, however, it is the permanent and internal changes which interest me more, particularly because, as a portrait painter, I effect them.

I see your eyebrows rise, or rather, I do not, but I sense them doing so, and I have caused that too, although not observed it. QED again, I think.

Let me explain. As a painter I bestow immortality. I change the imperfect living flesh before me into art; I mutate the man and give you an object of wonder – sometimes, of course, even one which becomes an object of devotion.

A boy comes to me, greasy of skin and spotted yellow like a pustular pard, and begs a portrait for his mother to admire in her declining years, of her boy as a young man. I paint it, toning down the grease and, with the medicinal magic of a few brush strokes, curing him of his acne. I work the miracle of transmutation, and the boy as he never was appears on the panel to the evident delight of himself and his mother. I am paid, and my life changes temporarily; he has been made immortal, and his life changed for ever.

When, later, his head is removed by the judicial stroke of an axe, his family have the solace of being able still to gaze upon his countenance, alive and pimple-free, and think him still with them. Maarten, or Jan, or Pieter becomes not the living, breathing man, but the portrait; it is referred to by his name. Those who knew him in life see it and remember him, while those who knew him not see it, and feel they know him.

Here lies your power. Have you, painter, laced his fingers together? Why then, he was a pious man. Are his eyes closed? A saint of God, then, always at his prayers. The folds of his cloak betray him as a pilgrim, hiding his scallop shell in his modesty.

And so forth. His human imperfections are forgotten; what remains is the truth of art, which may be no truth at all in philosophical terms; the transformation is complete. To confer immortality is a god-like thing, just by the act of observation.

And, incidentally, QED.

Of the Revelation of
the Strangers

(December 1470 to January 1471)

Ned and Dick and their friends returned to Bruges several times over the next few weeks, begging a night's lodging for any number from four to fourteen. I always found space for them.

Soon after the feast of the Epiphany of Our Lord Jesus Christ they arrived for what turned out to be the last time, once again very late at night, and once again Cakkeston went through the motions of begging me to take them in. As ever, I made no objection, and in fact found space for even more than before, all of them dog-tired and simply grateful for a place to lay their heads, although it was clear that there was something in the air.

I was up at dawn, and roused Simonelle to prepare some breakfast before tripping over the bodies strewn over the floor on my way out. I took my morning swim alone. The English guests were still dead to the world, and I in the process of planning my day, when I heard the fanfare in the street. I threw open the shutter, and the rain blew in. Outside there was a cavalcade of nobility, so I went to the door for a better look. At first I did not recognize the man dismounting from his horse at my door, but when he turned to face me there was Duke Charles himself.

'Your Grace,' I said, dropping to one knee.

Two of Ned's men filled the doorway behind me, and on seeing my genuflexion they too knelt.

'So once again it appears that I am in your debt, Mynheer Memling,' the duke said, taking my hand and lifting me up.

'Your Grace?' I repeated, this time as a question.

'Your kindness to my brothers-in-law will not go unrewarded,' he said.

There was a movement behind me, and then suddenly the duke bowed his head and knelt. 'I crave forgiveness, Your Majesty,' he said. 'I was unaware of your arrival in my lands.'

I looked around, but could not see whom he was talking to. In my doorway there were only Ned, Will Hastings and Ned's brother, Dick. The three stepped into the street and Ned walked over to the duke. 'Get up, Charles,' he said. 'There is no need for this pretence. We both know why you refused to know me; we bear you no ill will for your temporizing.' He laughed, a great guffaw that echoed round the street. 'Why, if the positions had been reversed I would have done the same – might still, if they ever are.'

It was Dick who explained, sauntering towards me. 'I am sorry we were forced to mislead you, Mynheer Memling. Allow me to present King Edward IV of England, who has so often been your guest these last weeks.'

'Dick and I have been made wondrous comfortable,' Ned said. 'I am pleased to say that our host took us at face value, and stretched out a helping hand to one in need, and I thank him for it.'

Well, he might have thought that, but when Ned had taken off his soaking shirt on that first night I had seen the gold pendant flash in the firelight, and recognized the dead sheep of the Order of the Golden Fleece hanging around his neck. It's true that a man can disguise himself, but he cannot disguise the deference that others show to him, willy-nilly, no matter how much they try to hide it, so Cakkeston and the others did not have me fooled for a moment. It had taken me a while to work out exactly who he was, but the fact that he was of the Order of the Fleece would itself be enough to ingratiate me with Duke Charles. Nor indeed could the tallest monarch in Europe disguise his height or his colouring, both of which were famed far beyond his realm.

Thus I was fully aware almost from the outset of who he might be and of the risk I was taking in letting him in and pulling the wrath of the rival faction around my head. On the other hand he was a king, and even a deposed king has influence and friends, and he was the brother-in-law of Duke Charles. All in all, I thought, it was worth the risk, and as I have said, in that instant I became a merchant venturer in men's souls, a venture that paid off manifold, as shall be shown.

'I will have you moved to a safer place,' the duke was saying. I made to kneel to Ned, but Dick's hand in my armpit prevented me. 'Louis de Gruuthuse has agreed to place his house at Your Majesty's disposal,' the duke went on. 'It is a fine house, fit indeed for a king, although he perhaps needs a day or two to prepare it. You will be more comfortable there.'

'Let it be so,' Ned said, 'if you wish, but there is no rush. This house has warmth and friendship aplenty, if, that is, Mynheer Memling can bear to have his neat and tidy home ravaged by such as us for just a few days more.'

I bowed my head. 'Your Majesty is surely welcome to my house for as long as he wishes to stay,' I told him.

'There are no titles between us, Hans,' the king said, and

threw his arm around me. 'Under your roof I am plain Ned, as I always was.' He turned back to the duke. 'I do not want to disrupt your courtier, Charles,' he said, 'so I will remain here for two or three days, and then come to him when I am dry and clothed. And you – will you now receive me?'

The duke inclined his head.

Ned pursed his lips. 'I shall be glad to see my sister Margaret again.'

'May we go inside, Mynheer?' the duke asked, and I ushered them into my house to the total consternation of Simonelle, who had seen and heard all from an upstairs window.

'He is truly the king, then?' I said to the man who was holding my elbow. 'And you are truly his brother?'

'He is, and I am,' Dick said. 'For my sins I am Duke of Gloucester – or was, once.'

'Your Grace,' I began, but he stopped me with a smile.

'Dick,' he said. 'Friendship takes precedence over title. I shall always be Dick to you.' I thought back; the conversation I had overheard was all true, then, except that for 'lands' and 'estate' I had to substitute 'England' and 'realm'.

'We are going to get our country back, Hans,' Dick went on. 'We have done the groundwork, and now we must build on our preparation.'

They stayed just two more days, long enough for me to get to know them better and to like them both even more. They were relaxed men, despite having lost the crown, and they were confident that they could win it back in their own time. Dick especially was excellent company, being witty and urbane and a youth who had the approbation of all who knew him. He was as honest as the day was long, a loyal brother who had accompanied his king into exile, and genuinely pleasant to all. Of them all, he was the one I liked the best.

After their few days with me, word came that the town house belonging to Louis de Gruuthuse had been readied for the king and his men, and they moved out with no ceremony, apologizing for having disrupted my household. A small bag of gold came from the duke, and this I gave to Simonelle to share with the other servants. She in particular was sad to see them go, having enjoyed some night sport with one of the Dicks or one of the Wills – neither she nor I was ever sure which.

Duke Charles's position was unenviable. France had made peace with the new regime in England, and promptly declared war on Burgundy. It was self-preservation that had brought the duke round to my house to court his brother-in-law – a Ned back in charge in England was his only hope.

In due course Dick's prophecy came true. They did win England back; from their landing, through two triumphant battles to their arrival in London and Ned's acclamation as king was barely eight weeks.

Another visitor had come to see me during that Christmas week that Ned and Dick were reconciled with the duke, that same John Donne, Will Hastings's brother-in-law, who had commissioned a work from me two and a half years before on the occasion of the duke's wedding, and then disappeared. 'My apologies,' he said, 'but my duties have kept me much away from Bruges, and are like to do so again for some time.'

He looked again at the sketches which were all that I had so far done, and reiterated that he still wanted the painting – but not just yet. 'The present state of my finances will not permit such expenditure,' he explained, 'and in view of His Majesty's plight I am unable to give you a firm date as to when payment can be made. When there is a revival in his fortunes, perhaps . . .'

I nodded my head in sympathy, made no attempt to return the deposit he had given me (and, to give him his due, he did not even hint at such a thing) and bade him farewell.

It would be another six years before I saw him again.

Of the Further
Sitting of My Lady

(June 1472)

At the end of one of our sessions at the palace Princess Marie asked me, 'Do you call upon all your models at their homes in this way?'

'Indeed not, Your Highness,' I told her. 'In general, they come to my house.'

'Then so shall I,' she said. 'It is not right that an eminent man such as yourself has to dance attendance upon a young girl such as myself.'

'Your Highness is a princess and a very great lady,' I began, but got no further.

'And you are a great artist,' she said. 'I have seen your work, so I know. That is why my father chose you above all other artists for this work.'

Still not having the power to say 'You may not' to her, I contented myself with advising against venturing into the streets, but she waved the objection away. 'It is my city,' she said, 'and I shall do as I please in it.'

It was certainly true that the city had taken its charming young princess to its heart. The citizenry saw only her public face, of course, the smiles and sweetness that she bestowed upon them, but for all that her keen intelligence was apparent to all who took the trouble to look deeper. Her quickness to anger was seen by none but those of her household, but it was said that like her father she could explode into a terrifying turmoil if her will was thwarted or a servant not quick enough to do her bidding. Fortunately, she also had a sweetness of patience that may have been reserved for court painters, for with me she was never other than charming.

The princess first came to my house on a bright summer's afternoon. Her harbinger had adverted me to her arrival two days in advance, and Simonelle entered upon a fury of dusting and cleaning, while the men in the workshop smartened their attire without bidding from me. When she arrived at my threshold the house smelled faintly of flowers, and my men, not knowing how to conduct themselves in the presence of a princess, stood stiffly to attention and tried their poor best not to grin inanely at her.

In her turn the princess was gracious and disarming, and after she had looked around the shop and nodded prettily at stock, work in progress and my troop of imbeciles she accompanied me into my own working area, her two shadows behind her. One of the women pulled the curtain across so that the princess was hidden from the idle gaze of the commoners.

'I have great news this day, Hans,' she said.

'My lady,' said one of the women in a warning tone, but the princess quietened her with a gesture.

'It is not official as yet, but it will be later today, and Hans is a friend, so there can be no harm in telling him,' she said, and turned back to me. 'I am to be married,' she said, tossing her hair back from her face.

'I am delighted to hear it, madam,' I told her. 'And may I ask the name of the fortunate prince in question?'

'It is my lord Nicholas, Duke of Lorraine and of Calabria,' she said.

'I have seen him here in Bruges,' I said. 'A most handsome young man, and of an age with yourself, is he not?'

'Older than me by only nine years,' she said, 'and as you say, a most handsome man, as well as being one of my father's most loyal allies.'

I nodded. 'Yes, both he and his father before him have always stood by Burgundy.'

'It will be a most excellent alliance,' she said. 'He will make my father a most excellent son-in-law and ally.'

'And yourself a most excellent husband,' I said.

'Yes,' she said after a short pause. 'That too, I suppose.'

My eyebrows rose of their own volition, but it was no business of mine to question her.

'Does love come after marriage, Hans?' she asked plaintively.

'It must, I suppose,' I said, 'if it has not had time to grow beforehand. Of course, in some cases it bursts into full bloom at first sight. In others, however, it will come when it is ready.'

'Have you ever been in love?'

'I have thought myself to be,' I said carefully, 'once or twice.'

'How is it possible to think yourself in love and yet not be?'

'Youth sometimes wishes so much to be in love that it convinces itself that it is so,' I said, 'or sometimes the love is real but goes unanswered. In either case the love is likely to shrivel and die if not watered.'

'Leave us now,' the princess said suddenly to the two chaperones. 'Go to the market if you wish. I would not have you bored with the work I have to do.'

'It is unseemly, madam,' one of them protested.

'The workshop is full of gallant young men who will dart to my rescue in the event that Mynheer Memling threatens me with violence,' she said. 'Do you know how ridiculous your bleating sounds? Now be gone. Come back at the angelus to escort me to the palace; until then your time is your own.'

Neither woman needed a second invitation. They bobbed curtsies and made their way out, and the princess grinned at me and sat on the stool I had placed in position. 'Come, Hans,' she said, 'let your great design be initiated.'

I asked her to look down and to her left, and gave her a doll to hold so that I could sketch her hands. 'Imagine that the baby is squirming,' I told her, 'so that you have to hold him firmly but gently. You don't want him to get away, but you don't want to hurt him either.'

'Babies are much like men, then,' she murmured, smiling slyly.

As I looked up in astonishment she dropped her eyes and became once again virginal and pensive. I sketched rapidly, knowing exactly what I wanted to achieve, and managed to catch her to perfection. When, later, I came to paint her face, I was able to do so without tricks – no foreshortening or unnecessary enlargement of any of her features. She is almost full face, her visage in repose, with just the faintest of dimples on either side of her mouth and in her chin. Her eyes are hooded and mysterious, and she looks fragile and vulnerable, younger than her fifteen years, and very beautiful.

This was a Virgin and Child, the central panel of a triptych for a German broadcloth merchant whose name now escapes me. He got a bargain, for of all my portraits of the princess this is the one which most closely resembles her as she was in the flesh. I kept the sketches, and occasionally used them again in the future, but none of the other portraits were ever quite as lifelike as this.

When I had finished the sketches I told her to relax. For a moment or two nothing happened, and then her eyes came back from that inward place whereat they had been gazing, deep in thought, and she looked at me.

'Will you do something for me, Hans?' she said softly.

'Of course, my lady.'

'Kiss me, Hans.'

I looked up sharply from my sketch. She was looking steadily at me. 'I am serious,' she said.

I shook my head. 'That is not allowed . . .' I began, but she interrupted.

'I am giving permission, Hans,' she said.

'May I ask why, my lady?'

'I am to be married to this prince of Calabria,' she said, 'and yet I have never experienced any feelings for him, nor any stirrings of love for any man. I have never kissed any man other than my father, and then only on the cheek. I want to experience a kiss, Hans, a real kiss, so that I may know what to expect of my husband.'

'A husband is likely to demand more than a kiss,' I said, and she raised her eyebrows and smiled. 'In any case, it is not the place of a painter of portraits to instruct a princess,' I objected, but this time she rose to her feet, stepped forward and placed her finger lightly on my lips.

Then she turned it around and put it on her own lips. 'That is all we do, Hans,' she said, so softly that I could barely hear her. 'As much, or as little, contact as that; that is all. What harm can it do?' She turned away and looked through the curtain into the workshop. 'And even if there were harm, all your men are working at their own tasks, so no one will know, and thus there can be no scandal.'

I shook my head. 'I may not.'

She smiled. 'As I recall,' she said, 'you may not say "You may not" to me, although I am at liberty to say "You may" to you. And so I do.' She stepped forward and reached up, and despite myself I lowered my head. Her lips brushed mine gently, and then pressed against them more firmly. I closed my eyes and responded, and so did she, and we stood enjoying what we were doing for some seconds, lost in the moment and in the wonder, and then she broke away and smiled up at me.

'Thank you, Hans,' she said, and resumed her seat.

I remember swallowing, and thinking that what I had just done was tantamount to treason, and thinking too that if the duke were to know of it I would be shorter by a head ere long.

But all that I could think of to say was, 'It was a pleasure, my lady.'

She smiled. 'It was, wasn't it?' she said, just as one of my journeymen came through the curtain.

Of the Correspondence of
My Lady

(August 1472)

'**D**o you realize what a valuable commodity you have before you, Hans?' she asked, an amused look on her face.

'It is merely a piece of wood, my lady,' I told her. 'It becomes valuable only after I have smeared paint on it and made it into potential art.'

'Why only potential art?' she asked.

'Because it is not art until it is sold,' I told her, selecting the brush I needed. 'Until then it is merely a storage problem.'

She had the grace to laugh at my joke, and then said, 'In any case, I am not referring to your miserable plank. I was referring to myself. I am the most desirable property in Europe, the ultimate in heiresses, the most fortunate of princesses, and because I am so rich, so desirable and so fortunate, I am of necessity the most beautiful of all women. What do you think of that?'

'Even if I were inclined to, my lady, I would be in no position to deny any one of those statements.'

'And, unlike most women, Hans, my value increases as time goes by. The longer my father goes without a male heir, the more desirable I become. I shall in the end have my pick of any man in Europe.'

'I am aware of your ladyship's desirability,' I murmured. 'None more so. I would have to be both blind and stupid not to be.'

'Do you know how many times my father has offered me in marriage?'

'I might hazard a guess to the nearest dozen,' I muttered, risking her wrath, but fully aware that she was in an easy-going mood this morning.

She smiled. 'I think we are well into the second dozen,' she said. 'I was being touted around before I was a year old, I believe. Let me see.' She counted them off on her fingers. 'Clarence of England, Charles of France, Ferdinand of Aragon, Philip of What's-its-name, you know, the one who is nephew to the Elector Palatine, Maximilian of Austria, Francis of Brittany, Philibert of Savoy, the Dauphin of France, who is but two years old even now, Adolphe of Guelders. That's nine, and there's a few more whose names I can't remember. Who else?'

I coughed. 'Your present fiancé, my lady.'

'Oh yes.' She coloured slightly, grinning through her discomfiture, and said, 'Fancy forgetting Nicholas.'

'You may sit if you like, my lady,' I told her. 'I have some minor touches to add for which I do not need your pose.'

She turned and sat on the cushioned chair at the rear of the room. I was working on a Standing Virgin with Child, but had had to adapt the symmetry because the painting was spread over two pieces of wood. I was forced to put the madonna and child into the left-hand half and the donor and his patron saint in the other to avoid unseemly cracks appearing in the faces of any of them should the wood separate at some future date. The potential for a charge of blasphemy was much too great.

The princess had recently come again to Bruges from Mons, and had called on me for a sitting.

'My father made me write to Nicholas,' she said.

'Made you?'

'It was not a letter of love.'

'Ah.' I looked up.

'It was a letter of policy.'

Her face had undergone a sea change from the earlier amusement to an abject misery. 'What is it, my lady?' I asked.

'Oh, Hans,' she said, 'do you now listen to what I wrote – what I was forced to write to the man I am to marry . . .'

'Madam, it is not meet . . .'

She rose and came towards me. 'Listen, Hans. I have it by heart.' Her brow furrowed slightly, and then she intoned, '"You shall not for whatever reason or on whatever occasion make any abstinence from war, truce or agreement or make peace for your person, lands, subjects and lordships otherwise than with the knowledge, leave, good pleasure and express consent of my lord and father, and you shall make and continue to make war against France with good will and with all your power, and you shall forever be well disposed, true, loyal and obedient to my lord and father, and I promise you that, while you are alive, I will never have any other husband but you." This is what I had to send, Hans, to the man who wants to marry me.'

'Madam,' I began, 'among princes it is not unusual . . .'

'Not a word of love, Hans. Not a single word of love or matters pertaining to love was I allowed to write.' Suddenly she burst into tears and buried her face in my chest. I heard 'I am a pawn on a chessboard' come from her before a further bout of sobbing, and she added, 'If I may be exchanged for a knight then 'twill be thought a good bargain.'

'My lady,' I said, 'if you were a chesspiece you would be a queen, too valuable to lose in any game.'

'Yet even a queen may be sacrificed, if the advantage be a good one,' she said, and her tear-stained face looked up at me. 'Oh, Hans.'

I sealed her lips with mine, a gentle kiss, for I have never been able to see a woman in tears without wanting to comfort her. I put my arms around her and held her, and she kissed me back, and even if I had wanted to say 'You may not' the words would never have escaped me. We stood a long moment holding each other until a sound without warned us that the chaperones were about to return. I stepped back and released her.

'Thank you, Hans,' she said, and resumed her seat, and then, when the door opened, said aloud, 'My gentlewomen are returned, Mynheer Memling. Need we do more today?'

'I think not, my lady,' I told her. 'I thank you for coming.'

She inclined her head and left.

I shook my head. She is a princess, the daughter of one of the most powerful men in Europe, and she is fifteen years old, I told myself, but the heart does not listen to reason.

Of Losses by Sea and Land

(May to August 1473)

Portinari came into my house looking as happy as a banker normally does, which means not at all. I did not mark this at first, having become used to his melancholy ways, usually to do with money, but as it happened this morning's bereavement touched me nearly. 'They have taken your picture,' he said.

'I know,' I said, as indeed I should, for had I not personally accompanied my work to the galley and seen it safely on board? 'It should be well on its way to Italy by now.'

'It should,' he said morosely, 'but unfortunately it is not.'

I turned to look at him at last. The galley, called the *San Matteo*, had sailed for England en route for Pisa about ten days before, with my Last Judgement on board along with another altarpiece that Tani had had done by Hugo van der Goes. Tani himself had already gone back to Italy, obsessed as he always was with death, and, I believe, had dedicated a chapel in Florence ready to receive my work.

'The ship has not sunk?' I asked. It was a newish galley, owned by Duke Charles but paid for by the Italian bankers, which meant that they had the right to utilize cargo space if they wanted.

Portinari shook his head. 'The galley was taken by pirates,' he said, 'or privateers, as I suppose they are technically. It had hardly left these shores when a galley hired by the Hanseatic League bore down on it and arrested all aboard before sailing the galley off to the edge of the world. In the Baltic somewhere. Danzig, I believe.' He paused. 'You seem unconcerned, Signor Memling.'

I shrugged. 'I have been paid for it, and the customer has taken delivery,' I said. 'Why need I concern myself?'

'I am out of pocket, His Grace has lost a ship, and Tani has lost a valuable painting,' he said glumly. 'Could you reproduce the painting if necessary?'

'I suppose so,' I told him, 'although I do not have the time at the moment. And of course I would have to be paid again.'

'You would insist on that?' he asked.

'Of course.'

He grunted. 'I have asked the duke for help,' he said, 'and of course my masters will contact the Pope. His word may release our goods.'

'I see,' I said, and made as if to continue my work.

'You would really want paying a second time?' he asked suddenly.

'For work done a second time, yes,' I said.

'Even . . .' he began, hesitated, and then, seeing that that way out was closed to him, he went on his way.

Her entrance was as dramatic as it was violent. The door was flung back on its hinges and she strode into the room, her cloak a black swirl of velvet about her head as she hurled it from her to settle gracefully across one of my benches.

'I am inconsolable, Hans,' she said. 'Console me.'

I stared, unsure how to approach this clearly impossible task, and as I did so I realized that she and both her ladies were in the black of mourning. 'My lady,' I said softly. 'What is it? Whom do you mourn?'

She looked up at me, her eyes red with crying. 'It is my husband who has been taken from me,' she said, a slight quiver to her voice. 'My brave and noble husband-to-be is dead a month since, and not yet twenty-five years of age.'

'Forgive me, but of whom does my lady speak?' I asked.

'Why, Nicholas, of course.'

'My lord Nicholas of Calabria?'

'The same.'

'My lady, I was under the impression that your engagement to the noble lord was ended in December last—'

'A detail, Hans, a mere detail. He was the last man I was engaged to marry, and it is meet that I mourn him.' She paused, took a breath, and went on. 'Taken,' she said, 'and I am a widow before I am a bride. He died of a fever in Nancy, and my father is at his wits' end to keep the alliance good and at the same time find me a new husband.'

'A new husband?' I said.

'Yes, a new husband. Stop repeating what I say, Hans.' She paused, and then added, 'One of an appropriate rank, of course. Louis the Spider is already at work weaving a web. I think my father has Maximilian in mind again. I suppose I would not mind that.'

'My lord Maximilian,' I said. 'He is younger than my lady, is he not?'

'He is a child of fourteen,' she said, 'with a face like a horse, like all his family, but he is about the best I could wish for.'

My surprise must have shown too clearly, for she said, 'Do you not know how hideous I am?'

'Madam?'

'Louis the French Spider is anxious that I should not marry

anyone. He is terrified of my father making a powerful alliance against him, so he is putting out rumours about me. I am unable to bear children, I hear, although how Louis can be expected to know this I cannot fathom. I also have a hereditary disease, but whether 'twas from my father or my mother's side I am unable to say.' She turned to the women. 'Go and leave us, ladies, and let Mynheer Memling do his work in peace. Return at the angelus, as normal.'

They bustled out, unquestioning by now, and she came to look at my painting. 'It looks nothing like me,' she said.

I was startled, never having had any criticism from her before, and must have allowed my surprise to show on my face.

'This lady is quite attractive,' she said, 'and I am not.'

I saw that some tease was coming, and remained silent.

Seeing that I did not rise to the bait, she smiled. 'I am a consumptive hunchback,' she said, 'according to the various ambassadors of the good King Louis. Moreover, I am mad. I see that none of these attributes appear in your depiction of me, sir.'

'I have disguised the hunch with a capacious cloak,' I said, 'and although the lady is interestingly pale, I pride myself that the consumption is not obvious. As for the madness, it does not always show on the exterior, but is inward only.'

'Thank you, Hans,' she said, and came into my arms. 'I need you so much.'

'Your eyes are much abused with tears,' I told her, and kissed each of them before moving to her lips.

'Oh, Hans, if you had only seen me play-acting this day,' she said when we broke off. 'What do I care for Nicholas of Calabria, a man I've never met? I have carried onions in my kerchief the livelong day.'

That made me laugh, and we shared another cheerful kiss. We had grown more intimate during her frequent visits to my house, and no one had suspected anything. Our relationship was chaste still, but I knew that she would soon give herself to me, and I was happy to bide my time and have a beautiful young princess kiss and fondle me.

'One thing is missing from your portrait,' she said. 'I would not be misrepresented by you, sir.'

'And what is that?'

'Louis says I am scrofulous. Come, paint me as a scrofulous virgin.'

'You know I may not,' I said. 'Such warping of the truth would be unacceptable, especially for a commission such as this one.'

'Mmm. I suppose not.'

'This one' was an altarpiece for the high altar of the chapel of St John's Hospital, here in Bruges. The irascible abbot of that other St John's, where my painting career had been reborn, had never claimed the diptych I had promised to him, and Duke Charles had reminded me of the fact about a year before. The abbot having died in the meantime, no doubt of an apoplexy, His Grace had suggested that in its stead I might like to offer an altarpiece to the hospital, which cared for the maimed soldiers of the duke's many wars. I thought it politic to agree. No one was sure to which of the many St Johns the hospital had been dedicated, and thus I was commissioned to paint, without fee, a triptych featuring the two most powerful, the Baptist and the Evangelist. The master of the hospital, the prioress, the bursar and the larder mistress were to be featured as 'donors'. It was a huge painting, with much detail, and had taken up a great deal of my time. In view of its importance and where it was to be placed, Charles had again insisted that the Madonna be represented by his daughter.

She sauntered around the studio. 'Are these the side panels?'

she asked, pointing at the two large pieces of wood with the eight figures lightly sketched on them.

'Yes.' I pointed to the four kneeling donors and their four patron saints standing behind them.

Her face lit up with mischief. 'So this is to be the prioress?' she asked, pointing.

'Yes.'

'So her patron saint will be Agnes?'

'Of course.'

'That must be me, Hans,' she said delightedly. 'You must paint me there. I shall be her patron saint for eternity – oh, how that will annoy her. She used to beat me when I was a child, and now I can watch over her.'

I shook my head. 'I don't think so,' I said, but she pounced on me.

'You must, Hans,' she said. 'I insist. If you do nothing else for me, at least give me this revenge on her.'

'You are already the model for the mother of the babe,' I pointed out. 'I cannot have you all over the painting in different places.'

'It is on the reverse,' she said. 'No one will be able to see the two at the same time. And it is most appropriate, for is not St Agnes the patron saint of virgins, and am I not still a virgin, Hans, despite everything?'

'Madam,' I muttered, 'such words are unseemly . . .'

'No pious comparison with a saint of God can be unseemly,' she said, 'and I command that I be the model.'

I shook my head, but of course complied with her request, and as a result she appears twice on the painting, once as the Queen of Heaven, and again on the reverse as a demure St Agnes.

Portinari had no success with either the duke or the Pope. Both protested at the theft of the galley with my altarpiece aboard, but to no avail. I heard later that my Last Judgement was installed in the Church of Our Lady in Danzig, where it remains as far as I know, illegally but securely.

The banker did not finish out of pocket, though, as the city of Bruges itself paid him compensation in order to avoid an expensive clash with the Hanseatic League, but I fear neither he nor Tani ever saw the painting again, and Tani's new chapel remained short of an altarpiece.

Cakkeston came to see me at about this time, bearing a gift and an invitation. The gift was a copy of the first book he had produced, something about the war at Troy. Truth to tell, I could not read it, for at that time I had very little English, but it was a kind thought.

Ned, he told me, was secure on his throne now, with the various rebels having been dealt with; he administered the south of the realm and Dick the north, and England was beginning to settle.

The invitation was to a feast given by the English merchants, for Ned's queen had given birth to a second son that very month, and the succession was guaranteed. The child had been called Richard, after his uncle, so with his brother Edward there was a second pair of brothers named Ned and Dick to administer the realm.

As for the other altarpiece, that for St John's, the princess was quite correct. As she had predicted, the prioress was not at all amused when she discovered who I had used as a model for St Agnes. No one else saw the significance, however, and the elderly lady finally told me that she would offer the torment up to God as yet another burden that the mischievous little girl had forced her to bear over the years.

Of the Princess and the Painter

(1473 to 1476)

I cannot say with certainty how many times I painted the princess in those years as she grew into womanhood, but it must have been in the region of a dozen or so. I recall that one was a small seated Virgin and Child, with the babe's right hip resting on a cushion and the Virgin in front of an embroidered cloth of honour.

Later she was the Madonna in an Adoration of the Magi and a standing virgin with St Anthony as well as a seated one with St George. There were others, too, although I cannot now call them all to mind or the patrons who paid for them. Suffice to say that if I painted a Virgin Mary at any time during the five years before my lady turned twenty then she was the model. Without having been asked, I even included her in John Donne's portrait, which was still hanging fire, having been neither finished nor paid for.

I think the best of them was the smallest and the first, which I have mentioned before, the central panel of a triptych done for a German broadcloth merchant not long after the princess's fifteenth birthday. It is perhaps most successful because she was present throughout the entire process, from first sketches to final touches, and I was able to amend as I wished with the subject before me.

After that she was in Bruges less and less; as she became of a womanly age she had official duties to see to, and was not always available.

Her unavailability went beyond painting, too. Her kisses and caresses were fewer but as ardent as ever when they came, and it was clear to me that she wished our relationship to progress beyond that simple stage, but the opportunity did not arise. It was no great hardship for me to keep myself in check, especially as I could imagine the reaction of her father if he learned of our love, and I bided my time and waited for the announcement that the duchess had conceived, at which point the whole of the focus of Marie's life and my own would change.

It was an announcement that seemed never destined to come, however. The fifth anniversary of the duke's wedding to the Englishwoman came and went, and there was no sign of a male heir, and the sixth and then the seventh anniversaries passed. While he was waiting the duke saw fit to promise his daughter yet again, this time to a previously unsuccessful suitor, Maximilian of Austria, who had first come into the picture some ten years before, when Marie was a child of but six years old, and had reappeared periodically since as the duke's interest in the estates of the Holy Roman Emperor, Maximilian's father, had waxed and waned.

'Now I am once again to marry the horse,' she told me.

'The horse?'

'Foal, then,' she amended. 'His jaw precedes him into any room by several feet, and he is a baby – two years younger than I am. However, my father thinks that such an alliance will eventually lead to his being elected emperor when Frederick dies.'

'An engagement of convenience, then,' I told her. 'When your stepmother conceives then all such arrangements can be forgotten, surely? Your new brother will become the focus of your father's ambitions.'

'Would that such a happy day would come,' she said, and sat on the throne of the Virgin I had prepared for her.

'Amen to that,' I agreed.

'Amen?' she said. 'How can such matters be of concern to you, Mynheer?'

She often teased me in this way, pretending that there was nothing between us.

'Your Highness is well aware that I concern myself with her welfare,' I said formally. To speak thus pleased her and gave me a frisson of pleasure. In addition it ensured that were we to be disturbed, the formality would warrant that nothing untoward would be observed in our conduct. 'To find another model would be doubly difficult, for none would be fit to stand in Your Highness's place, and even were I to find one, my patrons would accept no other model but Your Highness's own self for the Virgin.'

'What will you do, Hans, when I am no longer a virgin?'

I looked quickly up at her, but she was pretending it was an innocent question, and I played along. 'Perhaps I may look forward to such a day.'

'How curiously you answer,' she said, and busied herself with the mammet that stood for the babe, but we knew each other's meaning.

'It is decided, then,' the princess told me on her next visit. 'The papal nuncio has issued the dispensation and arrangements are being made. I shall be married within the year, either in Cologne or in Aachen.'

I smiled and selected a crayon with which to make my marks.

'You take the news somewhat coolly,' the princess commented – slightly put out, it seemed to me.

'Your Highness will forgive me, but there is a certain element of crying wolf about His Grace's marital arrangements for you.'

'I think he means it this time,' she said. 'It has never gone this far before.'

'And may I ask how Your Highness feels about the matter?'

I thought the question might give her the chance to unburden herself, but perhaps it was not the time yet, for she equivocated. 'I am becoming used to the idea,' she said. 'Maximilian is somewhat grotesque in looks, but he is intelligent, and has a good heart, and I think he does love me. If I have to marry, then the son of the Holy Roman Emperor is as good a catch as any.' She smiled. 'And I may learn to love him, in time.'

'A suitable match, then,' I said, probably pouting; I was never happy when she teased me in this way.

'Oh, eminently so,' she said, apparently oblivious to my feelings, but I knew differently, of course. All I needed was time, which had always been my ally in the past.

Of Perspective

I come now to this most difficult of concepts for the apprentices of today. Perspective is no more than the method of depicting spatial relationships, especially depths, on the flat surface of the painting. We are able to represent depths and volume by means of lines converging on a point or points on a horizon line. To put it simply, the use of perspective enables us to depict objects at the size they appear to the viewer when they are at a distance.

Even the most casual glance will tell you that things appear smaller the further away they are. In order to draw them at the right scale (a technique much ignored in the past) it is necessary to have some system for gauging their distance from the viewer.

One such system which I have always found effective is the use of a tiled floor. I have long been an avid sketcher of tiled floors, for they hold a great advantage for the painter of interiors. As will be readily apparent, the tiles appear to get smaller as they recede from the viewer, whereas common sense tells us that they are in fact the same size.

It becomes a simple matter, then, to establish a floor pattern on which one can overlay the underdrawing, so that each item of the painting has an established place, and hence an established size relative to the other items in the room. This gives a more natural feel to the picture.

I long ago established the practice of laying down a tile pattern on the surface of all of my paintings, even those of outdoor scenes, the better to ensure that those painting the background had the proportions correct from the outset. The pattern (plain squares, of course, for exteriors) would extend to the horizon, and it is then a simple matter to block in vegetation or dwellings of an appropriate size.

With internal pictures the tiling need only run to the rear wall of the building (although a subsidiary pattern might be necessary for objects seen through an open window, for example). The internal tiles may be patterned in any way that you wish, as long as the painter is able to discern the distances and spatial relationships that he needs.

If you observe even a few of my paintings, you will note that I frequently use the same ornate and complex tile pattern (one copied, I have to say, from the ducal palace in Bruges some twenty-five years ago, and which has done me sterling service since). This provides the ground plan, over which the persons and objects of the painting can be superimposed, and which permits even the most incompetent apprentice to sketch objects at the correct size more or less accurately. Anything that helps him achieve a modicum of competence is a bonus, I suppose, and of all men, painters especially must keep matters in perspective.

Of My Intimacy
with the Princess

(October 1476)

The wedding preparations continued despite everything. If I had not known better, I might have thought that the duke was actually going to go through with it this time. I knew he would not, though, for his daughter was completely unconcerned. It was simply a matter of waiting for him to return from his latest campaign. At this time he was still in France, no doubt smarting from the defeats inflicted on him, but now laying siege to the town of Nancy.

'The wedding is fixed for August,' the princess told me on her next visit. 'Maximilian sends me information in great detail; posts arrive almost daily, and I am required to send him a likeness of myself. He says he has sent me a likeness of him; either it has not arrived yet or it carried his last messenger.'

I burst out laughing. Her disparaging comments about her husband-to-be's prominent chin were becoming more frequent.

'Could you do me a small, quick sketch?' she asked. 'I shall satisfy him in that if in naught else.'

'Of course, my lady,' I replied, 'but it may disappoint him. No likeness, however accurate, could live up to his memory of the reality, surely.'

'What memory?' she asked. 'He has never seen me.' She looked across as I goggled at her. 'No, Hans, we have never met. We have seen pictures of each other, but no more. It is our parents who fell in love for us.'

'But your descriptions of him . . .'

'Based on likenesses, as are his descriptions of me – unless Louis the Spider has a court painter who has sent him more accurate ones than you can manage – based on Louis's own descriptions of me, of course.'

'Any accuracy is impossible,' I said. 'The painter's hand shakes uncontrollably at the contemplation of the beauty before him, and makes the straight line curved and the curved straight.'

'You are a disgraceful flatterer,' she said, but smiled anyway. 'Begin, Hans. How do you want me?'

'If my lady would turn her head slightly to the left . . .'

'I wonder if you would mind doing me another small favour, Hans?'

'Anything, my lady,' I told her absent-mindedly. I was concentrating on getting the angle of the turn of her jaw exactly right.

'I think that if you call me "My lady" again you will have to find another model,' she said.

Now she had my full attention. 'I beg pardon, my . . .' I began, but stopped myself in time. 'I . . . my . . .'

'With my father away and my stepmother so often away at her own estates,' she said, 'there is no one who will call me by name. Everyone is so formal; I have no name any more, just "my lady".' She paused, and then said softly, 'When we are alone, Hans, like this, will you call me "Marie"?'

'Madam, I cannot presume . . .'

'As I have made the request, it is no presumption,' she said. 'I ask you as a friend.' She saw that I still hesitated. 'I would rather not have to command you,' she said. 'I hope that you will indulge me as a friend.'

'For my friend, anything,' I told her. Then I stood in silence for a moment and thought back over the sixteen years I had known her and watched her grow in beauty, intelligence and character, and for the last four years of her caresses and kisses, freely given and freely accepted. Then I said, 'Yes, Marie.'

Instantly she relaxed. 'Good,' she said. 'A little to the left, you say?'

'Yes, and with your glance angled downwards.'

She complied, and then said, 'Like this?'

'Yes.'

'May I talk while you sketch?'

'If you can keep your head still.'

'I'll try.' She took a deep breath, and then said, 'Mind you, nothing has changed. I am said to be still open to offers, like a pie in a marketplace late in the day. In this case, however, the pie has the power to choose its purchaser, and what this pie wants is a good man who will love her and cherish her.'

'But if you were to fall in love, then you have the power to marry where you will, surely?'

'I do not,' she said. 'I am helpless and at the mercy of my father's whim. My choice will be his choice, whether I like it or not.' She paused a few moments, as if gathering her thoughts, and then went on, 'In truth, Hans, I have seen a man that I would wish to marry, but he is not available to me.'

'How can that be?' I said. 'You have power to command any man in Burgundy to . . .'

'This man is not a Burgundian,' she said.

'A foreigner, then?'

'Yes.'

I looked at her, wondering whom she could mean or, rather, hoping that I knew whom she might mean. I essayed an exploratory question. 'An older man, perhaps?'

'Yes,' she agreed, 'although not so old as to make the match unseemly.'

'Without wishing to probe, Marie,' I went on, pausing now in my sketching, 'I wonder if this man might be known to me?'

'I see you have guessed my secret,' she said. 'The man we speak of is known to you – well known, I think.'

'Not, then, a man of great estate.'

'Of no estate at all when I met him,' she said, and then smiled again, 'although he had reason to hope for a better future.'

I looked at her and saw a smile play about her lips. Then she said softly, 'You do know, don't you?'

I nodded, and she added, 'Let us have no name, then, but share our silent secret.'

I busied myself with the sketch for a time, and then asked, 'If this man were to make an offer, be he however poor, you would consider him as a suitor?'

'Indeed,' she said. 'If I were able to choose. In such a case, I could choose where I will. I could even be a painter's wife, for instance.'

'And would you, Marie?' I asked, not daring to look directly at her.

'Would I what?'

'Be a painter's wife, for instance?'

'If I loved him, most certainly.'

I felt a surge of hope. 'If you were to find this good man to love and cherish you . . . ?'

'Show me such a man, Hans, and you shall be richly rewarded.'

I moved on to outlining her eyes. All was not lost, I thought, despite these wedding plans – but Charles the Bold, as always, still had one more card to play.

Of My Last Campaign

(November 1476 to January 1477)

As I enter the final years of my life, I can say with certainty that I have never enjoyed being cold. I still try to enjoy an invigorating swim in the canal most mornings, but I am careful that upon emerging from the water I place myself before a roaring fire and towel myself down, pouring a warm wine inside me the while.

Apart from this exercise, I care not to go abroad in the cold, and never have done. I am happy in the corner of the fire, with perhaps a sustaining jug of the aforesaid warm wine, and then to a warm bed with a wrapped brick at my feet against the night's frost.

One late November morning, with definite hints of a cold winter to come haunting the atmosphere, I received a summons to the ducal palace. I traipsed through the streets, not too pleased, to find out what His Grace had in store for me. I had thought him to be on campaign somewhere in France, and so it proved. It was his secretary who received me and handed me a document, the reading of which displeased me greatly.

It was His Grace's pleasure to make a novel appointment, the first such in the history of Europe. I was to be the official war artist, and to record the events of his battles with precision instead of using my fancy, as other artists, who worked far from the action, were wont to do.

I looked up from this document with some trepidation, and saw that I had guessed aright. Mynheer Secretary was much amused. '"Other artists,"' I said interrogatively, '"who work far from the action." What does my lord have in mind, exactly?'

'He intends that you should be there, during the battle, to record what goes on, and then to make a painting of the events of the day, in the same way, he says, as you did for the events of the Passion of Our Saviour.'

'And where is my lord at the moment?'

'He is, I believe, besieging the town of Nancy.'

'Nancy in France?'

'Indeed.'

I waited. I was not going to put what I feared into words lest I thereby put an idea into his head, but it was to no avail. The idea had already been placed there by the duke.

'You will join him post-haste at Nancy,' he said, 'to begin your duties.'

I opened my mouth to protest, but he waved a parchment at me. 'It is a ducal order,' he said, 'which neither you nor I have the power to countermand.'

'I am getting old,' I said lamely.

'You are seven years younger than His Grace, Mynheer.'

'I have not been in the best of health,' I continued.

'In which case a bracing journey to the south can only improve matters.'

Then I lost my temper. 'For God's sake, Jehan, I'm a portrait painter, not a soldier to be dragged off on campaign. I've done my bit. I've contributed to his war chest. I can't be any use to him there, and I wouldn't be able to work in the open air anyway, freezing to death.' I waved his parchment aside. 'No, send someone else. Send one of my journeymen.'

'The duke was most specific,' he said. 'He wants you. He named you in the letter, saying that you have military experience.'

I shook my head. 'A couple of months as a pikeman, and that a dozen years ago.'

He shrugged.

'And, Jehan,' I added, 'there's another thing. After what happened at Grandson and Meurthen, I'm scared. I'm not a brave man. I don't want to die.'

'None of us does, Hans, soldier, statesman, secretary or painter of portraits,' he said, 'but when the Duke of Burgundy sends for you by name it is the man who refuses to comply who is brave.' He placed the parchment on his desk. 'Reinforcements will be leaving Bruges for Nancy in three days' time. The duke has made ready a horse and the appropriate passes for you and for a servant, should you wish to take one. All expenses will be met. Be here at dawn on Thursday.'

I nodded miserably and turned away. 'And, Hans,' he said.
'What?'

'Make sure to wrap up well.'

I forbore to answer him, and went to break the news to the workshop.

It took us a week to get to Nancy, through countryside that had already begun to suffer the ravages of winter, and was dangerous and hostile, with enemy patrols everywhere and gangs of peasants looking for revenge on those who had ravaged their land. I travelled alone; none of the men in the workshop had wanted to accompany me, and I didn't have the heart to force them. I stayed as close as I could to the centre of the column and spoke to no man.

When we reached the camp, on the Pope's new feast day of the Immaculate Conception of Our Lord's Blessed Mother, matters were worse than I had expected. The captains were in open revolt, loudly disagreeing with Charles's decisions and in some cases arguing with him face to face, demanding that he abandon his siege and take them into winter quarters. Charles, already known as 'the Bold' to his admirers, had in the last few months, following Grandson and Meurthen, become 'the Rash' and worse to his enemies, and the epithet was being bandied around the camp even by men of low degree. He would not raise the siege, however; Nancy, he felt, was close to falling.

Morale was low. The defeats of Grandson and Meurthen had hit hard. The duke had lost all his treasure in the retreat from the first of these, so even apart from the shortages of food, weapons and powder, the men had not been paid since September, so had not the wherewithal to buy food, even if any had been available. Rumours were rife that some of the contingents were ready to change sides, with most speculation concerning the intentions of the Italian, the Count of Campobasso. One of the duke's junior officers had suggested that if Duke Charles was so keen on getting into Nancy perhaps they should load him into a bombard and blow him there; it had been meant as a joke, but the duke was in no mood for humour that undermined his position, and the unfortunate officer had paid for his jest by swinging from a tree by his neck.

Not long after I had arrived, perhaps a week before Our Saviour's birthday, our lines of supply were cut, and what meagre rations the men got were reduced to virtually nothing.

Amid all this, the arrival of an official war artist and the detailing of his duties were naturally pushed into the background, and I saw nothing of the duke. I attended each day at his quarters, and as part of his official entourage found that I was entitled to my ration of food and wine and to find a space in the huddle round his fire at night, for which I was extremely grateful, but I sensed that the real soldiers resented my presence as one using up precious resources and giving nothing in return.

I had never known it so cold. Men of the watch who leaned against a tree found themselves frozen to it and were unable to remove themselves without help; others less fortunate sat in ice which melted beneath them and then refroze, chilling them from the seat upwards and killing them where they sat. Men who sat at fires found that their backs froze, and their muscles gave up the ghost on them. One man, in attempting to help lift one of the cannon, took off his gauntlets and his fingers froze so fast that three of them snapped off when he exerted pressure on the metal.

On the eve of Our Saviour's birth, four hundred men of my lord's army froze to death where they lay, and in the morning confirmation came that the Count of Campobasso had gone over to the other side, and that his troops had abandoned the siege of Nancy and were dangerously positioned between the camp and the city.

But still my lord would not abandon the campaign. We were running dangerously short of powder, and Charles had written to his commanders in Luxembourg to send money, artillery, powder, bows, arrows, pikes – anything and everything to ease the situation. The only thing that he did not ask for, which could not have been supplied anyway, was the one thing that we could not last without – warmth.

Of Nancy

(5th January 1477)

O n Sunday, the eve of the feast of the Epiphany, we heard
that the Swiss were approaching at last from the south,
and the duke swung his army round to face the threat. At
least the movement kept us warm. The river was on our left
flank, the forest on our right; in front of us a stream flowed
from right to left through a ravine with thickets of wood
around it, an excellent first line of defence. To the right of our
line the stream came from dead ground through a small row
of low hills before draining into the river. At our back was
another stream; it was an extremely defensible position. Our
artillery was stationed on the left, covering the road along
which the enemy would approach. Light snow was falling,
being blown from our backs.

I was warming my hands at the fire outside the duke's tent
when he appeared. 'Ha!' he cried, apparently well pleased to
see me. 'I heard you had arrived, Hans. Too busy to talk
to you, unfortunately, but glad you are here, all the same.'
He pointed at the troops. 'A grand sight, is it not?' he asked.

Frozen and bedraggled men, ill-fed, badly clothed, huddled
together for warmth and suffering from dysentery and fever did
not constitute a grand sight to me, and I remained silent. The
duke seemed to be overconfident, but that is not the sort of

observation that one makes to princes at any time, least of all on the morning of a battle.

'I think I would like a sketch of this,' he said, 'and possibly of the enemy too, as they approach. Do you go up there, Hans, and make a start. There will be little time for sketching once battle is joined, or in the aftermath. Give me a view from there.' He pointed up the hill, away to our right, where the trees began.

'Your Grace,' I said, 'there is thick snow and no path, and I can barely hold the charcoal . . .'

'Of course,' he said, 'forgive me,' and I relaxed.

But too soon. 'Hubert,' he called to one of the servants. 'A scarf and a hot stone for Mynheer Memling. Best give him some warming drink, too. He may be gone some time.'

The man brought the items and there was nothing for it but to obey the duke's whim. I set off, trudging slowly up the hill, the snow crunching beneath my boots, always at least ankle-deep and more often up to my knee. At least my fingers were warm though, from the hot stone I carried wrapped in the scarf the servant had given me.

The position the duke had indicated was no more than three or four hundred paces away, but it took me a considerable time to get there, time in which I was able to reflect on the duke's folly. His army was much reduced by cold, disease and desertion, and yet he was allowing it to face a force of skilled, fearsome volunteers, many of them veterans of Grandson and Meurthen, and all of them men who had been well fed and billeted in warm quarters while we had been freezing in the open. I looked back down the hill. Truly, our men were a sorry sight, standing in small clumps and unenthusiastic; the very flags echoed their attitude, for they drooped at their poles, sodden wet. If I sketched realistically Charles would have my head. Shaking that valuable appendage, I moved to the tree line and unwrapped the stone. I took off my own scarf and wrapped it around the stone and put the scarf warm from the stone around my neck. The stone itself I placed on the ground against a tree and sat upon it; it still held some warmth, but had cooled enough to be comfortable.

The snow had become much heavier, and although I could make out the right wing of our army, there was nothing else to see. Ahead of them was a blank wall of white; if the enemy were there, they were invisible. I decided it would be politic to draw something, and made some broad swathes, sketching in as far as I was able, but without any detail. It was too cold for art.

By now it was about noon, as far as I was able to judge, and I began to think about cooked food and some warm wine. The snow had started to swirl down in ever thicker clouds, and even the comforting sight of our right wing was lost to me. I decided that I had suffered for my art long enough. I tucked my charcoal into the bag at my waist and was about to rise when a movement seen out of the corner of my eye checked me. A man carrying a sword and wearing a helmet stepped out of the wood no more than twenty paces from where I sat. He glanced quickly from right to left and then advanced a few paces. I kept stock still, watching him, not daring to breathe, and then felt the hair stand up on my head as the wood began to bristle. At first I thought the trees were moving, but it was a forest of pikes that began to emerge and form up along the edge of the wood, the men stepping out of cover and forming ranks no more than five or ten paces in front of me.

This meant that Charles's army had been outflanked, and the men below me on the hill were about to be taken by surprise. Though I was no soldier, my duty was to warn them. But how? I peered through the ranks forming in front of me and could see nothing. The Burgundian left flank was lost in the heavy snow. There were now several hundred men milling about in my vicinity, and I still had not moved. Then a soldier coming out of the woods aimed a vicious kick at my leg and I rolled over and away from him.

'Wo ist deine Waffe?' he asked.

I gaped at him, waiting for the thrust to the belly, and then realized what had happened. 'Da,' I told him, pointing vaguely back into the woods. 'Zerbrochen.'

'Krieg doch noch eine andere,' he said, then 'schnell,' and turned away.

'Ja,' I said to his back, and retreated into the forest, where hundreds of pikemen continued to wend their way through the trees and past me towards the places where their units were forming up. Not a man of them gave me a second glance. I squatted beneath a tree and took off one of my boots, pretending to have a stone in it, and then spent some considerable time shaking it and running my hand around the inside.

Soon the forest was free of Switzers, but then after a minute or two I saw one limping along, wet through. I stepped up to him and took hold of his pike, foolishly thinking that he would surrender it to a fellow soldier without hesitation, but instead he cuffed at me and delivered himself of a number of oaths and imprecations, suggesting that I should look after my own weapon, and that the only way I would get his would be if he inserted it into my fundament.

Being mistaken for a Switzer had bought me some time, but not much; they had a tendency to execute stragglers, and the truth about me might be revealed at any moment. As soon as it was I would not be long for this world.

I had with me a small knife, the sort that is used for eating. I looked about, but there was no one at hand, and no man in that forest glade but me and the Switzer. I stepped up to him and plunged the knife into his neck, slashing across and up. His face barely had time to register his shock before he fell forward, gurgling, and then went quiet. I looked down at him where he lay, and then picked up his pike.

The forest was still silent, with no man to observe what I had done. With the pike at the trail, I set off through the forest in pursuit of the phalanx.

I strode out of the forest as if I owned it, veering away from the direction the man who had kicked me had gone in, and walked with an assurance I did not feel through the blizzard across the back of the pike formations. The Swiss were milling about, getting into formation, and I was not the only one whose wanderings seemed aimless, and no one challenged me.

Then three things occurred to me at once: first, that I was the only one, thanks to the snow, who knew where the Burgundian flank was situated, second that I knew of a track down the hillside and they didn't, assuming that I could find it in the storm, and third, that a man crawling on all fours with a cow on his back can outpace a Swiss pike phalanx. I looked around. There were no handgunners or bowmen that I could see, just hoards of pikes, and my mind was made up.

When I saw a larger gap than normal I went straight through it and continued down the hill, waiting for the shouted challenge to come.

But it didn't, and by the time I had gone thirty paces and risked a look back I could see nothing but vague forms in the swirling storm. I cast away the pike I had killed for and, unencumbered by equipment, I broke into a stumbling run and blundered down the hillside. In my haste and panic I overshot my mark, and had actually run some distance across the face of our troops when I realized it and turned towards them. I began yelling, 'Don't shoot! Friend!' as soon as I could make out figures, and when they saw that I was only one man they made no aggressive move. I was exhausted by my unaccustomed exercise, and at first could not make myself understood by the officer I encountered. 'Swiss,' I gasped. 'Swiss on the hill.'

'Yes,' he told me. 'That is why we are here.'

I shook my head desperately. 'Outflanked,' I told him. 'Up there.'

This disturbance in what had been a tranquil line attracted the attention of a couple of mounted officers, who came jingling over. One of them recognized me from the duke's tent, and I gasped my news out to him.

'You're sure, Mynheer?' he said, and then reached down and pulled me across the pommel of his saddle. 'Forgive the undignified position,' he said, 'but this news must reach my lord of Savoie with all speed.'

The ground behind the front line was flat and well trampled, and the horse sped across to where the duke had placed his cavalry, slightly behind the right flank. I slid to the ground in front of a lord I did not recognize, although he may well have been Jacques de Savoie. I did not notice his coat of arms, as I was too busy gesticulating and telling him what I had seen.

He was furious. 'I told the duke,' he said. 'I told him not to leave that wood unscouted and unreconnoitred. The man would not listen, and now look. We will pay for his folly with our lives.'

Then he realized that there were men-at-arms within earshot, and reined in his tongue. To give the man his due, he wasted no further time but turned his troop and began to advance up the hill. Even I knew that speed was essential: a unit of Swiss pikemen is a shambles and easily destroyed at any point before it is formed, but then it becomes a formidable weapon which is almost impossible to stop.

A second troop of knights appeared and while they disappeared into the driving snow, our captains began to pull the Burgundian line back to face the possible threat from the right. At that moment there was a blast on a horn, held for as long as the air in a man's lungs can last, followed by another and then another of the same length.

Then there followed that eerie silence that sometimes falls over battlefields, a perfect stillness that is begging to be broken, and each man strained his ears, and we looked at each other, our eyes on our companions but our minds, with our ears, higher up the hillside.

Then at last we heard the shouts of men and clashing of arms from up the hill. They were much nearer than I had anticipated. That meant that the Swiss had formed up and were advancing down the hillside – a bad sign for us.

And it proved. Soon riderless horses began to appear out of the snow, swerving their way around the men that stood in their path, but then beaten knights too began to appear and made no pretence of rallying but rode past to the rear. They streamed past in huge numbers, some batting aside men-at-arms in their haste to be away. From up the hill there were more horns and then loud cheers, and once again the silence fell.

We waited, and for a few minutes all was still except for the occasional shouted command coming faintly through the swirling air. 'They're dressing their ranks,' the nearest man to me said. 'We're next.'

Then our artillery opened up, far off to our left, and for a moment hope leapt into our hearts, but it was a false one. I learned later that the enemy had appeared out of the storm so close to the artillery that they had had no time to bring their pieces to bear, and a couple of shots loosed into the air, with the pieces too highly sighted to do any damage, was all that they could manage before the Swiss frontal advance overran and silenced them.

Then we heard the crunch of feet on snow, heard it before we could see them, but the sound was enough, and from all around me men began to melt away, until when I turned to see I was almost alone, not enough of a soldier to know that all was lost.

A knight came cantering out of the gloom, dragging his lance behind him, and seeing me directly in its path the horse halted. 'Help me, sir,' the knight said, and I took hold of the reins as he fell out of the saddle, over the beast's head and into my arms. I crumpled under his weight and the horse, affrighted, tried to run. One of the knight's feet was still in its stirrup, though, and the animal pulled us round in a circle. The knight died noisily, coughing a cloud of blood into my face. I averted my head, and as I lay on the ground, my head upside down, I saw the Swiss pikemen bearing down on me, in perfect step and with their weapons levelled before them. Apart from my dead knight, there was not a Burgundian in sight, and I closed my eyes and prayed for a swift end.

I heard the feet as they reached me, but the phalanx did not break step, and no one turned aside to finish me off. For a long minute they tramped past, and then there was a moment of peace before I was dragged from under the body by two pairs of hands and lifted to my feet. I looked at them – two Swiss. One of them dragged the lance from the knight's grasp, and I saw that it was not his lance at all but a pike that had wedged itself under his armour and been pulled out of the grasp of its owner. The two men handed it to me and said '*Gut, gut. Komm*' before continuing on their way and leaving me alone on the field. Once again being mistaken for Swiss had given me my life.

From where the cavalry troop had disappeared into the storm I could hear the screams of wounded horses and the groans of dying men, but the sound of marching came only from the other side, where the Burgundian army had once stood.

Of the Aftermath of Nancy

(5th to 8th January 1477)

By the time the Swiss had completed their two-pronged attack the Burgundian army was either cut down where it stood or thrown back in confusion. It was converted into a ragged collection of desperate fugitives, myself among them.

Most made their way across the hill at our rear and set off for the road to Nancy, but after what the officers had said at the council of war I knew that escape by that route was unlikely. I chose well, for the road was blocked by the traitor Campobasso and his men. I heard later that any wealthy fugitive was taken prisoner for ransom. Anyone else was killed, while those who tried to escape by crossing the river were either drowned or froze to death in the water. Bodies were floating past the Porte de la Craffe at Nancy weeks later.

I carried my pike for a few hundred paces to avert suspicion, but then threw it away and moved away to the north-west, at right angles to the direction in which the Swiss were driving the remnants of the duke's army.

Being thus behind the line of the advancing Swiss but heading away from them, I was able to avoid both the road and Nancy, which was just as well, as any fugitives who had escaped the attention of Campobasso were slaughtered by the peasants, who had no reason to love any man who had fought for Burgundy.

I lost all track of time and eventually, after perhaps three or four days, I found myself with a host of other fugitives outside a friendly town; I was not even sure which one it was, although I later found it was Metz.

We were huddled together in the moat, begging the watchmen on the wall to open the gates. Those who could show that they were knights and nobles were allowed access, but the rest of us were left to fend for ourselves, and as the night wore on more and more men froze and died where they lay. The cold had not abated. There was not a man who could say where my lord of Burgundy was, or even if he was alive.

The cold became worse in the early hours of the next morning, with a bitter frost, and more fugitives arrived to swell the numbers of the freezing and starving and, eventually, the dead.

Just before dawn two men appeared on the wall and began to shout questions down at us. It was difficult to hear what was being asked, because the moans of the crowd were so piteous, but I managed to catch some of one question, which was asking if anyone had seen the duke on the day of the battle.

'I saw him, sir,' I called. 'I saw him with my own eyes and spoke to him.' I rose to my feet, and around me the noise died down as his former troops waited to hear the fate of Charles.

'Was this before or after the battle?' the questioner shouted.

'Before, sir, only minutes before the Swiss swept the army away.'

Several other men came to the edge of the parapet and looked down at me. 'Where did you last see His Grace?'

'For pity's sake, I will answer all your questions if you but let me into the castle,' I said.

'We have no room in here for refugees,' one man answered,

holding up a torch which served to illuminate him better than it did the miserable frozen wretches below.

But it was enough; for by its flickering light and the grace of God I recognized his face. 'Mynheer Bay,' I said. 'You are Mathieu Bay.' It was the merchant who had hired my window to watch the duke's wedding procession.

That gave him pause. 'I am Bay,' he said. 'Do I know you?'

'Yes, sir, you do,' I called. 'You are Mynheer Bay, and I am Hans Memling. You sat in my house on the duke's wedding day, sir, and I painted your portrait.'

He turned and spoke urgently to the other men, and to my delight a squad was sent down to single me out from the crowd and take me into the quarters of the commander of the town, Lord Andrieu de Rineek.

I was given clothes and a warmed drink and made to tell my story. An Englishman was brought in to listen, the English ambassador to the court of Louis XI, and this man too was known to me – that same John Donne who had commissioned a triptych from me nearly ten years before, now Sir John, knighted by Ned himself on the battlefield of Tewkesbury, and much risen in the world. 'We think the duke is dead,' he told me. 'There is a page here who claims to have seen him fall, which is itself a wonder, for the whole army was running pell-mell from the field and no man taking note of anything beyond his own survival. None from the duke's entourage saw fit to return to verify his fate. It was an abject defeat.'

'It was indeed, sir,' I said. 'I know not if the duke be dead, but of his army there can be nothing left.'

'I am negotiating a truce,' Rineek told me. 'A small detail will go and collect His Grace's body, if it can be found. As you knew him well, you will make one of the party for identification purposes, along with his physician and the page who can locate where he fell. As an Englishman, Sir John is a neutral in all of this, and has graciously offered to lead the search. Rest tonight and tomorrow, and then I must ask you to return to Nancy.'

He made it sound like a penance. For two nights of sleep, warmth and wine I would have gone to Hell.

Of the Last Service

(mid-January 1477)

We followed the page along the path, where the grass was just beginning again to rise up after being thrust down by the retreating Burgundians and the Swiss pikemen following up hard on their heels, leaving dead men strewn across the landscape. 'The ditch begins here,' the boy said, pushing his way out of the forest onto a small plain with the towers of the city visible a short distance away. As in the forest, bodies littered the ground, stiff in the awkward attitudes of death, their faces and hands tinged faintly with blue. 'Somewhere along here,' the page said. 'I cannot be certain of where exactly.'

'Hmm,' grunted Sir John irascibly. 'It's always difficult to observe well when you're sprinting so hard in the opposite direction.'

'I was not alone,' the page said defensively. 'And anyway, no one could have stood against those Swiss. They came . . .'

'No matter,' Sir John said, turning away. 'Along here, you say?'

'Yes, sire.' The page skirted me and the Portuguese physician, Lope, who was clearly not a man used to the outdoors, especially in winter, and trotted up alongside the Englishman. 'He was wearing his silver-chased armour, sire, and the helm that he had as a gift from . . .'

Sir John spun sharply on his heel. 'Stop your prattling, you stupid boy,' he said angrily. 'Do you think to find the body of His Grace fully clothed a week after a battle? Do you not know what happens to a body left on a battlefield?'

'I did not think, sir.'

With another grunt, John turned back to the path and strode on. The frozen sedge crunched beneath our feet, our heels settling slightly into the light covering of snow and occasionally breaking through into the odd shallow puddle that lay beneath the thin ice. The number of bodies was greater the further we went, and suddenly the page pointed excitedly ahead to a small rise. 'There, sire,' he said. 'I think that was where His Grace fell.'

It was clear that there had been much fighting around that part of the battlefield. Everywhere we looked there were men, all without boots, most without even the tiniest of meagre shreds to cover their modesty. We began to quarter the rise, on the lookout for even the smallest clue.

Soon we had one. 'There are household troops here,' Sir John shouted over to me, and held up the remains of a blue and white halved surcoat. I raised a hand in acknowledgement and went on searching, moving from one body to another, turning them with the toe of a boot and staring into the faces of those that still had them, each frozen into a rictus that it would retain until the spring thaw or until the wolves removed it.

We found no trace of the duke on the hillock, and moved back, following the line of retreat down the slope and towards a narrow open space that ended where the forest began. Here again, the bodies were thicker on the ground, and there was evidence that they were in the main Burgundian. At the bottom of the incline was a ditch, perhaps four feet deep and five across, and this was so filled with bodies and gnarled parts of bodies that it was possible to cross over it by stepping on them.

Up and down its length we went, pulling, peering, wrestling one aside to look at the face of the man underneath him, wiping the rime frost away to get a better look. Going up one side of the ditch, I encountered the page coming down the other, and nodded at him. 'There's another ditch over there,' he said, encouraged by this recognition, 'fuller if anything than this one is. It might take us weeks.'

'Still has to be done,' I said. 'This isn't just any man we're looking for; it's a royal personage, and that means that there's protocol to be observed and rules to be followed.'

I looked across at the physician, who was taking no part in the search. His task was that of identification alone, he said, and he would do no more. I straightened up, my back beginning to hurt with so much stooping, and at that moment Sir John called out: 'Mynheer Memling!'

He was about twenty paces away, bent over a body, and he beckoned urgently.

I trudged through the frozen tussocks, almost tripped, then regained my balance and advanced on him a little faster than was comfortable. He stretched out an arm and fended me off, and then used it to right me and help me become steady.

'What do you think?' he asked.

I followed his gaze downwards.

It had been a man once, of course, but was no longer. It was the body of a man in his middle forties, with the beginnings of corpulence about what there was left of him. He had been wounded a number of times, it appeared, once on the temple, a wound which stretched across his face and then along his throat under the jawline to the left of his head, and the other times in the bowels, from which two broken spears still projected.

The page came up beside me and looked, and I saw him turn pale. 'Stand back,' I said to him, not anxious to do what had to be done through a film of vomit, and pushed him away.

The physician sauntered over and looked down dispassionately.

'Is it the duke?' Sir John asked.

Lope shrugged. 'It could be,' he said. 'It is impossible to be sure. It's as likely him as anyone.'

'Can't you examine him to find out, man?'

The doctor thrust out his lower lip. 'The man has no face,' he pointed out, 'nor anything else to identify him. What can I tell you?'

It was easy to see his point. After the man had been stripped, but before he froze, and for his sake I hope God had been merciful enough to ensure that it was after he was dead, the animals had feasted. You could see where they had ripped and torn at the body. The flesh of the belly had been stripped away, the wolves gorging themselves on the soft inner organs and those vital ones which are carried outside the body. From his chest cavity downwards there was a gaping hole. Heart, liver, lungs, kidneys and genitals had all gone, and the ground around the body was frozen a deep, marbled red. At the tops of his thighs there were bite marks, as if later animals had tried to take chunks of the frozen meat away after the early arrivals had eaten their fill. There was nothing to learn there of who he had been.

The eyes were gone, as they always do in these sad circumstances, but so had everything else. The throat wound had given the beasts the access they needed to the soft tissue in that area, and they had burrowed and pulled, torn and dug until the skin had been ripped away from the face – cheeks and lips had been gnawed, and the ears had disappeared completely. There was still some hair attached to the scalp, but that was the only thing by which the body might have been recognized.

'I think this is His Grace,' Sir John said. 'Right hair colour, right age, right build, and cleft through helm and head, as they said. What do you think?'

'It could be,' I said, 'but it's difficult to be sure.' I bent and forced myself to look more closely, and then straightened up. 'It could be him . . .' I repeated, but left the rest of the sentence uncompleted.

'He had no distinguishing marks,' Sir John said.

'Wait.' I dropped to one knee and tried to roll the body, but it was frozen into the ground. I grasped one of the arms and pulled, and it moved a few inches away from the body. I had to put my foot into the elbow in order to get the arm to bend, and it resisted before giving with a crack.

'I've broken his arm,' I said to the Englishman unnecessarily. 'I'm sorry.'

'No matter,' he said. 'He can't feel it now.'

The other arm was frozen into a more convenient position, and I was able to look at what I wanted to see simply by bending close and peering. When I had seen all that was necessary I got back to my feet and wiped the mud from my knees.

'Well?'

'I think this is His Grace,' I said.

'Why?'

'He had very distinctive fingers,' I told him. 'Long and supple and always well manicured. Like this man's.'

'Hardly convincing, though. So did many men.'

'The duke also had a habit of gnawing at the nail of his left thumb,' I said. 'No other finger – just the left thumb. I have often observed him doing it in times of stress.' I pointed downwards. 'This man's thumbnail has been gnawed almost to the quick. Not unusual in itself, but when added to the evidence of the wounds, the hands and the general resemblance that you yourself have noted, I think it's fairly conclusive. Add to that his location and the fact that he has been completely stripped, which suggests fine clothes, and I think we have a strong case.'

'I think you're right,' the knight said, and then suddenly took command in that way that nobles have, confident in who they are and what they are worth. 'You will stay here with me. The page and this useless lump will go back and return with the coffin detail, and then we will take His Grace back to Bruges.'

The page went off to do his bidding, the physician trailing glumly behind, and Sir John and I bent to the task of removing the duke's body from the ground. By rocking it we were able to loosen the grip of the frozen earth, and each effort shifted the body a little more, so that before long we were able to release it completely. We lifted the duke clear of the ground and placed him so that the coffin party would be able to manoeuvre him. By the time we had finished I could hear them trudging through the fringes of the wood.

'Hallo, what's this?' Sir John said behind me.

Frozen into the ground in the dip from which we had removed the duke's body was a smashed silver frame with a long chain attached. The looters must have missed it in their haste. From it had fallen a piece of polished wood about the size of a man's palm, with a crumpled scrap of paper still partly attached. Sir John picked up the frame and I the wood.

'What is it?' he asked.

I smoothed out the paper and looked at a charcoal drawing of the face of a little girl. 'Confirmation,' I told him. 'This is the duke.'

*

It was a melancholy journey, that trek from the battlefield to the city of Nancy. We made solemn procession the whole way so that the church was ready to receive him. Each night that he lay in state four of us were told off to stand vigil around his bier; there was never any shortage of volunteers.

For five days we stood guard while the news was taken to his wife and daughter and they waited for their last sight of their lord on this earth.

Even that was to be denied them, though – we all knew that it would be the case, and the victorious Duke of Lorraine ensured that they would not have to face it. We washed what was left of the body in clean water and wine, but after it had thawed it began to stink, so it was wrapped in lead which had been taken from a church roof and beaten out thin, and then the coffin was sealed. Charles the Bold was buried with the ducal dead before the high altar of the church of St George in Nancy.

Of the Work of the Painter

Think what it is that we do, we painters.
        Ponder on it.

We deal in the creation of that which is not. What we make is a fiction, which may contain within itself a truth. We are the manufacturers of counterfeits; masterly ones, sometimes, which can cause the viewer to say 'That is she, to the very life' or even move him to tears. A painting is a subtle deception that lies like truth.

To paint is to feign; it is to make an artifice. We colour our pictures in the sense that we colour a story; to put it bluntly, we lie.

We present in two dimensions that which exists in three, and yet we force the viewer to 'see' their three dimensions in our two. All is lies, all is artifice, all is fake; and yet the viewer sees all as true. Strange, is it not?

It is all a matter of technique, of fooling the eye, of turning the falsehood into something truer than truth.

The stock-in-trade of a painter is trickery, so you must be warned. Do not believe any thing that a painter tells you.

Especially when he swears that it is the truth.

Of the Suit of
Milord of Clarence

(March 1477)

'Think not that I am the thing that I was,' Marie said loudly as she swept through the door. 'I am no longer the daughter of the Duke of Burgundy – I am myself Burgundy. I am a prince in my own right, and I make decisions in my own interests, not Louis's or Edward's or anyone else's. I am happy for you to advise me, my lady, but you will not presume to dictate to me.'

Behind her trooped the dowager duchess, my lady Margaret, and an entourage of courtiers and servants. I rose to my feet. I had not expected to see so many people.

'Leave us, Mynheer Memling,' my lady Margaret told me. 'Your services will not be required today.'

Obediently I began to pack up my things, but Marie's voice stayed me. 'I have called you here, Hans, and it is God's work you do, so pray stay.'

I was in Ghent, where the new duchess was staying (reluctantly, it has to be said) as the guest of the city fathers. I went to the palace to catch a likeness of her for a nativity piece for Mynheer van der Straaten, for which once again the duke had insisted that the Madonna be represented by his daughter. She no longer needed to be advertised, of course, but Charles had owed the man a large sum of money, and this was one way of paying part of it off.

After his death I had offered to use some other model, but she would not hear of it. 'If it was my father's wish,' she said, 'then it is mine too. I shall sit for you.'

She repeated those words to me again now. 'I shall sit for you, Hans, and no man' – and here she flashed a venomous look at her stepmother – 'or woman, shall gainsay me.'

'Surely,' Margaret said, 'affairs of state should take precedence over such frivolity?'

'Frivolity? You call an inspirational painting, a gift of love for God's church, a frivolity?' Before the dowager could reply, Marie went on, 'If there is any frivolity in this room it is in the minds of those who wish to marry me off to a toad.' She moved to the chair I had set up and sat in it. Then, more composed, she said, 'No doubt affairs of state will demand our attention in due course, so there may not be many more occasions left to us to sit for Mynheer Memling.' Then her temper overcame her again and she turned to her stepmother and shouted, 'And if some have their way we fear we will soon no longer be qualified to represent the Virgin. Therefore leave us.'

Margaret stood for a second, furious, but then turned and swept out, the courtiers trailing behind her. Marie sat glowering, and then looked at me. 'What do you think, Hans? Was I impressive?'

'You blazed like a comet in the night sky, my lady,' I told her, 'both brilliant and furious, beautiful and dangerous, close to us and yet unattainable in your glory.'

'You are fawningly honey-tongued today, Hans,' she said, and then smiled, enjoying the compliment. 'But what is this "my lady"?'

'Marie,' I said softly, and she gave me her hand to kiss.

'It is worse now than before my father's death,' she said. 'Now that I am duke there is no one who will call me by name.

Everyone is so formal; I have no name, just a title. I am become Burgundy.' She paused, and then said softly, 'There is only you left, Hans, to call me Marie. Until I marry, anyway.'

'It would surely be the best solution for you,' I said.

'Hans, your business is painting, and I do not presume to advise you on how best to go about it.' I raised my head, and she must have seen my eyes, for she went on, 'I'm sorry. That was the duke speaking, not Marie. I know I have to marry. But I am going to choose for myself, and it's certainly not going to be that slimy English duke whose alleged excellent qualities my stepmother has been touting.'

'English duke? Not the Austrian prince?'

'No. Clarence, the King of England's brother. Yet again he dares advance his suit. And he's my stepmother's brother too, of course. What sort of man is he? He has three times risen in rebellion against his brother the king. He plots against both his brothers, he sided with Louis against both his own brother and my father, and he has been a widower no more than a few weeks. He is charming on the surface, but as slippery as a greased pig, and his temperament is like him, unreliable in the extreme. He is an unstable man, and untrustworthy, and greedy as a gannet. I could not in all conscience put Burgundy into his hands. On top of that the King of England insults me, too.'

'Edward? How?'

'In suggesting that instead of Clarence I might want to marry his wife's brother, Rivers, a lowborn upstart of no pedigree.'

'You would not hold a man's birth against him?'

'Not as a friend or an advisor, no, but I could not take such a man as a husband, not if I wanted to keep Burgundy free of France. The country would be a laughing stock if I did such a thing. I would be forced to abdicate. Already I will have to make great concessions if I am to retain my power.'

I moved some paint around, almost aimlessly.

'Will you lose power?' I asked.

'Most certainly, unless I make a brilliant marriage.'

I could feel misery flooding into me, like a misapplied pigment into a well in the support. I stopped in surprise, with the sudden realization not only that something was wrong, but that I knew what that something was, and that in addition I had the cure to it, if only I could snatch the opportunity. 'If you do not make the brilliant marriage . . .' I began, and she finished the sentence for me.

'Then I might as well be dead, for I would be lower than the lowest of my own subjects, and with as much value. Less, in fact, for I am trained to nothing, and I would have no value in the marriage market.'

'Except,' I said, placing my brush on the easel, 'to he who truly loves you – loves you not because you are a princess but because you are a beautiful and spirited woman, and loves you for yourself and not for the power you can bring to him.'

'Oh, Hans, could I but find such a man,' she said.

I took her hand. 'Marie,' I said, 'there is such a man, and he stands before you, ready to be yours in every way, no matter what the future may hold.'

'You have always been my man, Hans, and a most faithful one,' she said, 'and I thank you for it.'

I fell to one knee and took her hands in mine. 'Then marry me, Marie,' I said.

She was silent. She cast her eyes downwards. 'Hans,' she said at length. 'To marry a man of ability and genius like yourself is a thing that I wish for so devoutly, and so humbly. Your offer is as flattering as it is surprising to one of no skills and little prospect.'

I felt the elation surge in me. 'It is all I have ever wanted,' I said, 'everything I have ever hoped for. Marie, I shall make you so happy that you will forget that you ever were anything other than the wife of a painter, and you shall never pine for your former status while I live.'

She shook her head. Softly, she slipped her hands out of mine. 'You misunderstand me, Hans,' she said. 'If I were Marie and only Marie, then I might be able to accept your offer, but I am not Marie, and never will be again. I told you – we are become Burgundy, and are thus in no position to negotiate marriage with any man other than our peers. It is not to be spoken of ever again, Hans. In any case, my mind is made up. I shall marry Maximilian, who can take care of me personally, but more, who will defend my realms against their enemies, having as he does the forces of the emperor at his disposal.'

'But you do not love him,' I protested.

'Hans may love Marie,' she said, 'and Marie may not love Maximilian, but when Burgundy marries Austria love is a minor consideration; my duty now is to Burgundy, not to myself or to anyone else who may love me, Marie, as opposed to me, Burgundy. And, indeed, as for Maximilian, it is not impossible that I shall grow to love him, and even he to love me, in time.'

'Marie,' I protested.

'No, Hans. I forbid you to speak of it again.'

The elation was replaced by confusion. 'You said you could marry a painter,' I said, and even I could hear the fear in my voice turning into a whine. 'You have given me so much reason to hope. You kissed me – you told me to call you Marie, and that I was the only one to do so.' I reached again for her hand, but she pulled it back and stepped away from me.

'Marie,' I said again.

'"Your Grace" it shall be henceforth,' she said, her voice

turning cold. 'We are sorry if we gave you the wrong impression, Mynheer Memling. We meant nothing by it. We neither thought nor intended that you would take our childish ways so seriously.'

'But, Marie . . .' I protested. 'You gave me such hope . . .'

'Will you be silent?' she snapped. 'Have we not made ourself clear enough, Mynheer? Surely you cannot have failed to understand?'

I made some gesture, I remember, my hands reaching out to her.

'You practically told me of your love for me,' I said.

'What? When and how did I say such a thing?'

'In Bruges,' I said, remembering our conversation. 'You told me you were in love with a man you could not marry, a foreigner, an older man, one of no estate but with good hopes for the future, and well known to me. Then when I guessed you confirmed that I was right. Our "silent secret" you called it.'

'You thought I meant you?' she said, incredulous, and then she laughed in my face. This was not the shared laughter of friends, but the laughter of contempt or of mockery. 'Oh, Hans, you are a fool. The man I meant was the Englishman, Richard of Gloucester, and I could not marry him because he was in love with Anne Neville, who is now his wife.' She shook her head and then she must have seen my feelings in my face. There was a moment of coldness, and then she drew herself up. Her voice had changed perceptibly when she spoke again. 'Be aware that the royal house of Burgundy does not ally itself with master painters,' she said. 'Your offer is absurd, Mynheer Memling, and is as far beneath our consideration as your station is beneath our own. You presume too far even to think of us in that way. Henceforward, you will not presume to enter our presence unless we specifically send for you.' She stepped back, for the first time putting an unbridgeable gap between us. 'You have our permission to go.'

Of Divers Matters Concerning
My Lady and Myself

(August 1477 to February 1482)

She married Maximilian in the August of that year of 1477, and never sent for me or spoke to me again in the meantime.

Maximilian's erstwhile rival Clarence was already dead, having offended his brother Ned once too often, and he had been executed in London, thereby ruining his chances of becoming either Duke of Burgundy, King of England or anything else that he might have been drawn to.

I was cast down, and cast out. No one knew why I had suddenly lost my royal favour, but the mere fact was enough, and my studio began to languish from lack of custom; I was no longer fashionable, a fact which I laid at the princess's door.

The princess herself had little time for anything other than her new husband and his devices to maintain Burgundy's independence, and in her turn was forced into compliance with various demands by her cities, and then she fell pregnant. A son, Philip, named for her grandfather, was born the following year.

Against all the odds, it seemed that it became a love match, and a little girl, Margaret, followed soon after.

*

There was no longer any need to advertise the charms of the princess, as the original object of a suitable marriage had been accomplished, but old custom dies hard, and I found that I could not prevent my madonnas taking on her form. For five more years she haunted my paintings and my dreams and intruded into them both. Her face was everywhere. I even played with her image and painted her as St Wilgefort with a beard and as the reformed prostitute St Mary of Egypt in a triptych which I did for Adriaan Reins to commemorate his induction into the Order of St John's Hospital. If she saw, or knew of my lese-majeste she gave no sign and she took no action against me, although I recall some tutting from the burghers and their wives when it went on display in the hospital.

That proved to be my last religious commission for some time. With no patrons, I made a virtue of necessity and swore off religious paintings altogether.

I also took the advice of St Paul and married a small, perfectly spherical dumpling of a young woman half my age who proceeded to drop children at the rate of one per year until I called a halt after three boys. Tanne was a pleasant, bland, undemanding girl who filled my belly and bed with equal gusto. I miss her. She died of a fever not long after Claykin was born.

Although the princess and I no longer had any contact with each other, I was not kept frozen out for ever. As part of his introduction to his new territories Maximilian held a number of receptions to which members of different guilds or fraternities were invited, and at that which included the members of Our Lady of the Snow I met him for the first time. I was surprised to find that he spoke not a word of either French or Hollandish, and became his interpreter for the day. He was a pleasant, cultured man with many intellectual interests and, it turned out, an eye for a painting. Despite his grotesque appearance (his jaw proved to be every bit as huge as Marie had described) he was an excellent companion. He made a point of coming to see my studio soon after and then asked me to the palace. Within a short time I became a member of his circle, although I was never as intimate with him as I had been with Duke Charles. Truth to tell, I think he cultivated me largely because I was one of the few people he knew in the Burgundian lands who could speak his language.

Gradually, as the duke had done, he began to include me in matters of the court. He knew that I had painted his wife many times, of course, but knew nothing further of our former feelings for each other, and neither she nor I was inclined to enlighten him. More and more, therefore, I found myself invited on outings or to court events.

The duchess was at first more than cool towards me, but when I made it clear by my demeanour that I accepted without question our relative positions, she relaxed and began to tolerate my presence. It was, I think, not until the third year of her marriage, when she was big with her second child, that she spoke to me, and then it was a mere acknowledgement of my presence in a room she entered. I could not bring myself either to look at her or to talk to her, so I avoided her when possible. She may have forgiven me, but I did not have to do the same.

Nonetheless, slowly my stock began to rise again. My relationship with Maximilian prised open doors that had not been fully ajar for some time, and I was besieged by fashionable young men, many from the Italian banking community, who would give me any amount of money for a portrait.

Once again I had the Medici bankers to thank for much of this; Tommaso Portinari sent his two nephews, Folco and

Benedetto Portinari, to me to have their portraits painted, and they were followed by every young blade in town. The Portinaris paid for an old-fashioned plain background for their matching portraits, but subsequent subjects were not to be outdone. At first the fashion was for background landscapes glimpsed through pillars or from a loggia, and then nothing would do but a full landscape behind the figure. Before long each young man went a little further, and some personal attribute was added to each – a letter, perhaps, to denote his importance in business, or a rosary or breviary to show his piety. One man, I remember, had me paint him with a palm tree in the background, a laurel leaf to the fore and a coin of the Roman emperor Nero in his hand to identify him for future generations; his name was Lorenzo Nero Palmieri.

Despite all, they were years that were good to me, those few while Maximilian and Marie reigned in Burgundy.

Of the Sadness
Concerning My Lady

(March 1482)

I do not see the pleasure in hawking, and never have done, despite the many times I have hunted in this fashion. To deliberately set a large, fast bird of prey against a smaller, slower, defenceless one strikes me as cruel in the extreme, but sometimes we must damp down our own feelings and indulge those of our betters – at least if we wish to continue working and painting. Maximilian lived for the hunt, and perforce dragged Marie and the court with him whenever he could. Even when he was out of the country administering his other territories the chase had to go on, and if summoned, one had to attend.

This, and no other, was the reason why I happened to be one of the party that went out to the forest of Winendaele at the beginning of March in the year of Our Lord 1482. All Burgundians had been breathing more easily since the previous November, when Louis XI had suffered an apoplexy at Chinon. For the moment, his pursuit of Princess Marie and coveting of the lands of Burgundy had relented, and the prospect of his imminent death and a permanent end to the persecution made the future a lot rosier.

With Maximilian away in Vienna, Marie was bored, and one of the courtiers had the bright idea of organizing a heron hunt in the forest. Never mind that it was freezing, never mind that the princess was pregnant, never mind that the ride to and from the forest was through the least interesting part of these lands – in spite of all of this, a-hunting we would go. We could have stayed home and had music or dancing, or just drunk lots of mulled wine, but no, we were summoned to attend upon Her Grace. I went with some resentment, as I was preoccupied, surrounded as I was with half-finished portraits of young Italian blades. All the same, one does not ignore a ducal invitation, even if one suspects it was sent in error.

Of course the princess threw herself into the chase wholeheartedly, as she did with any activity she took up. Her falcon on her wrist, she hurtled through the morning, launching attack after attack upon the heron, and fussing over her bird when it came back as if it had done something extraordinary, like delivering a sermon in Spanish or something.

At about midday a meal was announced. Fires had been lit at the edge of the forest, and the cooks had been busy since early grilling meat, baking bread in portable ovens, and warming up wine mixed with herbs and brandy so that those of us who were starved cold could regain some semblance of life.

The party all dismounted to prepare, but Marie was exultant, pink in the face and beaming with the exertions of the morning, and she decided to keep her seat in the saddle until all was ready. The other horses were led away so that their sweat and noise did not disturb the royal party, and the scent of roasting meat wafted around the site, almost, but not quite, as pleasing to me as the respite from bashing my backside against a saddle for hours on end.

Naturally I had been bringing up the rear of the cavalcade, resentful at being kept from my brushes and easel and muttering to myself, not for the first time, that hunting was literally a pain in the arse. I reached the site just as the princess began to move away. She had seen a pair of heron on the outskirts of the forest, I think, and was idling her horse over to get a better look. The food was almost ready, and I walked my horse up behind hers.

'Perhaps you had better not wander too far, my lady,' one of the courtiers hinted. 'They will begin serving as soon as you wish it.'

She looked round to see who was speaking, and then turned away again. 'They can wait a moment or two longer; it won't kill them,' she said dismissively, and then returned to scanning the horizon. Suddenly she craned forward and said excitedly, 'Can you see those two . . . ?'

At that moment the heron took off, flapping into the air, and she could restrain herself no longer. She flung her hawk into the air and set off for the forest, determined to see her bird bring down its prey.

The movement of her horse excited mine, and I tried to bring it under control, but it was anxious to join in the chase. I realized too that no other courtiers were ready to go with the princess. I was the only one mounted, and all the other horses were perhaps a hundred yards away to the rear. Someone had to chaperone her, so I gave my horse its head and spurred after her. She was perhaps a furlong ahead of me, and a much more accomplished rider than I, so I was in great danger of losing her.

She followed the path into the forest, and I saw that right where the deepest part began a fallen tree was lying across the way. Instead of going round it, she urged her horse into a prodigious leap and took the tree in her stride. As the horse landed I distinctly saw her saddle lurch forwards, as if the girths were loose, and she began to sway dangerously.

I took the more secure way, veering round to avoid having to jump the tree, but I still had her in sight as she entered the forest. It was clear though that the saddle was dangerously loose, and she was having a great deal of difficulty staying on the horse's back. She was heaving on the reins, but the horse was not responding. She turned to the left, following the path. Within a few seconds she had vanished from sight.

Just as I entered the forest I risked a look around; none of the rest of the party were yet mounted – I alone could reach her. I rode as fast as I dared along the forest path, but there was no sign of her mount or its rider. Then, a short distance after I had passed the place where I had seen her disappear, I saw her horse's head, apparently on the ground. As I approached I realized that the beast was standing in the dry bed of a stream.

An icy hand gripped my heart, and I slowed my mount to a walk. She was in the stream bed some way off the path, lying flat on her back with her arms outstretched. I dismounted with some difficulty, and my horse moved away and was soon lost in the trees as I jumped down from the bank into the stream bed.

I dropped to my knees, and saw that she breathed yet. There was matted blood in her hair and on the ground from a wound in her back.

Along the path I could hear the sound of voices, and hooves drumming, and the approach of courtiers, too late. I rose and called to them, although I could not see them nor they me: 'Here! Here! My lady is grievously hurt! She has been thrown.'

They forced their way through the bushes, the first few leaping one by one into the dry bed. One of them went to collect her horse. Each tongue was stilled as her people crowded onto the bank and saw, those at the rear peering through the throng to get a glimpse, some kneeling on the edge, and every face appalled.

They made a litter out of what would have been her eating cloth, and took her up alive and gently bore her out of the forest and into the care of the holy sisters. One of the better riders rode ahead to warn the nuns to expect a patient, and the sisterhood were ready when we arrived. They took the princess through the gate and then all of us, men and women, nobles and commoners alike, were told to go home and pray, and the great gates clanged shut.

Of Happy Tidings

(March 1482)

'God be praised, Mynheer Memling,' the old woman cried as I opened the window and threw the first piss of the day onto the cobbles. She capered nimbly enough out of the way, given her age, and I drew back my hand with the chamberpot in it.

'Indeed so, Dame Heylie,' I answered automatically, and waited for her to move on so that she would not get splashed when the remnants came down.

'Have you just risen, sir? Do you not know the glorious tidings?'

'Indeed I have, and I do not,' I told her. I got as far as 'What tidings . . . ?' when it struck me what she must mean. 'The princess . . . ?'

'The same, sir. I have just come from the fish market; to be sure you must get there right early for the freshest, or they shall all be gone, and nothing left but yesterday's . . .'

'The princess,' I said curtly. 'What news of the princess?'

'That she did wake, sir, in the night, and called for water, and did remain awake some hours before falling into a most peaceful sleep. God be praised, sir, that she is restored to us.'

'God be praised indeed, dame,' I said. 'Such good news deserves recompense. Wait till I come down.' I made my way down through the workshop and out into the street, still in my nightshift, and gave her a few coins.

'Take these for tomorrow's fish,' I told her.

'No, sir, I cannot take it. No one expects a reward for gossiping.'

'In the ancient legends of Greece and Rome,' I told her, 'a messenger bringing glad tidings was always rewarded, and it was bad luck on the house if he refused to take the recompense, so you would be doing me a great favour by all the pagan gods if you would but accept this small token of my gratitude.'

'What it is to have learning, sir,' she said, and then added unsurely, 'pagan gods, though . . .'

'Our Christian God would never begrudge a poor woman a few pennies,' I said. 'Remember the widow's mite.'

She had no idea what I was talking about, of course, but agreed, saying, 'To be sure, sir, the widow's mite,' and secreted the money somewhere in the capacious folds of her garments.

'So. What else can you tell me?'

'Well, Dame Herzog is delivered of a fine boy . . .'

'I mean of the princess,' I said, perhaps too sharply, for she drew back a little and looked at me warily.

'Truly nothing, sir, except that there will be a mass at Sint Salvator's this day to thank the Lord for her safe delivery. You must go into the town to find out more.'

'And be assured that I shall,' I told her, and stepped back into the house to complete my toilet and make myself decent, for of a surety I had never expected to look upon her face again in this world.

Later that morning there was a joyous peal of bells to celebrate the survival of the princess, and the people began to gather outside the béguinage to hear if there was any further news.

The great ones were going back and forth, and each that entered or left was greeted with cheers and applause, no matter how popular or otherwise he had been at other times. The bells stopped their ringing after an hour or so, apparently in order not to tire the princess, and the crowd became more serious, standing in silence. At midday I found an inn where I enjoyed a meat coffin and a flagon of ale, though in truth I had little appetite, and then determined to see if there was any news, and if not to return to my work.

I was wending my way back along a narrow street when the call came to make way for some nobleman. I pressed back against the wall, but there was barely room for the horse. I pressed further, and then looked up into the face of the rider.

'Hans?' he said.

It was Maximilian. 'My lord,' I said, and waited to hear what he had to say.

'Take my stirrup,' he said. 'Come.'

I hesitated, but then did as I was bid and the horse half carried me towards the béguinage. 'Is it true, my lord?' I asked. 'Has my lady recovered consciousness?'

'She has indeed, the Lord be praised,' Maximilian said. 'She has been asking for you. You were there when she fell, she says.'

'Yes, my lord.'

'She cannot recall much else. It was a fierce blow.'

For a few moments I could not find my breath, but at last we reached the convent and I released his stirrup and helped him down. 'Come with me, then,' he said, 'and you shall surely see her, if the good sisters will allow it. They are ferocious women, Hans, and a bar even to royal husbands at times.'

It was clear from his good humour that the princess was truly recovering, and I asked him no questions as we strode along the corridor. The sisters made no demur at my presence, and we went into the room where she lay. She was in a huge bed, her face as pale as the best linen, and with her head heavily bandaged. Despite her obvious frailty, she made a frantic attempt to rise as her husband came in, but only her head moved, and that soon fell back on the pillows. 'You must not attempt to move, my sweetness,' he said. 'Your recovery has still a long way to go before it is full. I met Hans on his way here.'

Her smile was once again as warm as it had ever been, but she made no move towards me. I must have hesitated, for she said, 'I am unable to greet you, Hans. My body will not yet obey my will. The doctors say that the bruising is too severe. It will take much time.' She smiled across at Maximilian. 'You followed me, Hans, to save me, did you not?' she said. 'Thus much I remember.'

'I did, my lady.'

'Thereafter I remember nothing,' she said.

'Your Grace must not . . .'

'Who am I, Hans?' she asked, and when I realized what she wanted of me I found tears springing all unbidden to my eyes.

'You are Marie,' I told her, and was rewarded with another smile.

'Thank you for your help, Hans,' she said, and her voice was fading into a whisper. 'You are a true friend.' Again I felt the tears pricking my eyes at her innocent words.

One of the sisters decided that the duchess could take no more of my presence, and I was ushered outside with promises that when my lady was stronger she would no doubt call for me again, but until such time I was not welcome, this all delivered sotto voce as I was marched to the door.

I waited outside for Maximilian, and when he came out some

half an hour later he drew me to one side. 'I must add my thanks to those of my wife,' he said.

'Sir, I did but follow her, as any servant would do.'

'And had you not done so and thus provided a trail for the rest, my wife might not have been found for days. No, Hans, we owe you more than you know, and more than we can ever repay.'

I was much troubled by his words, but said only, 'My lady's recovery is the only recompense I could ever ask.'

He nodded, his thoughts somewhere else. 'She is not yet well, Hans, and there are more wounds than men know of.' He lowered his voice and said, 'Our child is no more. She miscarried him in the night following the fall.'

'I am sorry, my lord.'

He squeezed my arm. 'I shall supply you with a warrant,' he said, 'so that you can enter the convent as you wish.' He smiled. 'Although I cannot of course guarantee that the sisters will allow you to see Marie. Come, I shall escort you out. I must return to matters of state. Louis does not stop his scheming just because neither he nor Marie is well.'

Outside I was recognized and delayed some time on the bridge, telling those gathered there what I had seen of the duchess and how she had been.

She was not well, for all that. The news the next day was that she was troubled with a pain in her bowel, and only Maximilian and the children were admitted to her chamber. The day after that only Maximilian himself was allowed entry, and when he left his drawn and hollow face betrayed his strain.

The days turned into weeks, and there was no improvement. I had not been allowed into the bedchamber a second time, and had to glean what information I could from those of the servants who recognized me. The duchess, they told me, was in constant pain, and none of the doctors' physics were effective. The faces in and around the béguinage became more sombre as the people waited, and spirits drooped when the news got no better.

Of Unwelcome Tidings

(March 1482)

By the last week in March it was clear that matters were more serious than anyone had suspected. Public prayers were ordered in all the churches of Bruges, and the Blessed Sacrament was processed through the streets, all of the prayers of the populace being offered to God for the recovery of our lady.

Towards the end of the month I was crossing the Markt on the way to the béguinage when I encountered a procession of priests moving slowly from the Chapel of the Holy Blood, bearing the relic in its shrine. I stood, head bowed, as they passed, and then asked a bystander what was happening.

'The duchess has asked for the Blood of Christ to be laid upon her person,' he said, 'that it may work a miraculous cure.'

I hurried after the priests and joined the back of the procession. We were admitted to the béguinage – no one asked me if I was a cleric or not – and then the bedchamber.

I could see immediately that she was worse. Pale though she had been before, she was much paler now, and lay back exhausted on the pillows. The bandages covered less of her head than before, but her body beneath the sheets appeared to have shrunk. The fingers which held her rosary beads were like small peeled sticks, and they moved not as the prayers were intoned. Her eyes were closed, with heavy black semicircles beneath them as if drawn by the finest charcoal, but her lips moved as she repeated the Ave Marias along with the sister who was leading the prayers.

Maximilian knelt at the side of the bed, his head bowed.

At the end of the last of the mysteries the sister cleared the room of all non-clerics except for Maximilian, but as I had entered the room with the priests she did not give me a second glance, and I remained where I was, wedged in a corner.

The old priest who had carried the reliquary bore it to the four corners of the bed, intoning prayers in Latin that was too fast for me to follow, and then placed it on a chest at the foot of the bed and opened it. Everyone in the room knelt as the Holy Blood was produced. In a small phial of clear rock crystal encased in a filigree golden container was the Blood itself, just visible now as a crystallized solid, mainly clear but flecked here and there with hints of black and brown amid the coagulation. The priest solemnly wiped the phial with a white cloth and then approached the bed.

'Your Grace,' he said softly.

She opened her eyes at once, fully alert, although the pain in them was clear.

'The Blood of Our Saviour,' he whispered. He held the phial out to her, and when she made no move Maximilian took her hands in his and put the phial into them. The priest's hands were hovering anxiously around in case of a slip, but her husband's grip was firm. Maximilian moved the relic first to her lips, allowing her to kiss it gently, and then lowered her hands until the phial was resting on her abdomen. Still the abbot remained ready to grasp at it, but Maximilian's hands were steady. He moved them from beneath the Blood and rested both of his wife's on top of it.

Then I saw her face clench, as she tried to press the Blood into her stomach as if to drive the phial through her skin and into the area of pain, but there was no corresponding movement of her hands, and her husband reached over and pressed his hands on hers. Through her pain I heard her say, '*In nomine domini Jesu Christi, custodiat animam meam in vitam aeternam.*'

We all joined in the 'Amen' and then she whispered to Maximilian, who moved the phial slightly to the left, and again pressed. She repeated her words, and once again we repeated the response.

This went on for some time, with the slightest movement of the relic to a new site, sometimes no more than a finger's breadth away and a repetition first of the clenching of the face, the pressing and then of the prayer. Her pain was so obvious that I am sure that I was not the only one in the room who imagined that he could feel it himself, and I am equally sure that I was not the only man who wished that the pain might pass from her and come into him.

While she was engaged in this, another of the priests stepped forward with another reliquary, repeated the prayers at the four corners of the bed and then opened the box, unpacking a number of slender objects covered in silver. I recognized these as the bones of St Donatian, brought from his church, and after saying a few words over them he distributed them around Marie's person, tucking some in under her torso and legs and placing others on her pillow.

Finally Maximilian delivered the Holy Blood back to the abbot, who raised the princess gently in the bed and touched the reliquary to the back of her head. This done, he placed the phial in her hands once again, and she lay back, still praying, the Blood resting on her bosom, clutched in hands which could not feel its weight. Her tongue crept out of her mouth, and instantly Maximilian leaned forward with a cup of water, wetting her lips.

As he set the cup down on the table, he caught my eye and, pausing, nodded. His eyes too were dark with new circles. Then he turned back to his wife. As he did so she drew a heavy breath, and a stifled cry escaped her. Her body convulsed involuntarily, and there was some movement of her legs. Then she relaxed again and whispered something to her husband.

In his turn he turned to the sister and she inclined her head and hurried out.

The priest finally allowed his fingers to take hold of the Blood and Marie gave it up. He whispered something to her and we all heard her reply as she pushed her head up from the pillows – 'Not yet. Not until the little ones have been.' Then she lay back again.

It was the children that had been sent for. Philip walked in, his eyes wide and frightened, but his sister was fast asleep. The nurse put her in her mother's arms and the boy climbed up onto the bed and put his arms round his mother, disturbing some of the relics as he did so. The priest who had brought them immediately began to gather them up, and the boy took advantage of the extra space to get closer to his mother. She lay there, her lips moving softly as she spoke to him, her fingers lying limply among the curls of the sleeping girl.

We all stood in silence, the only sound the faint brushing of the priest's robes as he placed the silver-clad bones in their reliquary. Then from the princess came a shuddering breath. Maximilian signalled to the nurse, and the children were quietly removed from their mother's grasp, the girl still sleeping, the little boy barely able to keep his eyes open.

The old priest began to pray, and I realized with a start that he was giving her the last rites. Now Maximilian began to sob, a plangent sound that tore the hearts out of those of us around him. It appeared that the duchess had lost consciousness, and the priest carried on anointing her and whispering the prayers for the dying.

Then, for a moment, barely the beat of a heart, he paused and looked up. His lips moved uncertainly, and then he recollected his duty and continued his prayers. Maximilian let out a great cry of 'No! No!' and then buried his face in his wife's hair, which lay on the pillow like a bloodstain.

It was finished.

Of Faces

Patrons are by and large interested only in the depiction of themselves and their family. There are, it is true, some devout few who take great pains to ensure that I get every little detail exactly correct, but they are very much in the minority.

Most will trust you to get the faces of the saints and angels right, but spend hours checking their own faces. They generally pronounce themselves satisfied, which is odd, when you consider the methods I have been using all these years.

Patrons look at their portraits, but they do not see them. They see only what they wish to see, and as long as this pleases them they are happy. There is not a portrait I have made in all my years which is an exact representation of the donor; further, every portrait I have painted has deliberately misrepresented the sitter in a most gross manner. I have always used distortion and ambiguity for expressive effect.

If you are disinclined to believe this, I suggest that you approach any portrait of mine with a straight rule and apply its dimensions to the painting, and you will soon see that what I say is true. I do not say that the paintings do not show the truth, but merely that they do not show the literal truth.

For one thing, I have always had a tendency to enlarge eyes, mouths and noses – partly because these are the most prominent features of any face, but also partly because they are the only features that a patron will notice. I discovered early in my career that serving the interests of the patron serves my own interests more completely than serving the cause of truth. The fact is that these are the most interesting features of any portrait, so it is only sensible to give them greater prominence. Of course, the distortion is not so great as to be obvious, but it is easily spotted, if you know the trick.

In most people, the distance between the eyes and the chin and the eyes and the top of the head is the same. Not so in my work. I increase the former and decrease the latter – only one patron has ever noticed, and he did not care. Thus the sitter gets more of the interesting part of his features and less of the flat and uninteresting forehead.

Measure, too, if you will, the width of a sitter's eyes and the distance between the eyes. Again, in most people these are approximately equal – but again, not in my sitters! The far eye is diminished and the near eye enlarged, as is the space between them, and the mouth is elongated to compensate for this.

The nose, too, is often adjusted so as to appear more in profile than it really should be. This has the effect of making it larger than in life. It also tends to move the nose further to the left or to the right (depending on which way the sitter is facing). This has the effect of moving the centre line of the mouth and the centre line of the nose away from each other, so that the centre of the mouth is never in true vertical alignment with the centre line between the eyes.

To disguise these anomalies it is enough to pay attention to the detail of the pupil or the eyebrow, or to ensure that the placing of the hat or the arrangement of the sitter's hair draws attention away. No man ever looks at the whole face in any case; by concentrating on one aspect he ignores another; if the eyes, for example, are slightly divergent then it tends to give the whole face a mobility of expression which is quite pleasing. The face seems to change aspect as the viewer concentrates on different portions of it – in effect, our sitters get two or three portraits for the price of one, as if they were being painted from several angles at once. Perhaps one day some enterprising revolutionary will begin to produce these three-dimensional effects without the necessity to disguise the fact! Whether or not such a portrait will be accepted into the world is another matter, of course.

There is a lesson to be taken from this, which is not to accept the meaning that you see in a face. There's no art to find the mind's construction therein, if you are an honest man, whereas to the cunning the face is a book in which man may read strange matters. Face value is no value at all, and truth is not to be found therein.

Of Mynheer Trimethius
Dixit Trethemius

(October 1482)

I was shown into the room by my lord's secretary, Arbelle, who raised his eyebrows and placed a finger across pursed lips to enjoin me to silence, and not without reason. I had never seen Maximilian so nervous. His hands were shaking and he could not stop pacing to and fro. I thought that at the very least the country was at war – but in that case, why had he sent for me?

He wasted no time in niceties. 'Hans, you must accompany me into Germany,' he said. 'There is no time to waste. We set off at first light.'

'I am yours to command, sire, as ever, but why?'

'Because you are a friend to me and were a good friend to Marie. And of course you speak German. And most of all because I can trust you.'

'Thank you, sir, but why must we go?'

He calmed down, seeing that he had explained nothing to me. 'There is a man in Haidelberg,' he said, 'who speaks to the spirits of the dead.'

'A necromancer?'

'A magician, yes.'

'The place is full of them, I hear, and most of them charlatans.'

'Precisely what I told my lord,' Arbelle put in.

'Most, yes, but this one has a good reputation, and he has written to me direct. One of his guiding spirits has told him that he has a message for me from Marie.'

I felt as if a cold hand had entered my body and closed round my heart. I opened my mouth, but no words would come. I had seen how this man had suffered after her death. He had barely healed, and to open the wound anew would do no good.

'There are many who are aware of your grief, my lord,' I said, 'and they play upon that grief.'

'But you do believe in an afterlife?' he asked. 'You believe that my Marie lives on in another realm?'

'Of course,' I told him, 'for our Father in Heaven tells us so, but as I said, most of these men are charlatans.'

'Indeed,' he said. 'Indeed, and it is that very word that gives me hope.'

'What word, sire?'

'Most,' he said, shaking a bent finger at me. 'Most, you see. Most are charlatans, as you say – but "most" implies "not all". Amongst them are some whose gifts are genuine.'

I remained silent.

'And this man, this Trimethius, is of excellent repute. I must give him his opportunity, Hans, and if he is a cheat and a liar, why then, I am no worse off. But if he is not – if his gifts are genuine – why then, I shall see my Marie again and speak to her.'

'Sire, you know that the most likely result is disappointment.'

'I do,' he said. 'I am not so gullible as you think. But if this man is genuine . . .' He paused, and a look of pure joy came over his features. 'You knew her, Hans; you understand, surely. I shall see her again.'

There was no arguing with him in this mood, and I returned

to my house to prepare for the journey, promising to return before first light to make sure that our departure was not delayed by as much as a minute.

Bruges to Haidelberg was longer than I had imagined. The journey took many weary days, riding on the back of a nag at the rear of a small cavalcade, spending the nights in inns that could not have been colder if they had been carved out of the ice that surrounded them, and bending our heads against the howling wind and blinding snow that lay in wait for us the moment we stepped out of doors. A cold coming we had of it, and no mistake.

The city of Haidelberg was quieter than I had expected it to be. The students had in the main been allowed to return to their homes for Christmas, and at least the inns were warm. I looked forward to a couple of days thawing out, but Maximilian had clearly not brought me along just for the ride, and I was sent out to earn my corn by locating this man Trimethius, who also apparently went by the name of Trethemius, which did not make him any the easier to find.

Find him I did, however, and when I finally located the house of this Trimethius/Trethemius, my knock was answered by a fresh-faced youth of tender years whose face was as yet innocent of any razor.

'I seek Doctor Trimethius,' I told him.

'You have found him,' he said gravely. 'I am he.'

I shook my head. 'You misunderstand,' I said. 'I seek the learned Doctor Trimethius, who has written to my master Maximilian . . .'

'I am he.'

'Ah. Perhaps then I seek the learned Doctor Trethemius, who has written to my master Maximilian . . .'

'I am he, also. My name is often confused.'

He stood aside to allow me to enter the house, and I blessed him for the warmth I found therein and explained that my master had arrived to put his skills to the test.

'Where do you lie tonight?' he asked.

'*Zum schwarzen Bar,*' I said.

'Good,' he said. 'Now, you must come to me two hours before dawn tomorrow, and by the route that I shall specify. No other route will do. Do you understand?'

'Yes.'

'His Majesty must come alone, or with two companions, or with four. Not with a single companion, or with three or five, and certainly not under any circumstances with any greater number. Do you understand?'

'Yes.'

'For breakfast he and his party may eat fish or eggs or milk, but no meat and no vegetables. Water and wine are permitted, but not beer. Do you understand?'

'Yes.'

'On your journey to this house no one of the party may speak to any man whatsoever, not even by way of giving him good day. Do you understand?'

'Yes.'

'And, finally, not this night or indeed any other should you allow into your inn a man who calls himself Johannes Faust, a charlatan of the first water who will mislead in any way he can. Do you understand?'

'Yes.'

'Tomorrow, when I open the door your master and his companions must enter by each placing his left foot across the threshold first. Do you understand?'

'Yes.'

'Then I shall see you tomorrow.'

I weighed him up. He had a mien of seriousness, and therefore was either genuine or demented. 'And do you understand?'
I asked. 'Do you understand what you have undertaken to do?
This man who comes here tomorrow in all hope and expecta-
tion was widowed of the foremost lady of the world, a paragon
among princesses, the nonpareil of women, and you have
convinced him that you will raise her so that he may see her
and speak to her in the flesh.'

'Her spirit,' he said. 'I raise her spirit, not her flesh. That is
the work of God, not of man. And your lord may not ask questions of the spirit, nor may the spirit speak to him.'

'She may not speak,' I said. 'I understand. And you can do
this thing?'

'I can give no guarantees,' he answered, 'but I have been
successful in the past.'

'I understood the title of "doctor" to be given to learned men
who have spent years in the study of their craft,' I said. 'Are
you not rather young to be so titled?'

'It is a courtesy title,' he said, 'applied to me by those who
know and admire my work.'

And with that I had to be contented.

When he opened the door the next morning Trimethius pointed
down at Maximilian's left foot, and His Majesty obediently
crossed the threshold in the approved style, followed by Arbelle
and myself.

'You took care, Your Majesty, to come by the way I enjoined
you?' was the first thing the magician asked.

'I did.'

'With two companions, good. And your breakfast?'

'As specified.'

'Good.'

The Master of Bruges

'And you spoke to no man during your journey?'

At that time of the morning there was no sane man abroad, but His Grace did not think to tell Doctor Trimethius this. 'We kept silence, as you told us,' was all he said. I felt pity for him; still, in despite of everything, he was taking the matter seriously.

'And yesterday, did you avoid the company of that Johannes Faust?'

'We know of no Faust.'

'Good. He is a liar and a debaucher of young boys,' he muttered, darkly. 'All, then, is ready,' and he led the way up the stairs into an upper room the like of which I had never seen before. It was windowless and was entirely curtained in black, the material layered with each piece stretching from ceiling to floor and embroidered with signs of every conceivable kind – Egyptian hieroglyphics, Greek letters and Russian characters, Arabic symbols, the new arithmetical signs, cabbalistic drawings, scribbles which I took to be Chinese writing, things that looked like naught of this world and in the midst of it this wild man, crazed no doubt by what he was doing if he were not crazed before that and dressed in a long gown, black too but with red showing beneath the slashes. 'Do you still wish to proceed?'

Maximilian solemnly nodded his head. The good doctor, who jerked about so much that he made a St Vitus's sufferer look like a marble statue, was very much on edge. I suppose it wasn't every day that he got the heir to an empire in his chambers asking for the impossible, but it has to be said that although he was polite enough he showed Maximilian little deference; I suppose he was too engrossed in his work. He told us to sit on a row of stools, Maximilian in the middle, while he made preparations for the visitation.

He treated us to an incessant analysis of his actions. 'You need to go to a lapidary,' he said, 'and acquire a good clear pellucid crystal, of the bigness of a small lemon, without any clouds or specks. Then get a small plate of pure gold to encompass the crystal round one half and let this be fitted on an ivory or ebony pedestal.' He produced such a crystal, with various signs and names engraved on the pedestal. This he placed on a table whereon he had drawn a triangle and two concentric circles.

'The table is made complete,' he told us. 'Now I may proceed.' He surprised me by beginning with a prayer: 'Oh, God! who art the author of all good things, strengthen, I beseech thee, thy poor servant, that he may stand fast, without fear, through this dealing and work; enlighten, I beseech thee, oh Lord! the dark understanding of thy creature, so that his spiritual eye may be opened to see and know thy angelic spirits descending here in this crystal: and thou, oh inanimate creature of God, be sanctified and consecrated, and blessed to this purpose, that no evil phantasy may appear in thee; or, if they do gain ingress into this creature, they may be constrained to speak intelligibly, and truly, and without the least ambiguity, for Christ's sake. And forasmuch as thy servant here standing before thee, oh, Lord! desires neither evil treasures, nor injury to his neighbour, nor hurt to any living creature, grant him the power of descrying those celestial spirits or intelligences, that may appear in this crystal, and whatever good gifts (whether the power of healing infirmities, or of imbibing wisdom, or discovering any evil likely to afflict any person or family), or any other good gift thou mayest be pleased to bestow on me, enable me, by thy wisdom and mercy, to use whatever I may receive to the honour of thy holy name. Grant this for thy son Christ's sake. Amen.'

This had a strengthening effect on Maximilian, who had feared (as indeed did I) that the spirits might have been invoked by forces other than those of good.

Now Trimethius placed a silver ring on the little finger of his right hand, hung a pentacle round his neck and took up a black ebony wand. He traced a circle around the four of us, saying, 'In the name of the blessed Trinity, I consecrate this piece of ground for our defence; so that no evil spirit may have power to break these bounds prescribed here, through Jesus Christ Our Lord. Amen.'

We all gladly echoed his Amen in this desire. Then he threw some powder into a small oil lamp and waved it about, before intoning another prayer – 'I conjure thee, oh thou creature of fire, by him who created all things both in heaven and earth, and in the sea, and in every other place whatever, that forth-with thou cast away every phantasm from thee, that no hurt whatsoever shall be done in any thing. Bless, oh Lord, this crea-ture of fire, and sanctify it that it may be blessed, and that they may fill up the power and virtue of their odours; so neither the enemy, nor any false imagination, may enter into them; through Our Lord Jesus Christ.'

This ended the intelligible part of the procedure. What went on over the next few hours was enough to drive any man as mad as Trimethius himself. First he had to consult the spirit, who was to be found in the little crystal ball. He made passes above and around the sphere, drivelling away in some mumbo-jumbo language that he made up as he went along and making signs in the air. This went on for some considerable length of time, and the result was – nothing at all. No spirit appeared, no messages were conceived in the ether and written on the wall – nothing. My own view was that the spirits, like all honest men, were fast asleep and not of a mind to listen to the meanderings of a lunatic at that hour of the morning, but Trimethius was of a different persuasion.

There was a sandglass on a small side table, and when it emptied he turned it over and consulted a massive book on a nearby stand. 'It is now the hour of the moon,' he explained, 'and today being Tuesday it is necessary to conjure Gabriel.'

Apparently it was the wrong spirit we had been calling upon, the hour for that particular spirit having passed and that of another having begun. The spirits, it seems, work on a shift system, like a baker's apprentice. Maximilian, who had begun the day in a lather of hope, was becoming dispirited. Perhaps, in the circumstances, downcast would be a more precise expression; we were all, literally, dispirited.

Not a whit daunted, however, Trimethius set off again – the same passes, the same dyslalia, the same aery signs, although the necromancer insisted that they were subtly different, to those who had ears to hear. Nonetheless the result was the same – a deep spiritual silence.

Meanwhile the sun came up.

The sandglass was turned, and a new spirit, Cassiel, controlled the hour under the influence of a different planet, Saturn. The passes continued. Circles were drawn on the floor with the ebony wand, mumbo-jumbo uttered and candles lit at various prestigious points in the room, but still the spirits slumbered.

Then came a change. Trimethius fell silent and stared intently at the crystal ball. 'It is time, my lord,' he said. 'Cassiel leads the spirit of your princess to you. I enjoin you, sir, to remember that she cannot speak to you, nor you to her. If you have questions, you may ask them through me, but I cannot guarantee that you will be vouchsafed an answer. You may gaze upon the princess's form, which is like unto her earthly form, but you must not attempt to approach her or touch her, or the angel will take her away again. Perhaps your companions will restrain you.'

Maximilian nodded his agreement and we each took one of his hands in our own. I could feel the tension in his fingers as he waited; no doubt he could have felt a similar tension in mine, had he been alert to such matters.

'Then behold!'

There was a flash of bright light, and when our vision cleared we saw the figure of a woman dimly, as seen through a mist. 'Stand not so far off, good lady,' Trimethius called, 'but approach nigher to your husband.'

The figure advanced a step, and the vision cleared for a moment before misting again. It was a young woman in a blue dress, her features indistinct but her hair clearly the reddish hue of the princess's.

'Marie,' Maximilian said hoarscly, and twisted his hand, forcing it out of mine. Then, as he rose to his feet, the vision disappeared.

'My lord!' Trimethius said, 'I did forbid you to approach my lady's spirit. The angel has taken her away.'

Maximilian was stricken. 'Bring her back,' he said. 'I command you to bring her back.'

'The spirits will not be commanded by man,' the magician said. 'I can only ask if they wish to return.'

'Then do so,' Maximilian said. 'I promise I shall not move again.'

The ritual began again, but before Trimethius had got more than a few minutes into it the sand ran out of the glass, and he announced that the hour of that spirit was over, and that he would have to begin again with another one.

'I must tell you,' he said, 'that it does not happen that the same spirit you call will always appear, for you must try the spirit to know whether he be a pure or impure being, and this you shall easily know by a firm and undoubted faith in God. Now I must call upon Sachiel.'

And off he went again with the wand and the ball and the muttering of spells and incantations. Finally all was ready again, and for a second time he gave his instructions. Maximilian prepared himself and again grasped our hands, and again Trimethius called out, 'Then behold!'

There was the same flash of bright light, slightly more subdued this time, and the same dim figure of a woman. Again Trimethius called out loudly, 'Stand not so far off, but approach.'

Again she advanced a step, and again the vision cleared momentarily before the mist closed in.

'Do you have any questions, my lord?' Trimethius asked.

'Is she well?' Maximilian asked.

'This is not a question to be asked, my lord. She is a spirit, not a corporeal body. Spirits are indeed well if they are in the bosom of Our Lord.'

'Is she happy?'

Raising his voice again, Trimethius called, 'My lord asks if the spirit of his lady is happy.'

In answer, the vision nodded its head emphatically.

'As you see, my lord, she is so.'

'And shall we meet again in the next life?'

Again the vision inclined its head. Through his hand, I felt all the tension go out of Maximilian. 'Her spirit lives,' he said. 'She is happy and with the Lord.'

The vision expanded and darkened. 'Take warning, spirit,' Trimethius called, 'approach not too closely the corporeal sphere, lest you do damage to those of us still here.' The darkness held for a second or two, and then the woman reappeared. She passed a hand across her brow. 'The spirit tires,' Trimethius said, 'and must return to her realm.'

The figure pressed its hand to its lips and then to its heart before holding out both hands towards us. Then, as Maximilian mouthed her name and began a prayer of thanks, the tears coursing down his cheeks, Trimethius sank exhausted to his knees. At that exact moment the vision vanished and the room was plunged once again into darkness.

'Mynheer Trimethius, are you unwell?' Arbelle asked.

'No,' the magician said. 'Do not touch me, please. Elements of the spirit may still be attached to me and may do you harm. I pray you, stand afar off. Or go below, into my chamber, and wait for me.'

The three of us rose and waited while the man composed himself and Arbelle found the door in the darkness. We descended the stairs, and when he was fully recovered Trimethius joined us. 'My apologies, my lord,' he said, 'but I am tired. The summoning of spirits is exhausting work. Did my lord find it satisfactory?'

'I did,' Maximilian said. 'It was my lady, and she told me what I wanted to hear. I am content. I thank you, Master Trimethius. What fee shall I pay you?'

'The amount of the fee is a matter for you, my lord,' the doctor said. 'It is determined by the means available to the person paying it and the level of satisfaction he has experienced. Will there be anything else, my lord?'

Maximilian shook his head.

'I should therefore be grateful to be left alone, my lord, so that I may recover from the encounter with the spirit.'

Arbelle reached into his pocket and brought out a small

purse, presumably full of gold, and was about to hand it to the magician when Maximilian stayed his hand, inclined his head slightly and closed his eyes. Arbelle immediately pocketed the bag again and moved to the door.

'I give you good day, doctor,' Maximilian said.

'And to you, sir, and your gentlemen,' he said, and put the door firmly into place.

Towards the end of the afternoon, with the sun low in the sky, Maximilian sent for me. He looked and sounded happier than he had done on any day since Marie's death, and he beamed at me. 'Hans, will you oblige me by delivering this?' he asked.

'Of course, my lord,' I murmured in agreement, and took from him a large velvet bag containing enough gold for a man to live on for ever, if he were frugal.

'Just tell him, "Thank you."'

'My lord.'

I bowed my way out, and set off to find the magician's house, reaching it just before darkness fell. The door was opened this time by an old housekeeper, and hearing the chinking sound coming from my pocket she wasted no time in ushering me into the venerable presence.

Trimethius rose to greet me and offered me a glass of the mulled wine which sat in a jug on a small table at his elbow. 'His lordship was satisfied with what he saw?' he asked, with just a hint of anxiety.

'His lordship,' I said, emphasizing the words strongly, 'was well satisfied, as the weight of this bag will indicate to you.'

I handed it over, and he gasped at the weight and then at the contents as he checked that it was really gold. It had been obvious that he caught my hint, but he refrained from pursuing the matter, so it was up to me to do so. 'The spirit of her Late Highness showed some early disinclination to appear,' I observed.

'Necromancy is an inexact science at best, your worship,' he replied. 'Even the most expert of practitioners cannot guarantee how the spirits will react, and whether they will appear at his call.'

'She came, all the same.'

'Yes.'

'I imagine that with help and encouragement, almost any spirit can be called to appear.'

'I imagine so,' he said carefully, 'although the number of spirits in the universe is limitless. There is much research to be done, and His Majesty's generous donation will ensure that it continues.'

'Is necromancy the only science you practise, sir?' I asked.

'Why no,' he said. 'A man of science must have many interests and divers skills if he is to succeed. Mathematics alone requires . . .'

'Yes, I understand,' I told him. I had had enough of his exposition of his various skills for one day, and had another direction I wanted to send him in. 'Mathematics is, of course, an abstract science. What of those with more practical applications – do you practise those, too?'

'Of course – physics, alchemy . . .'

'Optics?'

Oh yes, it was there – the momentary hesitation, the instant composure, the almost infinitesimal pause before he continued: 'Naturally. You see we have many glasses in this room . . .'

Again I interrupted him. 'The Italians, in particular, have done much good work in this field, I believe?'

Again the slight hesitation before he decided to check my

credentials. 'Your worship is familiar, perhaps, with some of the developments?' he asked.

'I have some slight acquaintanceship,' I admitted, and then decided to reel in my fish. 'There is one in particular which is most interesting,' I told him. 'I cannot now bring to mind the name of the device . . .'

He was nodding enthusiastically.

'. . . But in the Italian language it means "dark room".'

The nodding stopped, started again, faltered, and stopped completely. Now there were two possible directions, and he knew it. He placed his feet tentatively on the path of truth. 'I have heard of the device, yes.'

'I think His Majesty has not,' I said conversationally. 'Its use is not yet widespread in the countries north of the Alps. Most will not have heard of it.'

'Whereas you, sir,' he began cautiously, and I completed his thought for him.

'. . . have most assuredly heard of it.' I sipped at the warm wine. I suspected his own might be cooling rapidly. 'In fact,' I said brightly, 'I saw a remarkable demonstration of the device very recently.'

His demeanour changed. Gone was the sophisticated polymath, and in his place was a shrunken, frightened youth.

'Really?' he said.

I smiled and nodded. 'And not far from here, either,' I told him.

The silence was long. 'What do you want?' he asked finally.

'Nothing.'

'Then what are you doing here?'

'I am merely delivering your fee,' I said, 'although it is difficult to say what you did to earn it.'

'Are you here to kill me?'

'No.'

He licked his lips and said quietly, 'Are you going to tell him?'

I shook my head from side to side, just a tiny movement. 'What you did made him a happy man,' I said. 'When a ruler is happy, his subjects are happy; his rule becomes lighter, and we his servants all breathe that much more easily. I have come not to blackmail you, but to ensure that my lord never learns the truth – that he cannot ever learn the truth.'

Trimethius took a moment to digest this. 'What then?' he asked.

I pointed to his bag. 'You have a lot of gold there,' I said.

'Yes. I am now a rich man.'

'Yes,' I said. 'Rich enough to afford to be able to dismantle the device, and to ensure that it is not used again in his lordship's lifetime, perhaps?'

'Sir, his lordship is yet an extremely young man . . .'

'Which is a misfortune, as the use of the instrument is thus likely to be denied you for many years to come. You do have enough gold to ensure that, I think? Assuming, that is, that his lordship does not learn of your room with the Italian name.'

After a moment or two to consider the position he said, 'If that were the case,' he said, 'then yes, I suppose I do.'

I nodded. 'As you have so rightly observed, you are a rich man. You can pass the remainder of your years in the pursuance of some authentic knowledge.' I rose to my feet to leave, and he made a final attempt to retain his dignity.

'My first few attempts – the unsuccessful ones – were genuine,' he said. 'It was only when I had no success and saw His Majesty's disappointment that I resorted to the device. I had prepared it beforehand, just in case. The king – well, he seemed like a man in need of solace.'

'Did you ever see the princess – in life, I mean?'

'No.'

'There is no solace after the loss of one such as she,' I said. 'None whatsoever, but it is possible that you may have begun a process of healing.'

He remained silent, and, standing, I ran my fingers along the curtain opposite where the vision had appeared and encountered a fine thread, invisible against the velvet, and with a tiny bead threaded onto it. I pulled gently on it and watched the velvet curtains parting the distance of the top joint of a man's thumb, the tiniest movement of the wall covering. I bent down and peered into the gap, and caught the reflection of Trimethius's fire in the lens embedded there. 'Remarkable,' I said, 'but too dark at this hour, I suppose, for another demonstration,' I said.

'It is, sir,' he said. 'It is.'

'And no doubt the princess has gone home.'

He made no reply, and I left him to reckon up his reward.

He left Haidelberg within a few days, and I heard later that despite his youth he had been elected the abbot of a monastery at Sponheim or Spanheim or some such, where he has since dedicated his life to the writing of books.

PART TWO

Of Filth, Artifice and Beauty

I invite you to contemplate what it is that we painters do.
Look upon our creations, and see that they are good.

The Lord made Adam from the earth and Eve from a rib; thus was the precedent set.

What of our own beauteous creations? Do they not follow where the Good Lord led?

They do. Contemplate the lovely face of the Madonna in the painting you have just taken delivery of. Is she not the epitome of beauty, with that bloom on her skin and the light reflecting from her hair, and is the single red rose at her breast not the most perfect of flowers? Step closer – can you smell its perfume?

Let us hope not. Would it surprise you to learn that the lovely red rose she wears at her breast is painted from a compound of alum and powdered wood, lye and urine? If you could smell it, the odour would be the stale of horses.

All is artifice. The lovely face of that Madonna is composed of no more than piss, dirt and filth, and the highlights of her hair are brought out with a wash of lye and soot in more or less equal parts. Such things may surprise the layman, but not the painter, for he deals in lies, lives lies, makes lies, tells lies and sells lies.

I have said before, but it needs to be said again, that a

painter's life is delineated by trickery. Again I say, 'Do not believe any thing that a painter tells you.'

And again I warn you to be especially wary of what he calls truth.

Of My Journey into England

(December 1482 to May 1483)

On my return from Haidelberg towards the end of that year of the princess's death I was saved from the abyss I had fallen into by a commission from a man I had last seen in similar miserable circumstances. Sir John Donne called upon me once again to remind me of the commission of his triptych. The painting had in fact been almost complete for some time, but since he had sent his wife and daughter back to England I had never been able to finish the work, and the fact that the girl was growing so fast meant that the painting would be inaccurate unless she came and sat for me. Sir John was now on the point of retirement from his post, and although he had said that the work was to be painted when and where I had time and opportunity, he felt that time was now pressing. He was no longer often at Calais, he said, but was prepared to make a trip to Bruges for sittings and to make arrangements.

'To make arrangements, sir?' I asked.

'For transportation. Even if the painting is not as we would both like it, it cannot remain here. With your permission, I shall ask some English artists to paint in the figures of my wife and daughter.'

I think he saw immediately that he had insulted me.

'Sir,' I told him, 'I alone paint my patrons.'

'Then do so,' he said, 'but make an end. It is now near fifteen years since I first mooted this painting, and my wife has given birth to a daughter who is now approaching marriageable age. I am grown old and grey in the service of my country, yet my painting is as youthful as I was on my lady Margaret's wedding day.'

'I can adjust your own image, if you wish,' I told him, 'to more accurately suggest your present age, and your wife, perhaps, would not mind being depicted as she was when first she sat, but can your daughter not come for me to sketch, at least, sir?' I asked.

He shook his head impatiently. 'She will not be returning to this country.'

'I am loth to leave a painting unfinished,' I told him, 'especially after all this time. Equally,' I added, 'I am loth to commit paintings to the sea for transportation.' He knew why – the whole of Bruges had heard of the fate of my Last Judgement.

'If you would consider it, Mynheer, there is an alternative,' he said. 'To save the costs and risks of transportation you could yourself make the journey to England and complete the painting while staying as my honoured guest. My estate is an attractive one on the sea far in the west of Wales.'

'Wales? Not England? Another country?'

'Another country indeed,' he said, 'but Wales is not so strange a country as all that.'

'But is there not constant fighting and laying waste of the countryside because of your eternal civil war?' I asked.

'Indeed not,' he said. 'The English do not make war in the same way as other nations. The aristocracy attack and kill each other, make captives and demand ransoms, but the ordinary people are left alone – after all, it is the land that they work that the great ones wish to own, so there is no point in devastating it, and the nobility will not work it, so they need the land workers to produce the land's plenty. No, you can work in peace and quiet at Kidwelly. My estate,' he added, seeing my confusion. 'In any case, all is tranquil for the time being. We have a strong king.'

He saw my hesitation, and added the sentence that decided me. 'You might also wish to take into consideration another invitation that I have been instructed to offer.' He had such a wide smile on his face that I had to respond in like manner; he was clearly going to enjoy whatever was coming.

When he made no effort to go on I bowed to the inevitable and asked, 'What is it, then?'

'I am informed that there are two gentlemen who wish to reciprocate your hospitality of a dozen years ago.'

'My hospitality?'

'You are invited to be the guest of Ned and Dick Plant,' he said.

My eyes must have lit up, but then I bethought myself. 'But the war,' I protested. 'You said . . .'

'I said that all is quiet for the time being because we have a strong king.'

Of course I could not refuse. The Dumpling raised objections, but it is not every day that one's husband is called to be the guest of a king, and it would enable her to lord it over the goodwives at the market, so it was agreed that I would go to England at the beginning of Advent and stay some four to six months, paying a visit to London before going on to Kidwelly and returning once the painting was completed. To help in the studio and take on some of the work while I would be away I recruited a second apprentice, a lad called Passchier van der Mersche, a young local boy who is still with me as a journeyman.

When it was time to leave I took all the care that I could with the painting. I had a special frame constructed by a carpenter, and filled the space around the picture with the softest duck down in case of knocks. The whole was then sewn into a canvas sack which in turn was sewn into an oilcloth covering. It was transported from Bruges along the canal by barge, and it did not leave my side from the time it was placed in the frame until it was delivered into the keeping of a king's messenger on English soil. As Sir John, who had arranged the messenger through Ned, reminded me, even I could not keep it safer than such a one, and with it out of my hands I was at last able to relax and begin to enjoy my visit.

I went first, as promised, to see Ned and to spend the Christmas season with him in London. I was shown into his presence late one November afternoon and halted in astonishment immediately I caught sight of him. He was not as I remembered. Although a year or two younger than me, just forty, he was an old man. Sir John had warned me to expect a change, as the king had taken to indolence and inebriate habits, but I was completely unprepared for what I saw. The enormous strength was gone, and his magnificent body had turned to corpulence and flabbiness. He breathed with difficulty, and he was no longer able to go hunting or riding. In fact, most days he did not move from his chambers at all, and spent the afternoon and evening drinking so much that he was normally carried to his bed in an unconscious condition by four strong menservants.

He raised me up as I knelt and put his arm around my shoulder in that familiar way of his. 'You are welcome, Hans,' he said. 'It is always a pleasure to greet an old friend.' Even these few words exhausted him, and he returned to his throne and sat heavily on it. 'Dick is not in London,' he told me. 'He is busy in the north, but he will be here in a few days and we will be able to talk of old times.' He introduced me to his two sons, the elder of whom, Edward, had been born at about the time Ned was in exile at my house. He was a sickly youth, with some deformity of the lower jaw which caused him to slobber saliva, pus and blood and gave his face a lopsided look as well as making him shy of being seen.

His younger brother Richard was a cutting from Ned's tree, however, with the same fair colouring and good looks, already very tall for his age and full of boyish fun. I took to him at once, particularly as he expressed some interest in drawing and painting. He dragged out of me a promise to teach him some techniques over the Christmas period, should his father permit, and that immediately led to a commission that for once I could have done without. 'Hans shall paint my portrait while he is in England,' the king declared, and out of the corner of my eye I saw Sir John Donne's face drop. It seemed that his painting was doomed never to be finished.

It is not politic to gainsay a prince, and before the day was out I was allocated a room in the house and told to expect a sitting each day until my work was finished. True to his word, Ned turned up each afternoon for sketches, always accompanied by the little Duke of York, who sat at my elbow and watched and learned.

Truth to tell, it was not one of my best portraits. Ned wanted it fast, and so the background became a plain striped material instead of the English landscape I would have preferred, and his habit of turning up each day in a different outfit meant that I had to devise a suitable robe for him to wear, and with it preying so much on my mind I suppose it was inevitable that I would copy one from the Donne commission. The king sits clothed in the same cloth of gold which decorates the rear of the Virgin's throne. In addition, it was necessary to soften the king's features and remove from them the coarseness and heaviness which had overtaken him. The result was flattering in the sense that it made him look ten years younger, and was accurate in that he looked more like the man I remembered from twelve years before, but it was not a portrait of the man before me.

It was sadly successful, though, in that it engendered another inconvenient commission. The queen, having heard so much from her enthusiastic younger son about the painting magically taking shape in the Netherlander's room, came along to see for herself, and then of course nothing would satisfy her but she too must have a portrait of herself. When I told Sir John he buried his head in his hands and rued the day that he had met me, but Elizabeth Woodville was not a woman to cross, and so my stay was extended again and a second portrait begun. Fortunately I had grown used, over the years, to working fast, and so the portraits took shape quickly. I also enjoyed the help of an enthusiastic assistant in the shape of young Prince Richard of York, who took great delight in mixing paint under my supervision and then diligently applying it to the backgrounds, to the equal delight of his parents. Fortunately, I was able to repaint it to my own satisfaction once he had left for the day.

Dick returned to London two days before Christmas. My pleasure in seeing him again was increased by the welcome he was given by his brother. In previous months Richard had conquered the Scots at a place called Beric, an English town long held by the Scots but now returned to English rule. Apparently it was of major strategical importance, commanding as it did the road to the north, and the king was delighted. For this and other services Dick was rewarded with the wardenship of vast tracts of land on the Scottish borders, an event which explained something to me and caused Sir John Donne to fall into an even deeper gloom.

Ned had insisted that his portrait should feature his hands toying with a gold ring, although he offered no explanation for this. Naturally I had fallen in with his desires and done as I was told.

All was revealed when Dick turned up. The ring, it turned out, was a symbol of this new stewardship, and was to be included (and I could hardly contain my astonishment at this next revelation) in the portrait of Dick which I was to paint once I had finished the two I was already working on. Sir John asked to be reminded never to commission a painting ever again. I gained some time by having the young Duke of York paint his own portrait of Dick, which kept him away from my own effort.

Naturally, Dick wanted a landscape behind him, as being more in keeping with what he understood a Memling portrait to entail. I could not argue with a king, but I was more at ease with his brother, and eventually prevailed upon him to allow me a plain background on this occasion, given the plight of Sir John. Dick laughed at the good knight's predicament but allowed the concession, although he demanded that I paint a 'proper' portrait later. I promised to do so, but of course the promise was never kept. As far as I am aware, my portrait of Dick, his fingers fitting his brother's ring onto the third finger of his right hand, is the only one ever executed.

By the beginning of March all three portraits were completed. I was able to relax in the company of Ned and Dick for a few days and bestow the gift of some pigments and equipment on my young assistant, and then, to the enormous relief of Sir John, I was allowed to plead pressure of work and to beg leave to depart from court in order to complete my commission. Permission was granted, and I travelled across England to a town called Hay, on the River Wye, where Sir John arranged to have me met and escorted to Kidwelly.

Although cold, the estate was as pleasant as he had suggested, and I enjoyed the work. The painting had arrived safely and had even been left unpacked, so I was able to take pleasure in Lady Donne's reaction and show her daughter, Anne, who was almost thirteen, the space I had left for her, behind her mother and kneeling at the feet of St Barbara. I spent the mornings walking around the estate and occasionally swimming in the sea, although the water was much colder there than at home in Bruges, and the afternoons having the members of the family come and sit for me. Sir John's daughter was startlingly slight for her years and much resembled her mother, and it was the work of only a few days to complete her section of the painting. As Lady Elizabeth was not averse to leaving her portrait much as it was I made rapid progress, adding to her image only the slight bulge which later in the year turned into her second daughter, Margaret, and thinning her face slightly.

I added to Sir John's face some of the years which had passed, and offered to add a few more in respect of the three royal portraits I had done, but he declined those, and finally the saga of the family portrait drew to a close. By the last week of March the painting had been completed to the satisfaction of all, and I thought that at last I would be able to relax.

It was not to be, however, for events moved fast. I had no sooner laid down my brush when a messenger arrived hotfoot from Will Hastings.

Sir John came to see me, the paper still in his hand. 'I must go,' he said. 'The king is dead, and there is treason abroad.

Those loyal to Ned and his sons must act now in their interests.'

He told me that Ned had died suddenly, and that Dick had been named in his brother's will as the new King's Protector. Ned's son, young Edward, now the fifth king of that name, was with his uncle, Lord Rivers, the queen's brother, at Ludlow. Somehow, the Rivers party had ensured that the news of his brother's death and his own new responsibility had not been conveyed to Dick – deliberately so, apparently, as the queen's family were anxious to shift him aside as soon as possible.

As an office-bearer under Edward IV, Sir John needed to go to London, and I accepted his invitation to accompany him there, hoping to continue home thereafter. While we were on our journey, things took a turn for the better. Dick rode south and intercepted the Rivers party on its way to London at a place called Stony Stratford. He confiscated several waggonloads of weaponry, arrested Rivers and his cohorts and took the young king into his protection. On arrival in London, the king was placed in the royal apartments in the Tower of London.

My work done, I went to see Dick for leave to return home.

Of the Ways of Princes

(May 1483)

Leave was not forthcoming. I thought I would simply be waiting for a convenient ship, but Dick asked for my help. 'I will need you here,' he said, 'at least until the king is crowned. I need people about me I can trust, and so does that boy. This realm is unstable enough.'

'What can I do?' I protested. 'I am a painter, not a soldier or a diplomat.'

'Precisely,' he said. 'You do something he has an interest in, and you're not political. You know boys; you're a father, aren't you, and you know His Majesty well enough. He will be interested in your work, and you can keep him amused and entertained. It will be for no more than a month, Hans, until I can get him safely crowned. What say you?'

Despite myself, I agreed. Dick was too nice a man to turn down, and a month was not all that long. I was missing Tanne and my own small boys, but on the other hand an extra month might even lead to a few more commissions. 'Will I be living in the Tower?'

'If you wish. It's not the most comfortable accommodation in England, but it's safe, which is why Edward's there.'

'And it is free of rent,' I added pointedly, but Dick took care to ignore the comment.

So it was settled, and I moved my meagre belongings into a room in the Tower. The young king looked, if anything, worse than he had six months before. Several teeth had fallen out and a few others loosened, and there was now a constant flow of a mixture of blood and saliva from the corner of his mouth, where there was wadding which Doctor Argentine, the king's physician, changed every hour. There was a foul stench about the unfortunate monarch emanating from the mess of corruption in his jaw.

The new king was miserable and bored, and was glad of the diversion that my presence brought. He knew, of course, of how I had served Dick and his father, and his mother too had had pleasant things to say about me, so he was well disposed towards me from the start. I also offered him diversion in that I wakened in him a skill in drawing that he had once enjoyed, and that helped take away the misery of being without friends or companions. He especially missed his little brother, and my stories of how Richard had helped me paint his father and mother made a firm bond between us.

I had been in the Tower no more than a week or so when Doctor Argentine thought it was warm enough to let the king into the garden. It was a bright day at the latter end of May, but Edward was disinclined to attempt any physical activity. I managed to get him to walk around the outer ramparts, and for a while we watched the ships on the river, but he was too tired to visit the menagerie.

Finally I set him to drawing an elderberry bush in flower. He had a good eye, and a control of line that was pleasing and betokened a skill in observation. When he was occupied in reading or drawing he tended to forget the pain of his illness, so we were both sat in the bright sun exercising our common skill when my lord of Gloucester was announced.

Dick knelt before Edward and kissed his hand. 'Forgive the interruption, Your Majesty,' he said, 'but I have pressing business that will not wait, and that concerns yourself and your brother my lord of York most closely.'

I rose and made to excuse myself, but the king stayed me with a wave of his hand. 'We are learning to trust the wisdom of Master Memling,' he said, 'and unless what you say is so secret that he cannot hear it then we would like him to stay.'

'The fewer that are privy to it the better, I think,' Dick said, 'but I too have good reason to trust Master Memling, as did your father. In fact, he may be able to help convince Your Majesty of the wisdom of what I am going to ask of you.'

'Matters of state are some way beyond my powers of comprehension,' I smiled. 'I fear I can be of little use to you.'

'It is not your diplomatic skills that I wish to draw upon,' Dick said, 'but your love and friendship for my brother, his Late Majesty, and for his children.'

'In that case all my puny skills are at your service,' I said, and at his signal resumed my chair and waited.

Dick drew up a bench that we had been laying paper and charcoal on, shifted them all to one end and straddled the bench.

'What I have to say, Your Majesty,' Dick said, 'may sound cruel, callous and self-serving, but I assure you that it is something that is as necessary as it is undesirable.'

He paused to ensure that the boy realized that a matter of some importance was to come.

'Firstly,' he continued, 'you must be able to trust me – trust me with your life and that of your brother, and with the kingdom. If there is the slightest doubt in your mind the matter will become extremely difficult, and probably impossible.'

'I trust you, uncle,' Edward said without hesitation, suddenly a small boy instead of a king. 'No man ever had a more loyal brother, and no king a more loyal subject than you were to my father, and I cannot think that you will be any the less to me.'

Dick shifted his position and leaned back. 'I thank you for those words,' he said. 'Such kind interpretations of my deeds will not be common abroad in the times to come, I fear, unless our victory is swift.' He paused, and then went on, 'Why, in the light of what you have said, do I ask you to stay here in this Tower, which many call a prison?'

'For our safety,' Edward told him. 'We are aware of the designs which Henry Tudor and the Lancastrians have on our person. It is the safest place. We know this, and we stay here willingly and will continue to do so for as long as Your Grace thinks fit.'

Dick sighed heavily. 'There is another consideration,' he said, 'and that is my own safety.'

'Oh? How so?'

'Your Majesty is aware that I placed your uncle Rivers and my lords Grey and Vaughan under arrest at the time I took you under my protection?'

'Yes.'

'What think you of that?'

Edward considered for a moment. 'I know that they did not mean for you to be Protector long,' he said. 'They said that once I was crowned I would not need your guidance any more.'

'And what would have become of me?'

'You would have gone back to the north, I suppose,' Edward said, and then a puzzled look came over his face. 'No,' he said slowly, 'that would not have pleased them, for there you would be just as powerful as in London. They would have . . .' He paused again, and his blue eyes looked across at his uncle. Then, clearly troubled, he said, 'They would have had to . . .'

His voice tailed away and Dick's eyebrows rose in a double arch. It was clear that this was the first time that the boy in Edward had thought the matter through to its inevitable end.

'Why did they have cartloads of weapons?' Dick asked.

'In case you resisted my accession, of course.' Then he stopped again. 'But you wouldn't resist my accession, would you? You are sworn to carry out my father's will.'

'Why did they not inform me of your father's death?'

'To gain time. Time to . . .'

'Yes,' Dick said. 'Time to make sure I could do nothing about it. In a word, Your Majesty, they planned treason. Not treason against your person, but treason against the governance of the realm and its Protector.'

'But why?' Edward asked. 'I will still be king no matter what.'

'King though you are, Your Majesty, you are in body still but a boy. Any man would find it easier to direct your wishes if you were alone and without loyal advisors,' Dick said. 'The country could be in danger. That is why no country is happy to have a minor as its king. The people remember the days of old King Harry, you know, king virtually from birth. That is why your father wanted me to take over as Protector until you are of age.'

'Which is when?'

'That is for Your Majesty to decide, although fourteen to sixteen years old would be possible – seventeen or eighteen might be considered more normal.'

'Not twelve?'

'Your Majesty might find the councils of state too much to take at that age,' Dick replied. 'Some of the barons can be very argumentative.' The king showed some disposition to disagree, and Dick added, 'I might also say that they are a great deal larger and fiercer than I am. It sometimes takes a brave man to stand up to them.'

That gave Edward meat for thought. 'So what is it that you have in mind?' he asked.

Dick leaned forward, placing a hand on each side of the bench. 'You are aware, I think, that in your father's time there were many rumours about his parentage. There were those who said that my mother played false with my father, and that your father was not his son.'

'I have heard such stories,' Edward said, suddenly cold. 'Surely you of all people do not intend to repeat them now?'

'I do not,' Dick said, 'but I do see a glimmer of hope in that we might be able to use the rumours to our advantage. But, as I said, you have to trust me.'

'I do,' the boy said, perhaps less certainly than before.

'And it is essential that you understand, too. Why is Your Majesty in danger?'

'Because we stand between ambitious men and the crown. We – and you too, uncle Dick. They will kill you if they get the chance.'

A servant approached with a jug and some cups. I had ordered some wine warmed up and brought out. As well as keeping the cold from His Majesty, the wine helped stop his blood from thinning. It is a drink much taken here in the Netherlands, and I had made sure that His Majesty had some each morning. Doctor Argentine said that it might do him good. The wine is warmed with hot water and then lemon juice and honey are stirred into it. It is most aromatic. I rose and began to pour it as Dick continued.

'The difference, Your Majesty, is that I am a grown man who can command armies, and you and your brother are boys – a king and his heir, it is true, but boys nonetheless. Many years ago, when you were a mere babe in arms, your father and I talked about this. Then, as now, the country was unsettled and in need of a firm hand to guide it. Henry VI was not the man, and your father came back to retake his throne. The same unrest exists now, and the country may not be ready to accept a child as king.'

As I sipped my warm wine and turned to look at him, faint memories began to stir.

'Your father, sadly, did not live until the old age we had all hoped, so that you would be a man at the time of your accession. Your father and I did not know then precisely who was likely to arise, but we knew that the red rose of Lancaster would not lie dormant, and between us we worked out a plan.' He paused, and then said, 'This is where the trust and understanding come in.' He looked directly at the boy, holding his gaze for a long moment, and then said, 'We agreed that in the case of your father's early death, in order to protect his children I should declare him – and thus you and your brother – illegitimate and claim the crown for myself.'

The protest was immediate and loud. The king rose to his feet and began to berate his uncle. 'It is impossible that my father should have agreed to such a thing,' Edward said. 'It defames my father and my grandparents too.'

'It does, my lord,' Dick said, 'but it was the only way that we could see of keeping you safe. My mother is privy to the plan, and has agreed to it. She will speak to you confirming this, should you wish. Your mother does not know of it, and never can, for I fear she would not be persuaded. I would not tell even you, sire, young as you are, except that you are king and have a right to know what is to be done in your name.'

'I gain my life, and so does my brother, but I lose my kingdom,' Edward said. 'I do not see much benefit in that.'

'There is more to the plan,' Dick told him. 'Hear me out. I shall not be king long. When you come to man's estate – two or three years, perhaps, as we said – I am to reverse the Act and thus the stigma of illegitimacy, resign the throne and retire to my estates in the north. By then you will be sole and undisputed king in your own right, the possibility of revolt and other claimants will be remote, all our lives will be safe, and all matters can be put right.'

The boy was silent.

I leaned forward and coughed quietly. 'Your Majesty,' I said, 'if I may crave a word . . .'

Edward turned to look at me. 'I apologize, Master Memling,' he said. 'You may leave. I am sorry to have forced you to listen to this.'

'Your Majesty,' I said again, 'I can perhaps shed some light on this matter.'

Now Dick also turned to look at me. 'I don't understand,' he said.

Ignoring him, I asked, 'May I speak, Your Majesty?'

Edward nodded.

'I think your uncle does not remember all the details of the conversation during which this plan was hatched,' I said.

'I think I do,' Dick said.

'I think you do not remember where and when you had the conversation,' I went on.

'What in the name of Heaven has that to do with anything, man?' Dick asked. 'These are serious matters we speak of here.'

'Your father was a good and loyal friend to me,' I went on.

'As you to him,' Edward replied, and I thanked him with a bob of the head before continuing.

Dick was looking exasperated, and I went straight to the

point. 'The conversation did take place,' I told them, 'and I myself was witness to it.'

'What?' Dick rose to his feet. 'What trickery is this? How could you . . . ?'

'It was the warm wine which reminded me,' I said. 'I did recall when first I had it made for you.'

And then Dick remembered. 'Oh.' He sat down again.

The king looked from me to him and back. 'It was the night Ned Plant and his brother Dick came to my house in Bruges without even a coat to protect them from the rain,' I told them, 'and drank my warm wine and talked in my bed in front of my fire of how to regain Ned's estate for his new-born child, and what to do if it did not come to pass.'

'So it was,' Dick breathed, and sat upright on his bench. 'I had forgot. It was at your house, before your fire, drinking warm wine, as you say, and laying in your bed while the rain beat upon the roof and windows, that night when you first showed us your kindness.'

'I did not know then that I was listening to the King of England and his brother, but I remember what they said. Thus I can confirm the truth of what my lord of Gloucester says of your father's plans for you, Your Majesty, in the event of his death, which sadly has come to pass.'

'You loved my father, and are not a man of lies,' Edward said. I felt my head bow, partly in acknowledgement of his compliment, and partly to hide my face. He looked back at Dick.

'Why should we accept your plan?' he said to Dick.

'It is dangerous,' Dick said, 'for only a few may be privy to the details, but if all goes well it will save your kingdom. And even if it goes badly it may save the lives of you and your brother.'

'How so?' asked the boy. 'How badly can it go?'

'Realistically,' Dick said, 'it is not impossible that Tudor will attempt to take the crown anyway, as the claimant of the House of Lancaster. If God wills it, he may defeat me in battle. If that happens then the only way you will be safe is if you are no threat to his accession. Two princes will lend his reign a spurious note: two bastards are of no importance. There is another matter – when my time as Protector is over, I will be of no further use to you. I will be pushed aside, and will no longer be able to protect you. If you are to be bastardized according to this plan then it must be done soon.'

'But it is a lie, is it not?'

'It is, my lord, but a lie for the best of reasons.'

'I will swear that no man has ever heard you say a thing that you know not to be true,' Edward said. 'Why do you now change your mind? Is it not a sin?'

'It is, my lord, but one which will soon be rectified. And it is only a small sin in a great cause for good.'

'My cause?'

'Yours, of course, and your brother's, and, I have to admit, my own too. But above all it is the cause of England herself. Your Majesty may recall my motto.'

'*Loyauté me lie,*' Edward murmured. 'Loyalty binds me. Loyalty to England and to me, as to my father?'

'Yes,' Dick said. 'That is what I have to do. Above all, remember that it is not always right which will conquer. It is power that makes the law, and he that has the power will be the law. I have to ensure that that power is in the right hands.'

Edward rose to his feet and walked a few silent paces towards the tower wall where he stood, his back to us. Dick waited while the king thought the matter through. Finally Edward turned and came back to his seat. 'Do you assure me in all solemnity that you do not wish simply to take my throne for yourself?'

'I do, my lord, in all good faith. I would not do this were there any other way.'

Edward pursed his lips. 'I am minded to let it be done as you say,' he said, 'but why do you not just have me crowned and take whatever consequences come?'

'You will forgive me, Your Majesty, but your Woodville relatives are not to be trusted, especially after Stony Stratford.'

'I trust them,' Edward said.

'And well Your Majesty might, for they mean you no harm. But you do know how the treasure of England was looted while your father still lay on his deathbed, how the news of his death was not relayed to me, the Protector, and how your mother's brothers conspired to ignore your father's will and have their own way with the realm, do you not?'

'I have heard so,' the boy said. 'I suppose you must do it, then. Make the plan as you wish.'

'I thank Your Majesty,' Dick said, and smiled for the first time.

Of Princes and of Printers

(early June 1483)

'It is a necrosis,' Doctor Argentine told me over a stoup of wine one evening a day or so later.

'Necrosis?'

'Death of tissue. I have some herbs and salves which slow down the process, but I fear it may never be completely cured.'

'Is it serious?'

'It is, but he could live fifty years with it. The pain will never really go away, though, and of course that is likely to affect his humour and his temper.'

And so it had. Edward's condition had deteriorated since his interview with Dick, and along with it his humour. The young king-in-waiting had little enough to be cheerful about. The pain was constant, and he was all too aware that he was no longer the handsome young boy he had once been. The missing teeth and the constant bleeding gave his face a curious look, and he was forced to wipe his mouth two or three times a minute. He was also going through one of those phases of piety that boys of that age are prone to, and thus had decided that God was punishing him for some slight that he was unaware of, or some sin committed by his late father.

Having been brought up more or less entirely by the queen's family, especially Lord Rivers, he had moved among men who were antagonistic to Dick, and despite his own inclinations he seemed to have become suspicious of his paternal uncle. Consequently he was never quite sure if he was in the Tower for his own safety or Dick's security. I told him that it was as Dick had related, something of both, but I think that although his heart wanted to believe me, his mind was still partly Woodville.

The worst aspect, however, was his belief that he was dying. He fell to his prayers as a glutton to food, and my own time with him became more and more limited. At first he had enjoyed the novelty of drawing again, but soon he was loth to go outside to be seen by the people, as he was embarrassed about his appearance. Sometimes I cajoled him into the garden so that he could walk about and get some exercise, and occasionally he even took to practising with bow and arrow, but it was clear that the pain took his mind too much away from the activity. In the end it was all that Argentine and I could do to get him out of bed each morning. He became less kinglike as the days went by.

'No one tells me anything,' he complained one morning a few days after the interview.

'Of what, Your Majesty?'

'Of anything. I have been here nigh on a month now, and I have no news of my mother or my sisters and brother, and no news of my uncles save that the Protector has them under arrest.'

'Your Majesty knows how slowly the news of these things takes to come through.'

'What of my mother?'

'As you already know, sire,' I said. 'She entered sanctuary at Westminster Abbey, fearful that my lord of Gloucester might accuse her of treason too.'

'Uncle Dick would not do that – not to a woman, especially

a queen and my mother. Of that I am sure, for all her brothers' suspicions of him.'

'She is not as sure of him as you are, sire,' I said. 'She has only heard what his enem . . . what your uncles have told her.' If he noticed my slip, he affected not to.

'Could I write to her?' he asked.

'I cannot think that there could be any objection to that,' I told him. 'If you do so, I shall ask permission to take your letters to her myself, so that they should not miscarry. If I might suggest, Your Majesty, your sisters and brother might also enjoy receiving letters from you.'

This cheered him immensely, and he began to write, in a round, childish hand, first to his mother and then to his younger brother, begging him to come and visit the Tower.

There was a Great Council meeting that morning, and I sent in a note asking permission to carry the king's letters to his mother, which was granted. Apparently some lords wished to read the correspondence before it was delivered, but Dick over-ruled that idea, saying that a boy's words to his mother and hers to him were as private as might be, and could harm no one.

Every second day, therefore, I moved between the Tower and the Abbey, waiting at the great cathedral while the queen penned her answer, which was often accompanied by an ill-penned note from Richard, the king's younger brother, or a rather more elegant one from Princess Bess, Ned's eldest child, or, more rarely, one of Edward's other sisters.

After the second or third occasion I found the time hanging heavy on my hands, and having visited the Abbey's precincts many times I was idling my time away at a nearby tavern when I saw something that sparked my interest.

A man entered the tavern and sat at a bench opposite me.

Then he reached into a scrip that he carried and withdrew a white rectangle of paper, which he began to peruse. At first I took it to be a letter, and thought no more of it, though men reading in taverns was as unusual then as it is now. Then, as he turned the page, I noticed that the letters were of different sizes, and of a fierce black. It was not handwriting at all, but printing.

'I did not know that the craft of printing had come into England,' I commented idly.

'It is but a recent thing,' he replied. 'This man is the first to practise it.' He passed the pamphlet across to me. 'He has a place at the old Almonery opposite the Abbey. Look for the sign of the Red Paling.'

With time on my hands, I strolled over to the premises, the outer part of which was a shop, with a hinged shutter, propped open so that passers-by could see inside and make their purchases. In the room was a huge flat machine of timber and iron resembling a cheese press, while in a further room I could see a man's back as he bent over a bench before him. Beside the machine stood a shortish man with grey hair. He had aged and both he and his hair were liberally bespattered with a black liquid, but I recognized him immediately.

'Cakkeston!' I said. 'So you did manage to produce books!'

He was smearing the liquid onto the machine, coating what looked like a metal surface. He completed his task before looking up to see who was addressing him, and even then had to peer at me. He took a step towards me. 'Hans?' he said. 'Is it Hans?' Then he clasped me to him, clapped me on the back three or four times and stepped back to look at me at arm's length, by which time quite a considerable amount of the black fluid had transferred itself from him to me. He seemed not to notice. 'Hans!' he said again. 'I can't believe it.'

Then he broke away from me and said, apologetically, 'Forgive me, but this must be dealt with before the ink dries.' He returned to his metal plate, scrutinized it in some detail, and then placed a piece of paper across the top. He began to turn a large screw which lowered another plate onto the inked one. Once it was screwed down, he counted aloud to ten and then reversed the process, with the upper plate rising. The paper was removed and subjected to the same scrutiny as had befallen the plate, and after a nod of satisfaction he laid the paper flat, the ink markings on the upper side, and finally turned his attention to me.

'What brings you to London?' he asked.

I explained about Sir John, whom he remembered, of course, the rescue of the king and the arrest of the three lords, which he had also heard of, and my subsequent role as tutor and companion to the boy king and bearer of missives to and from his family. I said nothing of the other business, and when William asked after the king's health I merely said that he was suffering from a toothache.

'It was his father and the Duke of Gloucester who helped set me up here,' Cakkeston said. 'When I came back from Bruges they advanced me the money to set up the shop. My wares are yet few in number and still beyond the means of the ordinary man, I fear, but they will become more affordable in time.' He turned away and hunted around on a shelf, returning with two books, one small and one larger, and a great sheaf of papers which he tidied as we talked. 'Will you be good enough to take these to the king as a gift?' he asked. 'The larger is the more recent, and may amuse and entertain him. The other he will have heard of, but it was printed some years ago, so he may not have a copy of his own. It was written by his uncle, the queen's brother, Lord Rivers.'

'He that is in detention?' I asked.

'The same.'

'And the other book?' I hefted it; it was of a considerable size.

'It is entertaining as well as instructive,' William said. 'It is the work of an English poet of the last century, Geoffrey Chaucer. It fits all moods, being in turn beautiful and bawdy.'

The work of tying the loose sheets was done. 'For this I apologize to His Majesty,' he said. 'For the state of it, that is, but not for the content. It is the tale of King Arthur and his knights, heroes all, who lived in England centuries ago. It was told by a knight named Malory, who died some years ago. It is not yet ready to be given to the world, but it will make good reading for a boy.'

The other man now came through from the back room, and Caxton (for thus I must now remember to spell his name) introduced him as his assistant Jan Wynkyn. 'A man of your own territory,' he added, 'being a Netherlander.'

'German, originally,' Jan said, thrusting out his ink-stained hand. 'I know your work, Master Memling. I too have been to Sintjacobskerk.'

'I too was German,' I said, and we tested out our native tongue while William wrapped his gift for the king in clean paper to keep the ink away and tied it firmly with string so that I might carry it all the easier.

I spent the rest of the afternoon there, discovering the details of the printing trade, and promised to return again before long. William was the most pleasant of companions, as always, and I was loth to leave his shop, although mindful of the time passing. In the end I tore myself away and crossed to the Abbey to collect the king's letters.

In his turn the king was delighted with his books. He enjoyed reading, and in the two volumes and the sheaf of papers he was able to find the romance, chivalry and adventure that any boy craves, along with the bawdiness that all boys secretly enjoy and, in the work of his uncle, not only the wisdom of the philosophers of old but also a connection with a man who had helped to bring him up, and whose arrest had been such a shock to him. The three works became his constant companions.

The gift also drew him closer to me again. He began once again to see me as a friendly face rather than as a servant, and the fact that I was also the go-between for himself and his family raised me a notch in his estimation. Quite how high my star was riding became clear to me later, in the first week of June.

'I would request that you do me another service,' he asked.

'Your Majesty has no need to request,' I told him. 'I am his to command, as he is aware.'

'In that case I would wish you to attend the Great Council each day as my representative, and bring me news of what is said and decided in my name. At present, no one tells me anything. My uncle Dick would do so, but has not the time. He is too busy, and there are no others whom I know well enough to ask.'

'I cannot attend the Council, Your Majesty,' I told him. 'I have no title or office. Those are noble and powerful men. I am but a painter of faces.'

'And a plain, blunt, honest man who will tell me what he hears and sees. That is all I want. You don't need a title.'

'The Council will never accept it,' I said. 'Those are men most jealous of their positions. They will not want an upstart foreigner eavesdropping on them.'

'That is not the way they will see it,' he said. 'I shall make the request, and their response will tell me whether I am king or not.' He sat to write it, and then looked up at me. 'There is one more thing you could do for me, Hans,' he said.

'Of course, Your Majesty,' I said. 'What is it?'

'Stop calling me that,' he said, 'at least when we are in private. No one calls me by my name any more – it's "My Liege" this and "Your Majesty" that. It makes me feel lonely and separates me from myself. I want to be called Edward again. Will you do that for me?'

Of course I had to agree, and the boy had no idea of the footsteps he was following in.

Of My Elevation
to the Council
(9th June 1483)

King Edward wrote it out for me in his own hand, and I have it before me now as I copy it down.

Whereas Our Lord in Heaven has seen fit to take our father, Edward, into his bosom in our minority, we must perforce rely upon our Council of State to advise us on decisions that we must take. The better to ascertain what is mooted and decided in our name, we appoint our beloved servant Johannes Memling to be our eyes and ears and to give daily report to us of our Council's deliberations. Master Memling, being neither a native Englishman nor a member of any family or faction, will report to us without bias. Notwithstanding this, we intend that he shall be solely an observer of the Council, privy to its thoughts and considerations but allowed neither voice nor vote. Given by our own hand this ninth day of June, year of Our Lord one thousand, four hundred and eighty-three.

He sealed it with his signet ring, and signed it 'Edwardus Rex'.

I went that same morning and bore the paper to Dick. 'I can see no objection to this,' he told me, 'although there may be those that do. Present yourself to the Council today and let us see.'

There were obviously some members of the Council who were uneasy about what was proposed and even some who were suspicious of my own motives, and these were not slow at coming forward.

'How do we know that Master Memling is not a foreign agent,' asked Bishop Morton of Ely, 'or worse, a spy for the Lancastrians?'

'It is our king who has commanded this,' Will Hastings pointed out, 'and it is to that same king that Master Memling will be reporting. There can be nothing that any one of us would want to hide from our king.'

'I cannot vouch for Master Memling's dealings with foreign powers,' Dick put in, his lips curling into a faint smile, 'but for these twelve years he has been a loyal friend to my brother the late king and to me, and I would trust him to carry out these duties His Majesty has charged him with.'

'If your lordships please,' I said, 'I did not seek this post; nor do I desire it. I want no more than to return to my home and family. If your lordships see fit to deny me my charge I shall not be disappointed. Perhaps you could suggest to His Majesty another name more pleasing to you to fulfil this duty, and I shall be glad to leave your realm.'

'It would not be a wise move to deny such a simple request from the king,' put in another lord, 'and those who sought to do so might find themselves marked men when His Majesty comes into his majority.'

'I doubt His Majesty would see the matter as being of such a seriousness as that,' Dick said, and then turned to me. 'Master Memling,' he asked, 'in your opinion, why does His Majesty wish to make this appointment?'

'I think, my lord,' I said, 'that he wishes to feel himself part of the process of decision-making, and also to be made fully aware, in simple language, of what is going on. It will also mean that each day that the Council meets His Majesty will be guaranteed some human contact on matters which are of interest and importance to him.' I paused, and then added, 'Your lordships must remember that apart from myself and Doctor Argentine, His Majesty sees no one but his servants, and his illness will not allow him to permit strangers to visit. He is in every respect a king, but he is also a lonely young boy, frightened of the pain, the issue of blood and the thought of death.'

One of the clerics leaned forward, a look of horror on his face. 'Surely His Majesty's condition cannot be that serious?'

'I think not, my lord,' I said, 'but the young have such vivid imaginations and so little experience to set against them.'

There was a moment of silence, and then Dick said, 'Do we then accede to His Majesty's request?' There were general signs of agreement from those around the table, and Richard nodded at me and gestured with his left hand towards a small group of chairs set back from the central table, from where I would be able to hear and observe, but whence I would not give the impression of being part of the Council.

The early business was all about the arrangements for the coronation, which was but thirteen days away, and concerned matters which were largely routine, and I scribbled idly in my notebook and considered that my lot for the foreseeable future was boredom and naught else, and that I would have little of interest to relay to His Majesty on that night or indeed any other.

I was in the midst of such thoughts when the door opened and in came Archbishop Bourchier, dragging behind him an older man in clerical robes. 'My lords, I apologize for my tardy arrival,' he said, 'but I have come post-haste from a meeting of the lords spiritual with tidings that must be heard by you all immediately.' He swept around the table to his seat, looked to see that he had everyone's attention and then pointed at the other man. 'Some of you may know the Bishop of Bath and Wells, Bishop Stillington. Speak, my lord.'

Stillington began to fumble around, producing documents and papers from beneath his robes. He took so long about it that Bourchier suddenly thundered, 'Speak, I bade you. All this can wait until your news is given.' Bourchier was normally such a quietly spoken, affable man that this outburst alone was enough to rivet all of our attention on Stillington, who immediately began to wilt under the attention.

'My lords,' he began, 'I know not where to begin . . .'

Bourchier began to rise from his seat, his face a bright red, and Stillington hurried on. 'The late King Edward,' he said, which words were enough to drop Bourchier back into his seat, 'did, in 1461, enter into a pre-contract to marry Lady Eleanor Butler.'

Bourchier slumped back in his chair, the clerics looked at each other in a wild surmise, and the rest of the lords, like me, waited for what was to come.

'This cannot be,' Bishop Morton said. 'It is impossible.'

'What is?' Hastings asked. 'What has he said? What does it mean?'

'It means,' Bourchier said, still slumped, 'that King Edward went through a form of marriage with Lady Butler a full three years before he married the queen.' He looked around the table, and then added, 'And that means that the marriage with the queen was bigamous and unlawful.'

I looked at Dick; he was staring at Bourchier, his mouth open in shock.

The Master of Bruges

This time half the table began to call out. 'No, no. It's nonsense,' I heard someone say, and then, 'Who is Eleanor Butler?'

'Lady Eleanor Butler entered a nunnery after the ceremony, and died there soon after,' Bourchier said.

Morton let out a long sigh of relief and flung himself back into his chair. 'Well, that's all right, then,' he said. 'You cause us concern for no reason, my lord. If she died, where's the problem?'

Solemnly, Bourchier said, 'She died in 1468. The king married the queen in 1464.'

Richard still had not moved or changed his expression.

'For God's sake, will someone enlighten me?' Hastings said. 'What is all this supposed to mean?'

'In the simplest of language, my lord,' Bourchier said, which was a relief to me at least, and presumably to most of the lords around the table, 'it means that King Edward was never legally married to Queen Elizabeth, and that all children of the so-called marriage are illegitimate.'

Dick spoke for the first time. 'This must be the work of an enemy,' he said. 'Where is the proof, where the witnesses? This is just hearsay, with no basis in fact.'

'My lord?' Bourchier said.

Dick looked at him, but the archbishop was looking at Stillington.

'It was I that conducted the ceremony,' Stillington said. 'I was sworn to silence by His Majesty, and have revealed my secret to but one man before now, and he the king's brother.'

All heads swivelled to look at Dick, but Stillington swiftly corrected the impression he had given. 'I mean my lord of Clarence, now deceased,' he said, 'not my lord of Gloucester. Do not rely on my word, my lords; I have proof of what I say.'

Once again he dug into his robes to produce documents. 'Here is the contract,' he said, 'and here the seals of the king and the Lady Eleanor, and here the seals of the noble witnesses to the ceremony.'

'Forgeries,' Dick said. 'Bound to be. I would ask you, my lord bishop, to examine these papers most carefully. I know not what you expect to gain, Bishop Stillington, but . . .'

'Nothing, my lord,' Stillington said. 'I am an old man, with nothing to gain and nothing to fear. I wish naught except that the truth before God should come out and prevent an error, indeed a sacrilege, of the most serious nature.'

The documents were being passed from hand to hand, each man having barely a moment to glance at them before his neighbour tugged urgently at them. Dick reached out and plucked the largest of the papers from Archbishop Morton's hand. 'This is certainly my brother's seal,' he said, 'and this, I presume, that of the Lady Eleanor. The witnesses; who was present?' He fell completely silent, and then his head came up, looking along the table. All our eyes followed his and converged on one man.

'Yes,' said my lord Hastings. 'I was there.'

Dick's face went deadly pale, the blood draining from it even as we looked, and again horror was written across it. 'You knew this, and said nothing?' Dick said.

'It was Ned's will,' Hastings said.

'If Prince Edward is not king,' someone asked, 'then who is?'

'My lord Edward of Warwick is next in line,' someone else said.

'Warwick is a minor,' said Rotherham.

'More to the point, he is a simpleton,' Lord John Howard said. 'The country would never accept him as king.'

'In any case,' Bishop Morton muttered, 'Warwick is attaindered because of his father's treason. He cannot succeed. So that means . . .' The sentence went unfinished as we looked across the table at the Protector.

His face was like that of a man stunned by a blow to the head, and then he began to shake his head slowly from side to side. Finally, a low moan escaped his lips. 'No,' he said, 'no, Lord God, no, not me. Please, no, not me.'

Of Marriages

(9th June 1483)

I returned with Dick to Crosby Hall, his house on Bishops-gate Street. All the way home he remained silent, but once behind his own doors a torrent of words flooded out. His eyes were blazing and the volume of language hurtling from his mouth made it impossible for me to follow what he was saying. His wife, the Lady Anne, came into the room and simply waited. After pacing up and down several times, flinging incomprehensible sentences in all directions, Dick caught sight of her gaping at him and stopped his rant. Then he flung himself into a chair and stared at the two of us. 'What am I supposed to do now?' he asked. 'Just what am I supposed to do?'

My Lady Anne, calm as ever, must have at the least raised an interrogative eyebrow, for he took a deep breath and told her the story, remaining for the moment as controlled as he could.

'Is that possible?' I asked at the end. 'Would your brother marry a woman in secret?'

'Where women were concerned Ned was the biggest fool in Christendom,' Dick said. 'He'd promise them the earth if they'd let him put his . . .' He caught himself and the Lady Anne's eye at the same moment, and adjusted what he was about to say.

'If they'd let him . . . you know. That's how Elizabeth came to be queen – she just held him at bay for a few weeks until he agreed to marry her. Oh, he was capable of it all right. Damn Ned, damn Stillington, damn Hastings, damn the whole bastard bloody country. I don't know what to do.'

'What does the woman say, this Butler?' Anne asked.

'Nothing. The woman is dead, and can tell us nothing.'

'I still don't understand, though,' she told him. 'What, after all, has changed? The plan you hatched with Ned can still work. The boys are still illegitimate, you will still be king until you decide to step down, as you intended. The result is the same, surely, whether Edward likes it or not?'

Slowly, Dick shook his head. 'No, you don't see. If my brother were declared illegitimate, then it would be a slight on my mother, but one which she is prepared to put up with to gain us the time we need. The result would be that the Woodvilles would have no quarrel with me or anyone else. They could be eased aside gently with no difficulty in an atmosphere of peace. In a few years' time the truth could be revealed and Edward take his place on the throne, a peaceful transition. You see that, yes?'

Anne and I both nodded. That much had always been clear.

'But if the boys alone are illegitimate, all that changes. The slight is now on Elizabeth and her family, and they will stop at nothing to avenge that, and fight tooth and nail to keep their positions and their power. They are probably plotting against me even now. If Edward is not king, then I am not Protector, so they'll see me as a legitimate target to be done away with, at least until I am declared king. With me gone, only our baby stands between them and power, or between Henry Tudor and power or, worse, between the two factions and another twenty years of war.'

'Oh, my God,' Anne said suddenly. 'I had not thought of that. Our boy will be king after you?'

'By God, I hope not. I don't want to be king,' Richard said, 'and I don't want him to be either. I have a good life, and work to do in the north. I want to be with my family.' He paused and gnawed on his lower lip, and then said, 'There's another thing; if the boys are bastards, then the girls are too.'

'What difference does that make?' I asked.

'I am told that Henry Tudor has long had his eyes on marrying one of the princesses to unite the York and Lancaster lines. It would bolster his feeble claim to the throne. If that happened during the reign of my nephew Edward or after Edward had sons of his own, it would mean little, but now it gives the Woodvilles a reason to unite with Henry Tudor against me. I can probably defeat them, even combined, but it will be a long and bloody job and a waste of the men and resources of England.'

'And if you lose?' Anne asked gently.

'If I lose, then I die, and if I have read this aright, then our son will die too.' Anne's hand flew to her throat as she tried to stifle a gasp.

'Henry will never support my Edward's claim once I am dead. The end result would still be to put Ned's Edward back on the throne, as I intended all along, but without the security I sought for you and me and the baby. That would serve Tudor's purpose, for by hook or by crook he will take the crown from Edward as soon as the opportunity arises, and take the throne for himself. Then he can do what he likes with Ned's children. No, this declaration of illegitimacy snatches peace from England's grasp in the very moment that it most seemed secure.'

'If this story of Ned's earlier marriage is true, you can

never hand the throne over to Edward – I mean, His Majesty Edward V,' I said. 'After all, if it is true, then you are the rightful king, despite all.'

'I don't want to be king,' he said. 'I have never wanted to be king. I want to stay at home and look after my estates and play with my babies and hold my wife in my arms in peace and safety – and because of the family of monsters that I had the misfortune to be born into I have never had a moment's peace just to do those simple things and have those simple pleasures that the meanest of subjects takes as his right. I don't want the throne, Hans. I only agreed to the original plan because it was Ned's will and to protect his children. It was bad enough to think of being king for a few years until Edward came of age; to be king for life does not bear thinking about. I am heartily sick of the whole bloody business.' He turned to his wife. 'Anne,' he said, 'Anne, my love, what can I do?'

'You told the prince,' I ventured, 'that power makes the law. If you are king you have the power, so could you not reverse any Act of Illegitimacy?'

'That is one small hope,' he said, 'but it will be a long struggle, taking several years – at least until Edward is of age. Changing Parliament's mind is easy, but changing the Church's mind is a difficult, slow process. Mind you, knowing Elizabeth, I think it most likely that she entered into the marriage faithfully and honestly, knowing nothing of Eleanor Butler. If so, that would help in any campaign to legitimize them again. In the meantime, though, England has to be governed.'

'And who is the best man to do that job?' Lady Anne asked.

Despite himself, Dick smiled, and she took his head in her hands and kissed him.

I still had work to do. It was necessary for me to go back

to the Tower, to report to the unfortunate Edward V what decisions his Council had made in his name this day. I rose to my feet.

'Don't tell him, Hans,' Dick said.

'What?'

'Don't tell the king what was said. If it's true he'll have to be told soon enough, but if by chance it isn't, then to keep it from him will spare him anguish. Tell him only of the routine matters. He has a big enough cross to bear, God knows, with his illness. I will tell him myself, when the time comes. I owe him that, at least.'

I saw the sense in this, and nodded my agreement. It was his family, after all, not mine. Mine was still beyond the seas and beyond reach, and I knew not when I would see them again.

Of Revolt and Insurrection

(13th June 1483)

Edward was still not well disposed towards anyone by the time of the next meeting of his Great Council on the following Friday, and he took himself off to the menagerie to stare at the sad animals there, so that anyone who wished to see him would have to search the precincts of the Tower.

Few took the trouble to do so. My lord Hastings was one who did, kneeling to him as monarch on arrival and talking to him for a few minutes before excusing himself for the Council meeting. Dick was late in arriving, unusual for him, and he too greeted Edward as king. I was not close enough to hear what he said, but he spoke gently to his nephew, and when he left his face was serious and troubled. Edward, who had spent the entire time shaking his head in negative responses to his uncle, was left in tears, with spittle and blood mingling as he tried to stem the flow from his mouth.

'I must go to the Council, if Your Majesty gives me leave,' I said.

'I have a riddle for you,' Edward said, smiling wanly.

'Your Majesty?'

'How am I like unto this beast?' he asked, pointing at the lion which was sleeping in the summer sun.

'I know not, sir,' I said. It was an easy question, truth to tell, and I could have had the answer with a moment's thought, but my mind was on the coming Council, and I did not try to think of it.

'We are both kings, and both caged,' he said.

'Your Majesty is not caged,' I said, and almost added that he was not king either, but that would have been a step too far.

'I would be free of all this,' he said wearily.

Not knowing how best to respond, I bowed and followed Dick, to take my place as observer at the Council in the chamber in the White Tower.

The trouble was not long in starting. I took my place, at the rear and discreetly away from the table, and before I had even inked my pen Dick had thrown two documents on the table and said in a quiet, calm voice, 'Can any man explain these to me?'

At first no one moved, and then the Bishop of Rotherham leaned over and picked up one of them. He squinted at it closely, his eyesight being none too sharp, and then put it down. 'It is a letter, that is all,' he said, 'pertaining to some minor grants to do with the coronation.'

'I did not ask that you identify them,' Dick said, 'but that you explain them.' I looked up at him – there was something in his tone and manner that betokened ill to someone.

No one spoke; most seemed genuinely puzzled.

'For those who, unlike my lord bishop, cannot identify them,' Dick said, 'they are, as he says, minor grants and dispositions of some of His Majesty's revenues.' He tapped one of them. 'This is to do with some cloth, and the other with five tuns of wine to be distributed at the coronation. The one bears the seal of Archbishop Morton, the other of my lord Hastings.'

'I do not see the point you are making,' Morton said, with a hint of nervousness.

'What neither of them bears,' Dick went on, 'is the seal of either His Majesty King Edward V or of the Lord Protector,' and his voice suddenly rose in volume: 'Richard of Gloucester, Defender of the King, myself.'

'Some oversight,' Hastings said. 'These things happen, Dick.'

'Oversight,' Dick repeated. He looked around the table. 'I have seen too many seals this last week, placed where they should not have been, have I not, Will? By one oversight you seal this, by another oversight you fail to inform the Council of a matter which renders all that we do and all that we strive to do pointless and possibly illegal. But are the oversights ended?' He raised his eyebrows and looked along the row of faces before him.

'I am sorry, Dick,' Hastings said. 'You know how things can get overlooked when a man is so busy with such matters. I shall be more careful henceforward, and I am sure that the same can be said for my lord Bishop of Ely.'

Dick did not reply at first, but reached inside his tunic. 'A firm purpose of amendment was ever a precondition for forgiveness,' he said, as he smoothed out another piece of paper. 'And the oversight on this one?' He placed the paper on the table, flattened it again, and then turned it so that it was the right way up for those opposite him. Men leaned forward. I had no possibility of seeing what it was from where I was sitting, but I noticed that neither Morton nor Hastings leaned forward, as if they knew already what they were being asked to look at. At the far end of the table two other men made no movement either; their names were Catesby and Howard, the one a lawyer and the other the noble landowner who had accompanied Ned and Dick to Bruges.

'I see your seal here, do I not, my lord bishop?' Dick said conversationally, placing his finger at the end of the document, 'and here next to it I find the seal of my lord Hastings. Nowhere, however, is there any seal of the king, or once again any seal of the Lord Protector, Richard of Gloucester, Defender of the Crown, myself.' He picked it up. 'Just another minor oversight?' he mused. He was quiet, but the menace was real. 'Oh yes, very minor, for I see that my two lordships have issued orders commanding Members of Parliament not to attend on the 25th of June, as they had been commanded by their king by the advice of his uncle Richard of Gloucestershire, Protector and Defender. Myself. His Majesty and I have been excised from our role in government as easily as a sheepdog cuts out the sheep his master wants. If the king and I are the sheep, which lord is my shepherd – and who are his dogs?'

Again his eyes traversed the table, and again, still conversational, he said, not even looking at the man he addressed, 'Come then, my lord Stanley, show us how well you bark.'

Stanley's reaction was instantaneous. He leapt to his feet and his hand went to his side, where normally his sword would have been. But he had unbuckled the belt and hung the weapon over the back of a chair when he had entered the room, and when he turned to look for it he found it in Lord John Howard's grasp.

'This is a mockery,' Morton said. 'You know he is no king. You have seen the evidence, as I have.'

'And yet, seeing that, knowing that, you plot against my life in order to put him on the throne?'

'You have no legal status,' Morton said.

'And you cannot have it all ways, my lord,' Dick told him. 'If Edward is not king, and you are plotting against my life, then you are plotting against him whom you proposed and recognized as king in this very room on Monday last, and that is a treasonous act. If Edward is king, as I hope he may yet be, then plotting the death of the Protector is a treasonous act. Edward my brother was lawfully king, and in his will left me in charge during the minority of his son. I am the lawful government of this land. Acting against the lawful government of the land is a treasonous act, my lord. I do not yet know whether your treason is against the king that was, the king that is or the king who might yet be, but it is surely treason against someone and against this realm.' He raised his voice. 'Captain of the guard!'

The door opened and an officer entered. Behind him a troop of men was arrayed. I saw pikes and swords. 'My lord?'

'Arrest and confine my lord Bishop Morton, my lord Bishop Rotherham, and my lord Stanley to await trial on charges of high treason.'

The captain did not flinch. 'My lord,' he said.

'This is all nonsense,' Rotherham said, in a belated attempt to bluster out of it.

'If only it were,' Dick said, 'I would be well content. But I have proof enough. Proof of how people stole from one bed to another, or had their wives carry messages to the queen – yes, that too I know, Stanley – and sent their servants to do their treasonous bidding. I know how you tried to wither and destroy my power as if to remove my right arm from me so that I could use it no more. I know all this, and more, and you shall answer for it before the courts.'

Morton pushed back his chair and rose, and Rotherham too saw that the game was up. Only Stanley refused to accept what had been said. 'You can prove nothing,' he said.

'When you come to trial we shall determine that,' Dick told him, and then Stanley shrugged and accepted the situation.

All this time Will Hastings had stood silent at the end of the table, but when the others had filed through the door he spoke to Dick. 'What about me, Dick?' he asked. 'Am I to be arrested too?'

Dick sat down, heavily, the chair scraping back on the flagged floor, and would not look at him.

'Well, what . . .' Hastings began.

'He knows everything, Will,' John Howard said slowly. 'Catesby told him, and I confirmed it with what I knew.'

'Catesby?' Hastings said. He looked at the lawyer, still in his seat. 'I trusted you.'

'Trusted? You trusted him?' Dick said savagely. 'You trusted him, Will? Did you trust him as Ned trusted you? Did you trust him as I trusted you? Did you trust him as that young boy outside trusted you to do right?'

'I was doing right,' Hastings said. 'I want Ned's lad on the throne, and no other.'

'So do I, Will, so do I,' Dick said. 'But if that cannot be – if he be barred because by Church law he may be a bastard, which of us carries most responsibility, Will? You, who witnessed his father's wedding ceremony and knew about it, or me, who knew nothing? You, who could have spoken out and put the matter right any time in these last fifteen years, or me, who knew nothing? And at the last, do you side with those working for peace in this realm, or those who would sow such discord as will curse the country for another generation to come?'

'I thought it all for the best, Dick,' Hastings said. 'I wanted to do what was best for Ned and for his lad.'

'And so do I,' Dick said, 'but over and above doing what is best I have a sworn duty to do what is right. Right for the lad and right for the country – and if it happens to save my life, aye, and the life of my son, too, well all the better. I am astonished, Will. I expect this sort of thing of Morton and Stanley

– treachery runs through their veins; it is their life blood. But not from you, Will – surely, not from you.'

'If I'd spoken out, said what I knew, then I would have had to die, too,' Hastings said.

'Too?' Dick said. 'Why? Who had to die because he knew?'

'Oh my God, Dick,' Hastings said. 'You really don't know?'

Dick stared at him, and Hastings' face underwent a change. There was some strong emotion wrestling within him.

'Who, Will?' Dick asked quietly.

Hastings licked his lips. 'Stillington told you,' he said. 'He told George.'

If Dick had not previously appreciated fully what his brother's knowledge had led to, it was clear that he understood now. From him came a howl of anguish the like of which I had never heard issue from a man. The hair on my neck crawled as I listened. His face crumpled, and tears started from his eyes, while a long moan turned into a barely recognizable, long drawn-out 'No'.

Hastings stood silent, but Dick had lost all control. 'You traded Ned's secret for our brother's life? The two of you forced me to watch as you executed him, and it was just because he knew a secret? And now you wish to destroy me and my family to keep that sinful secret?' He shook his head violently, as if shaking away the idea. 'Loyalty is a fine thing, Will, but in the name of Christ find something worth being loyal to.'

'I was being loyal to my king and my friend,' Hastings said.

'Ned is dead, and you and your carousing helped him on his way,' Dick said. 'His lad is alive, and needs our help. I know not which of us your treason was against, Will, but treason it was.' With an effort, he regained his composure.

'Don't arraign me for treason, Dick,' Hastings said suddenly. 'I was your friend once, though I plotted against you, and I would be your friend again. If I must die, do it now and leave me my dignity. Leave my family with that which was mine. I confess my crimes before all these lords, and will take my punishment this day, Dick. I could not bear to be found guilty of treason, whether to Ned or to his lad – no, nor to you, either. I beg you, do it now.'

'I do not execute men without trial,' Dick said.

'If I go to trial I will be found guilty, Dick, and I will lose everything, and so will my wife,' Hastings said. 'And if I live, then go to trial I must. And Dick, if I go to trial I must die, too. You can pardon those three, but you can't pardon me. To pardon an enemy is magnanimity; to pardon a friend is weakness.' He leaned over the table, the better to make his plea. 'Do it now, Dick, today. You are Constable of England. You have the power to condemn me without trial. Do it, Dick, and spare me the trial – for the love I bore your brother, if not for my own sake. Or do it for George.' He straightened up. 'And I ask too that you forgive me.'

'There is no sense in delay,' put in Buckingham, his first contribution to the debate. 'And if he is held for any length of time his men may move to free him, and that would make matters worse. He has a lot of men in London, Dick.'

There was a long silence, and then Hastings said, 'Do it, Dick.'

Dick looked at the papers which still lay on the table, stood silent for a long time, and then, his mind made up, called, 'Captain.'

The man appeared again in the doorway.

'My lord Hastings has confessed before all men here present to a capital crime, and has waived his right to trial. He is to be taken hence and executed within the hour. Let him be shriven first, if he wishes it.'

'My lord!' The captain began to protest, but Dick pointed at Hastings.

'It is so,' Hastings said. 'Let it be done.'

When the captain looked at Dick again, the Protector indicated with his other hand the rest of the lords seated around the table. As the captain's glance swept over them, each man gave a silent nod of assent.

'I forgive you, Will,' Dick said.

Hastings nodded, and the captain made way, politely allowing Hastings to precede him out of the room. As the door closed, I heard the condemned man say, 'I should like to see a priest.'

Dick laid his head on the table in front of him. 'Get out,' he said. 'All of you, get out.'

Of Trust and Nobility

(16th June 1483)

After the official news of his deposition had been broken to the young king, he fell into a grave melancholy, and those who loved him feared for his sanity.

Dick, as ever, found the humane answer. He asked me to accompany him and Archbishop Bourchier to the Abbey to see the queen. Like the archbishop, I was a neutral politically. Nor was I powerful enough to belong to any faction, but I was known to be both a friend to the late king and a confidant of the young one. The young Duke of York liked and trusted me too, and so did his mother, and I readily agreed. If nothing else, young Edward was pining for lack of company of his own age. He was not strong, nor was he the sort of boy who is happy in his own company.

At the Abbey the queen was greatly changed. Her face was much beset by weeping while her beauty, although as powerful as ever, was strained by the stress she had been under. She received us kindly enough, entering with all of her daughters. We knelt to her, and before we could rise the door opened and in ran Richard. 'Hans!' he cried, and threw his arms around my neck.

'Your Grace,' I began by way of protest, but there was such a torrent of words from him that I could say no more.

'Ah, you have come with my uncle Gloucester. Are you going to let me paint some more? Have you seen Edward? What do you think of the fate of my lord Hastings? Did you bring materials for drawing? Have you heard the news? I am a bastard!'

'Richard, that's quite enough,' the queen said. 'Have you no greeting for my lord archbishop and for your uncle?'

Sobered, the boy knelt before the archbishop and received his blessing in a most unusual silence. Then he greeted Dick, still outwardly sombre but with a hint of mischief about his lips until he caught his mother's eye, after which he stood quietly. 'Go and make your preparations, Richard,' the queen said, and the boy bowed and left, followed by his three youngest sisters, leaving only Bess and Cecily with their mother.

'You knew, did you?' Dick asked.

'About Ned and the Butler woman?' She shook her head. 'Not at the time we married. He told me later.'

'She was dead, Elizabeth. Why could you not have told someone? All it would then have taken was a simple ceremony, and an Act of Parliament to legitimize them all. It would have been so simple, and all of this could have been prevented.'

'Why can that not be done now?'

'The king's death has taken that option away from us,' the archbishop said gently. 'The Church may make a match where there has been some error, but not even she can make a match where only one of the persons is living. The best that might happen . . .' He hesitated, unsure.

'Tell her,' Dick said.

'The best that may happen is that the Church may be able to recognize your children as legitimate, as you were unaware of any sin. Not all the children, perhaps – it might be restricted to those born after the death of Eleanor Butler.'

'Including Edward?'

'Yes, madam.'

She looked at Dick, a faint hope growing within her.

'It would need to go to Rome,' he said. 'The archbishop would have to consider the case and all the evidence would need to be presented to the Pope.'

'It is too broad a matter for a mere ecclesiastical court in England,' the archbishop explained. 'The fate of a nation depends on it.'

'We can start getting the case ready,' Dick said. 'It's just possible that I may not have to do Edward's job for ever.'

'How long?' the queen asked.

The archbishop's shoulders moved within his robes. 'Who knows?' he said. 'Three years, if they rush it through. Perhaps longer.'

'And in the meantime?'

'The country needs a king,' Dick said, 'and, Elizabeth, it must be someone who has no taint of bastardy about him, whose legitimacy cannot be questioned.'

'How convenient,' the queen said.

Dick bowed his head. 'I don't want this,' he said. 'If you had spoken . . . Why did you say nothing, Elizabeth? Surely not just to keep your Woodville family in positions of power. You could not be that short-sighted.'

The queen examined the edge of her handkerchief. 'If only I had known what was going to happen,' she said. 'I had no way of knowing, Dick. I kept silent for the most selfish of reasons. I thought Stillington might die, and then no one would know – Will would never have betrayed Ned's secret. It was even more stupid than you could think.'

Dick stared at her, and a look of comprehension came over his face. 'Oh, God, no,' he said. 'You thought . . .'

She nodded. 'That if Ned were to find himself free he might find himself another queen.'

Dick turned away, shaking his head, and the queen unfurled a paper and half-spoke, half-read a speech which had clearly been well rehearsed.

'"My lord archbishop and my lord of Gloucester, I freely confess to you that I entered into a bigamous marriage with the late King Edward. I entered into the marriage in good faith, but in his last years he confessed to me of his previous attachment. The evidence produced by Bishop Stillington is, I believe, correct. I hope that the Church will realize the suffering that I have been through since I learned these facts, and that both Church and State will realize why I remained silent. In protecting my own name and those of my children I know that I have sinned grievously, and I beg both Church and State to show mercy unto a woman who had thought herself to be a wife, widow, mother and queen, but now realizes that through no fault of her own she may call herself none of these save one. I have lost all else, but I stand before you still a mother in defence of her children."'

'You have no need to beg of me,' Richard said. 'I would not for all the world have wished you into this pretty pass, nor your children, whom you know I love.'

'Though your marriage be invalid, my child,' the archbishop said, 'you yourself are guilty of no sin; no more are your children. Forgiveness is absolute.'

'My brother Gloucester has ever been a most loyal subject to my husband, and an exemplary uncle to my children,' she said. 'I am happy to give my son Richard as well as my son Edward into his care, for I know of no one who would treat them better or take more care of them. You, my lord archbishop, I know as a good and holy man, and Master Memling here is a loyal friend and servant to my husband and his family. I ask you all three to keep my sons safe from any that may seek to harm them.'

'That will be easier to do within the Tower than here in sanctuary,' the archbishop said. 'There have been times when sanctuary has been violated . . .' He stopped suddenly, acutely aware that the most notorious such violation had been that by Edward IV himself at Tewkesbury Abbey twelve years before. The queen smiled; she saw the irony of that.

'Richard knows nothing of the details of what Stillington said,' the queen told us. 'I kept it from him. Does Edward know yet?'

'No,' Dick said, 'not in detail. I did not want to tell him until it was certain, and that there was no help for it. I will have to tell him soon, I fear.'

The queen decided to keep her daughters with her within the sanctuary. There had been a plot to have them removed to the continent, but it had been uncovered and it was known that she had no part in it. Illegitimate girls were as powerless as illegitimate boys.

Richard, still for the moment Duke of York, returned with us to the Tower to settle in with his brother. Their first moments together were traumatic for both. They had not seen each other for some months, and it was clear that no one had prepared the younger boy for the change he was about to see. I cursed myself for not thinking of it. The upshot was that the little lad hugged his brother at first sight, and then recoiled from the smell. Edward drew aside his bandage to show Richard what had happened to him, and shock burst onto the little boy's face like a ripe grape bursting in the mouth. 'You too are repelled by me,' Edward said, and turned his face away.

'Ed, I am not,' Richard said. 'It was a shock, that's all. I did not know that you were losing teeth.'

'You had better go,' Edward said. 'Your chamber will be made ready.'

To give him his due, Richard of York was a brave little boy. 'Can I not stay here with you?' he asked.

I looked away. The stench in the king's room was horrific, a cloying, evil smell that hung in the air and would not dissipate no matter what perfumes Argentine devised. To spend five minutes in there was more than I could bear.

'May I, Master Memling?' he asked. 'My place is with my brother, even if he be no longer king.'

Of course I could not deny him, and that night and every night they were there together the two boys slept in the same foul bedroom, reeking of decay and festering corruption, but purified by one boy's love for the other.

Of Backgrounds

It is imperative that the aspiring young painter ensures that he gets his backgrounds right at the outset. Not to do so can cause anger and cost a great deal of time and money. It must be made clear to the patron that a plain background is cheap and a landscape is expensive; and that he gets what he pays for. As a young man I twice did not make this clear to the patron, and as a result was forced to deliver complex and expensive work at a price that was far too cheap, so I eventually learned my lesson.

A plain background is the cheapest of all; that is because the youngest of boys can, with care, be taught to paint it. Interiors are more expensive, as they involve much more detailed work, and more expensive again are exteriors with a part landscape view through a casement. Most of these can be executed by a trained journeyman, as can the uninterrupted vista of a landscape behind the sitter, but all must be paid for at the proper rate, which of course increases if you yourself are forced to be involved. The master's time is much more precious than that of boys, apprentices or journeymen.

The intelligent thing to do is to set up a scale of charges so that the patron is aware of what he has to pay. Then, a series of cheaply drawn patterns can be placed behind a rough sketch of a sitter so that the patron can judge the effect each type will have.

It is worth keeping these patterns in the studio and then showing them to any patrons that may have come along to discuss a portrait. This has indeed been my own practice for many years, and it has the advantage that the patron is under no illusions as to what he will get for his money and, as you have done no original work at the outset, is also under no obligation to purchase.

Of the Early Reign of
King Richard III
(from 17th June to 6th July 1483)

The younger prince settled happily into life in the Tower, and had a beneficial effect on his brother. Richard was always eager to be up and about each morning, and was usually, although not always, able to drag his brother outside to play at ball or archery. As far as his art was concerned, Richard was more talented than Edward, but was never able to settle for long, and thus was not so good at observing, although he did share Edward's skill in delineation and produced acceptable portraits. I think he preferred sports to arts.

On days when Edward refused to move, preferring to stay immured with his books, Richard prevailed upon me to take him abroad into the city to see the sights. One little boy looks much like another, and the people always expected to see two princes, so no one paid any attention to a middle-aged man wandering with his son through the town. Thus he was able to visit his mother and sisters, who remained in sanctuary, on a regular basis.

Edward always refused to join us in these sorties, pleading weariness or pain, but the fact is that the deteriorating look of his face deterred him from going abroad. Young boys of that age are extremely sensitive about how they look. It has been said by Dick's detractors that the princes were never seen in public after July 1483, which is true enough in Edward's case, but if anyone had looked carefully enough they would have seen the Duke of York in the streets two or three days a week. As I said, the people were looking for two boys.

Obviously our steps led us many times to the Abbey, and after Richard had visited his mother I would take him across to see Caxton and Wynkyn. He enjoyed helping them work the press and frequently returned to his brother covered in ink and full of stories, but Edward would not be swayed from his determination not to go outside the precincts of the Tower.

Meanwhile the business of government ground on. Will Hastings was buried with honour in the Abbey beside his friend, Ned. Rivers, Grey and Vaughan were executed; such was Dick's reputation for probity that Rivers named him in his will as executor of his estate – in itself, some said, tantamount to a recognition of his own guilt and Dick's innocence.

Bishop Stillington appeared before Parliament and his documentation and proof were investigated and proven to the satisfaction of all, and the boys and their sisters were declared illegitimate. As Dick had feared, the attainder against Warwick, the son of Dick's elder brother George, was not even considered for reversal, and the throne passed by default to the next in line. Dick was declared king and the coronation fixed for the 6th of July.

That same day Dick came to the Tower and asked for an audience with the king. He was pale, with a clammy sheen to his skin. Edward was still innocent of any knowledge of what had been happening other than that he and his brother had been declared illegitimate, as he had agreed with Dick, but not that it was through their father's fault rather than their grandmother's; both Doctor Argentine and myself had taken great care that nothing was said to Edward or his brother or in their presence to give away what we knew.

The day was overcast, and Edward granted audience to Dick in the room the boys used as a play and study area. He came down from his bedroom carrying the smallest of Caxton's three books, and Argentine and I took up our places by the door, ready to go or stay.

'Do you know what I read?' Edward asked.

Taken aback, Dick shook his head.

'It is the book my uncle wrote. I mean my other uncle,' he added hastily, 'Anthony Rivers. It is a book of philosophy and a great consolation to me in this time of trial. What news of my uncle. Is he still under arrest?'

Dick was stunned. He hesitated. 'Yes,' he said, 'that is, I . . . no.'

'What news of him?'

It was clear that this was not the way Dick had intended the interview to go. He looked across at Argentine and myself and licked his lips. Then he made a decision and squared his shoulders. 'It is with heavy heart I tell you, Your Majesty. My lords Rivers, Grey and Vaughan have confessed their treason to the Council. The messengers bearing the sentences have been sent forth already.'

'What will happen to them?' Edward asked.

After a moment's hesitation, Dick said, 'Your Majesty, the charge was treason.'

The boy stared at him, his mouth agape and a large red slobber emerging from the side of it. 'Death?' he said incredulously. 'Death? You mean to kill my uncle Anthony?'

'Not I, Your Majesty, although it was I that did call for his trial. It was a decision of the Council.'

'Are you not the presiding voice of the Council?'

'I am, Your Majesty, but I am but one voice.' He paused, and the space lent extra weight to what he said next. 'In honesty, I must tell Your Majesty that I saw no reason to dissent from the sentence. They were guilty.'

'You would not raise your voice to save my uncle?'

'I was not able to raise my voice to save my own brother,' Dick reminded him. 'And I did think Lord Rivers guilty.'

'And this is how you protest your loyalty?' the boy said. 'We are offended by it, my lord of Gloucester, as we are now offended by your plan to make a whore of our grandmother. You may take your leave.'

'My lord,' Dick began, but Edward would hear no more and turned away. He walked towards the door and would have opened it, but Dick's call prevented him. 'Edward, come back. You must come back and listen to me.'

Edward turned and answered stiffly. 'It is not meet to use the word "must" to a king,' he said. 'You are dismissed our presence.'

'No, Edward,' Dick said, and something in his voice made the boy turn again. 'Please come back and sit,' Dick said, and added, I think for the last time, 'Your Majesty.'

Edward thought for a second, and then returned to his seat. 'Very well,' he said.

What Dick had to say was said quickly – how Stillington had come forward with a story which made his own impossible to spread, how the man had been hailed before Parliament and questioned, how his story had been accepted, the princes declared illegitimate, and finally how Dick had been declared king.

'And you accepted?' the boy said.

'I could see no alternative.'

'You lied to me. You did want my throne.'

'I swear, Edward, I did not, and I do not, and if it lies within my power to render it safely to you, then I will do so. We have

begun to work on a petition to the Pope, and that is all I can
do for now – but these things take time.'

'You stole my crown,' Edward said. 'You pretended to be
my friend and to do my father's will, and now you have
murdered my uncles and my father's friend, and you call yourself loyal? Call yourself what you will, Gloucester, but I for one
will never call you king.'

'Edward, Edward,' Dick said softly.

The boy refused to look at him, and instead gazed down at
the book that was still in his hand. 'Not all philosophy is consolation, I think,' he said, 'for herein I read from Boethius, "Truly,
in adverse fortune, the worst sting of misery is once to have
been happy."' He closed the book and then, with a cry of 'Oh,
Uncle Anthony!' he burst into a flood of tears.

The Council met a few days after Parliament to discuss
events, but Dick absented himself. Lord John Howard summa-
rized how he saw matters developing. Like Dick, he hoped that
some grounds might be found for overturning the Act of Illegitimacy so that Dick could pass the throne back to Edward.

'In the meantime,' he said, 'England has the best possible
bargain. If Prince Edward were king, not only a minor but also
an illegitimate one, then there would be no end of plotting, a
return to Woodville dominance of the king, and ultimately
a return to civil war. With King Richard on the throne, we have
a respected adult whose legitimacy is beyond question. He is a
proven warrior in the field and known throughout his lands as
a fair and beneficent governor.'

This was accepted by all, and was my last appearance at a
Great Council, as my writ from King Edward V no longer ran
in the realm. I returned to my duties in the Tower, hoping that
at last I might be able to go home.

Dick's only contribution to the debate was a short note which he sent to Archbishop Bourchier. The archbishop showed it to me. It read, 'In the bowels of Christ, I beseech ye – let this cup pass from me.'

Nonetheless, Dick was crowned in the Abbey on the 6th of July, the most reluctant monarch in the history of that troubled land. Both Edward and Richard were given honoured places at the ceremony, but Edward sat with his face looking downward and buried in the upper portion of his cloak – he wanted no one looking at him, and refused to look at Dick. The two boys sat with their mother, who looked on disapprovingly as her brother-in-law that had been was crowned, but her confession of the knowledge of Ned's previous marriage had been published by Parliament, and there was naught that she could do.

Only Dick seemed completely aware of what was going on. He followed the ceremony intently, noting every move that the archbishop made, but his face was pale and set, and suddenly he looked much older than his thirty years.

The boys had been moved out of the royal apartments a couple of days before the ceremony, as the rooms were needed for Dick and Lady Anne. Their son Edward and the Warwick boy (also called Edward) were also in residence during the preparations, so all of the male line of the House of York slept in the same building each night. Sadly, the Warwick boy is feeble-minded, and was no company to anyone, while Dick's son was too young to comprehend what was going on. The former Edward V refused to come out of his new chamber, and my days were lightened only by the presence of Dick and his namesake, the former Duke of York, who still found time for each other. Unlike his brother, Richard seemed to bear Dick no ill will, and the two managed to enjoy each other's company when time allowed.

Of Travels and Travails

(July 1483 to August 1485)

Dick saw only too well that the young former king had fallen into a decline from which he was unlikely to recover while in the Tower.

'We are a sickly lot, we Plantagenets,' he told me one day while walking in the garden. 'Ned was an exception, and so was George, but look at the rest of us.' He shook his head. 'All these boys need more than they're getting, Hans. They need good country food and country air. They need exercise that they can't get in a city.'

I must say that he had a point. Young Edward was a sorry sight, alternately drooling and bleeding from the mouth, and his ill temper made his ill health seem worse than it was, while his too easy tendency to give in to his illness made him poor company for the others. Dick's own Edward was weak, and although a boy full of fun and ready for anything he was always outrunning his strength. The Warwick boy, yet another Edward, was cheerful and amiable, but his mind had gone dancing. Only young Richard and Dick's bastard boy John, who was a little older than the others, maintained rude health both physically and mentally.

'I am minded to move them to Yorkshire.'

I looked at Dick in some alarm. Here in London I was at

least no more than a short sea journey away from home, but I had no idea of Yorkshire. I knew it was in the north, but as to how far away or whether the people were friendly I had no inkling.

'I must be away soon on the royal progress through the realm,' he said. 'I think the boys should go to Middleham in Wensleydale.'

'What is it?' I asked, possibly somewhat tremulously.

Dick's eyes softened as he looked at the place in his mind. 'Home,' he said. 'It's home, Hans.'

We left London as part of the king's progress in mid-July, going with him as far as Oxford, where he paused two days to listen to disputations on theology and moral philosophy. This is no meat for little boys, and we passed on to the north.

Wensleydale was as different from southern England and the Low Countries as could be imagined. It was a place of castles and crags, and wild, windswept moors. It was a wilderness, but a beautiful one; a harsher countryside than the soft south, but much more magnificent – it was male where the south was female. As Dick said, it was a boy's country. He had spent much of his own youth there, had first met Anne, the love of his life, there, and saw it as a refuge from the cares of the world.

Some boys, alas, take the cares of the world and cherish and grow them. Edward the former king was one such. Unlike his brother, he was never able to accept his change in fortune; unlike his brother, he was unable to forget the cares of his estate and embrace the joy of the day.

'Edward, to be a bastard is no great thing,' I overheard John telling him one day. 'I have been a bastard since the day I was born and will remain one until the day I die. What does this mean? One thing only – that I will never in all my life have a tenth of the cares my father has. No man will ever want to make me a king, and in this I count myself lucky.'

'You know not what you say,' Edward told him. 'I was a prince at birth, and then I was a king for the length of a spring-time, and now I am a nothing. I prefer my former state.'

'And I prefer this one,' Richard told him. 'It is better to be a free bastard in Yorkshire than a prince confined to a fortress. In any case, we shall not be bastards for ever; Uncle Dick will see to that.'

The freedom he cherished was not to last, however, although the campaign to legitimize the former princes looked as if it might. The king had written to Rome, and the Pope had asked for evidence. This was being laboriously gathered and copied; Dick estimated that this exercise alone might take until spring.

Meanwhile the five boys enjoyed a summer of fresh air and exercise, the four younger ones following John as he showed them the countryside around Middleham.

Thus I was allowed some time of my own, and I wandered the hills, those strange hump-backed beasts which are not native to Flanders, and even found time for a few sketches to exercise what remained of my talent and remind me that I was an artist, not a politician. I had not lost my cunning, I found. The fingers still placed the paint where I wanted it to go, and mixed the colours to the degree I wanted, and when I did the preliminary sketches the lines found themselves in the right place. Perhaps it is a God-given gift after all, and cannot be lost or forgotten or taken away by mere man or an effort of will, or the promptings of a soul condemned to perdition.

In August they all went to York to meet the king and queen, leaving me, suffering from an ague, behind. In York, Dick's son Edward was created Prince of Wales and Earl of Chester; there had to be an heir, although Dick was reluctant to name his son when he hoped himself not to be king for long.

The other young Edward, Clarence's son, did not come back to Middleham, but went to live with his cousin John, the Earl of Lincoln. The queen brought her son and nephews back, and the cheerful days resumed.

There was a difference in feeling in Yorkshire. In the south Dick was tolerated at best, and at worst despised for his northern origins. In Yorkshire he was adored for his good nature, his honesty and his good government. Men of Yorkshire admire straight talking and appreciate straight dealing, but in the south of England these attributes are seen as naivety and leave their practitioners open to being cheated. Dick's reputation for fair dealing and generosity, like an Italian wine, did not travel.

Then at last autumn brought news of a revolt, and the cheerful days were gone for ever. Dick's cousin Buckingham, hitherto one of his staunchest supporters, rose in rebellion alongside the former queen's family, the Woodvilles, and the followers of Henry Tudor, an obscure nobleman who lived in exile in France.

Dick moved to a town called Lester and mustered his army, but the rebellion soon collapsed and Buckingham, completely isolated, was arrested and executed for treason.

Autumn turned to winter, a bleak but bracing season, but there were rumours of continuing support for Tudor, and Dick was uneasy.

It was a bright morning in April when Dick's lad John came to see me, his face pale as the snowdrops without. 'You have not heard the news, I think,' I told him. 'Ned's queen has come out of sanctuary together with her daughters.'

'Yes, I had heard,' he said distractedly.

'That's good news, is it not?'

He shook his head. 'Yes, of course it is, but that's not ... It's Edward.'

I thought he meant Ned's lad, the former prince, but it was Dick's son that concerned him. The boy had taken a fever a couple of days before, and as we entered his bedchamber I sensed the worst. He lay very still, the opposite of his normal lively self, and all the strength seemed to have gone from him. There was a rasping in his chest. 'We have sent for a physician,' John said. 'There is none locally, so we have sent to York, but ...'

There was nothing to be done. The boy was given the last rites, and died in the early hours of the following morning; he was simply not strong enough for the world. We sent word to Dick and the queen.

Summer came and went, and rumours grew of support for Tudor. Some of the nobles were unhappy with Dick's reforms giving rights to ordinary men and correcting economic injustices. Even the barons were required to obey the law, and some of them were unfamiliar with the concept. Overtures were made to Tudor.

The queen did not outlive her son a year. She had ever been a victim of the same weakness in the lungs, and succumbed, like her son, as the spring returned to England. I did not see Dick, who was said to be distraught with despair, but grief was a luxury he could not long indulge, and he was soon back working as energetically as before. He named John of Lincoln as his heir and sent me letters asking after Ned's boys.

Tudor had taken the hints offered to him by the malcontent nobles, and fresh rumours began that he was to invade England in the summer. More letters arrived from Dick; Middleham was not strong enough to withstand any sort of siege, and he wanted Ned's boys in the safest place if Tudor came, which meant a return to the Tower. On May Day he issued commissions of array calling his forces to muster, and included the former Prince Edward's name in them; meanwhile the depositions and evidence on the Eleanor Butler issue, two waggonloads, had set out for Rome, and he had high hopes that Edward and Richard would soon be legitimized.

In London, meanwhile, Tudor supporters began spreading rumours that the princes were dead at Dick's order, and he did nothing to dispel them, possibly thinking that if he maintained an ambiguous silence then no conspiracy could form around alternative rivals.

In mid-May our time at Middleham was at an end. Richard and I were sorry to leave, but Edward had grown more lethargic, and the heat of the summer suited him not at all. His younger brother rode happily all the way from Yorkshire to London, but Edward was carried in a litter, and his misery deepened as the Tower closed in around him.

We saw Dick briefly, in Nottingham on our way south. He was worn out by toil and worry. It was clear that the loss of his family had hit him hard; his paleness was exaggerated, and he was driven by some internal fire that looked to burn itself out swiftly. All these cares notwithstanding, he remembered to bid farewell to his nephews and myself before turning his thoughts once again to rebellion and warfare.

Of the Deaths of Princes

(23rd August 1485)

And then this snow rose of two summers was dead, killed by treachery in battle against Henry Tudor. The rumours began to arrive in London early in the morning of that August day, and I decided that my place was at the Tower where I might try to protect the princes and engineer their escape, should the news be bad. I was sure that Sir Robert Brackenbury would ensure their safety by any means at his disposal. At the very least I could take them to the Netherlands and let Maximilian and their aunt Margaret protect them.

The streets were paved with rumour that morning. Richard had been bought and sold by the Stanleys, the king was dead, Henry Tudor was dead, Richard had triumphed at the last, Henry had ridden across the body of the king, Henry had been killed by Richard in a final struggle, they were both dead, and every imaginable variation on these themes, and with every step I took the rumours changed again. The crowds thronging the streets knew for certain what had happened, but each had a different certainty, and not a man of them had witnessed a moment of the battle for himself. It was hard work fighting my way to the Tower, but eventually I found myself outside it. I stood and hammered on the gate and the boy came and opened the little flap. 'Have you heard any news?' I asked.

'Only rumour,' the boy told me. 'Mostly bad.'

'Let me see Sir Robert. If the worst of the rumours are true we must make plans. There is no time to lose.'

'You cannot see Sir Robert,' he said. 'He is not here. He rode to fight for the king.'

'And his deputy?' I asked.

'He too.'

'So who then is in command here?'

'I am, until someone comes with news,' the boy said. 'The maids and cleaning women I have sent home, and the men of the watch did not report this morning. I fear they too might have gone to the battle. The cooks and the boys are below, and I am here alone, with the princes and one servant, until Sir Robert returns.'

'Let me in,' I said.

'You have no business here,' he objected.

'You know my business here,' I told him. 'I am here to instruct the princes in painting and drawing. The daily business of the realm must continue, even when there is greater business about.' I held out to him my pass, signed by Richard himself, and that convinced him. He unlocked the gate and allowed me to pass. 'Allow no man to enter unless he bears the king's warrant,' I told him. 'No man is to be trusted this day.'

I found the boys pacing their bedchamber. They begged for news, but I could tell them nothing. 'There is nothing but rumour,' I told them. 'It has always travelled faster than truth.'

Outside the day was turning fine. 'Come down into the garden,' I told them. 'It matters not where we wait for news, and the fresh air can only do you good.' They saw the sense in this, and we trooped into the open. There was a small area where they had played with battledore and shuttlecock and we had sketched the flowers earlier that year, while Dick schemed and battled for their survival. I left them there and went to see the boy.

'It might be best if we took the princes to a place of greater safety,' I suggested.

'What place can be safer than the Tower?' he asked scornfully.

'Any place where the princes are not known to be,' I said. 'If Henry Tudor has won, this is the very place he would choose to keep them. Staying here is playing into his hands. If we move the princes at least it will buy us time; we can always bring them back if the news turns out to be good.'

'The idea is good,' he said, 'but I have no warrant to move them.'

'It is an emergency,' I said. 'Necessity is its own warrant. In saving the princes you will be doing the will of the king.'

'My life would be forfeit if I gave them up without a warrant,' he said. 'I dare not risk it.'

'What then if I were to take the princes into the town with me? It has been some time since they were both outside. It is the normal routine of the household, after all. No one could blame you for allowing that.'

He grudgingly allowed that this was a reasonable request, and I went back to the garden to ready the princes, and immediately encountered a problem. Edward refused point blank to go anywhere. 'I want to wait for news,' he said, 'and in any case I do not wish to appear before the people with my face like this.' His condition had admittedly grown much worse – the new physicians were not of the quality of Argentine. 'Your people do not know you, my lord,' I said. 'No one will recognize you.'

'No matter,' he said. 'I will stay home and read my books.'

'My lord, you know there are rumours abroad of a great

battle in the north. If the result has gone ill for the king then you may not be safe.'

'If the result has gone ill for the Duke of Gloucester then whom have I to fear?' he asked. Still he bore the grudge. 'My Woodville cousins will come and I shall be king again. No, I will stay here, Master Memling. Do you go out, if you will. I am sure my brother will accompany you.'

'I do beseech your lordship,' I began, but he would hear none of it, and by now Richard was so insistent on going that I thought it better to take the one and return for the other if necessary. If Richard were not with him, Edward might crave his companionship and be more ready to come along.

Richard and I went out afoot into the town round the Tower, and soon we were immersed in its rumours.

My first thought was to take Richard to his mother's protection, but Waltham was too far for him to walk, and I dared not reveal him as a prince with the country in such turmoil. In any case, it lay in Essex, to the east, and we would be walking away from the news that we wanted, so we turned west, hoping that we might meet men coming from the north road.

It was late afternoon when the riders appeared. We had taken ourselves to a pie shop and were lounging in the street outside listening to the gossip when someone shouted that armed men were coming, and an apprehensive crowd gathered. I had the idea of going into the ale-house across the way and buying a couple of jugs of ale. Sure enough, when the horsemen arrived they were thirsty and beckoned me through the press when I raised the jugs on high where they could see them. They were all stained with the mud of the road and with the blood of the men who had fought against them for control of England. They were all armed and armoured, but not a man of them was wearing any surcoat or helm that could identify them. The tallest of them pointed at the platter of pies borne by the man next to me. 'Is there more of this?' he asked.

'Yes, my lord.'

'Fetch it. Enough for all. We have had a long ride.'

'Come you from the battle, my lord?' the pieman asked.

'I told you to bring food,' the rider said coldly. 'One more catechism will cost you your tongue.'

The man backed away and went back into the shop.

'May we not ask about the battle, my lord?' cried a woman's voice from behind me.

The man smiled, his teeth full of gaps. 'My men need food,' he said. 'Perhaps we will trade information for sustenance.'

The platter of pies was replenished and emptied once more and the jugs twice more before he was satisfied. 'On, men,' he called, and a general wail went up from the crowd, disappointed at not getting the news they wanted.

Laughing, the rider reined in. 'You might as well know,' he said. 'The usurper is dead, and a new king reigns in England.'

'Is it Tudor?' asked another voice, bolder this time.

'God save King Harry, seventh of that name,' said the rider, and spurred off towards the centre of the city.

I returned to where Richard was waiting. 'You heard?' I asked.

'We'd better get back and tell Edward,' he said, but I shook my head. I had now lost two of the princes that I loved, and I had no intention of losing this third.

'It might not be safe to take you back through the city at this time,' I said. 'I will put you in a place of safety and return myself for Edward. Perhaps now he will be persuaded.'

'Where should I go?' Richard asked, suddenly full of interest.

'In that I may please you,' I said. 'I think you should spend the rest of this day practising your printing skills.'

The smile almost split his face, so one at least of my charges was happy. How easy it is to be twelve years old.

I had guessed aright; the riders I had seen were heading for the Tower, and by the time I got there as the sun was setting they had taken up residence in the Great Chamber. 'What news?' I asked the gateman.

'The king is dead,' he said. 'These men are here to secure the Tower for Henry Tudor.'

'And the prince?'

'In his room. They have not asked after him.'

'Was there any mention of my Lord Richard?'

'No – food and drink is all they have asked for.'

'Did you say anything about me?'

He shook his head. 'They didn't ask.'

There was a shout from the hall. 'They want more drink,' he said. 'I'll have to get them some.'

'Is no one else around?'

'Just the kitchen women still and some of the boys. I couldn't let them go – the horses needed attending to and the men wanted food.'

'You go,' I said. 'I can get the drinks and keep an eye on the prince. You go. I'll take responsibility when Sir Robert returns.'

'Oh,' he said, 'Sir Robert is dead. They told me he was killed fighting for the k . . . for Richard.'

I was saddened by that; Sir Robert Brackenbury had been a good and honest man.

'So no one will know if you go,' I said. 'Go home.'

'I'll just find out what they want first.' He went into the hall and came back a few seconds later, nodding his head at me. 'Yes, wine,' he said.

'I'll get it.' He handed his keys over to me and went out into the darkness, and I went to the kitchen for a tray, filled four jugs with wine and carried them back to the carousing veterans.

The leader was seated at the head of what had been the main Council table, and I started at the other end from him and began to pour. I was concerned that the sight of the jugs and myself in close proximity might send alarm bells clanging in his head, but he was quite drunk, and obviously didn't connect me with the man who had served him earlier in the day. He did want something else, though. 'Bring food,' he said. 'Meat, none of your namby-pamby cheese and bread.'

I lowered my head, whispered, 'My lord' and went back to the kitchen. The place was filled with women working away and boys awaiting orders. I gathered up some soiled clothing that was waiting to be laundered, and then piled bread onto a large platter with some hunks of cold meat and a cooked chicken that I found, and took that to the men.

They seemed happy, and none of them was bothered that I had replaced the doorman as a servant. When they were all served I came out of the chamber and went up to Edward's room. 'What's going on?' he asked. 'What's all the noise?'

I explained and told him about the battle, and he grinned broadly. 'Good,' he said. 'They have come to restore me as king.'

'They are proclaiming Henry Tudor as King Henry the Seventh,' I told him.

'It's probably just a mistake,' he said. 'Perhaps I should go and talk to them.'

'I do not know why they are here,' I said urgently, 'but if I were you I should place no reliance on them until they have proven themselves. I suggest, my lord, that you get out while the going is good. If they mean you no harm, you can return in a day or two.'

He considered this. 'There is no way out,' he said.

'Through the kitchens, and hide in the kitchen garden until I come for you,' I said, and gave him the bits of clothing I had found.

Edward pulled a face. 'They are dirty,' he said.

I pointed out that this was no time to be fastidious, and he stretched a point and got into the garments, with much noise of disgust and wrinkling of the nose, before following me downstairs. 'What do I do when we're there?' he asked.

'Just mingle. Here, take my tray. Look busy, but move toward the outer door. I shall find an excuse to throw you out at some point. You must forgive me if I box your ears, my lor ... and also if I call you by another name. You can be Will. And, forgive me, my lord, but try to keep your face hidden.'

'All right.'

The moment I walked into the kitchen I realized that I had done the wrong thing. Five of the men had come down from the hall and were moving through the kitchens. Edward was ahead of me, so to his astonishment, not well hidden, I cuffed him, grasped him by the arm and grabbed one of the other smaller boys at random. I thrust them ahead of me into a corner. 'Get those pots cleaned,' I said abruptly, and walked away.

One of the men-at-arms blocked my way. 'More food, my lord?' I asked. 'Or is it wine?'

He ignored me and brushed past. I walked to the other end of the kitchen and began scraping food off platters. When I turned my head I saw the leader of the riders there, standing in the doorway I had just come through, with the rest of the knights behind him. He looked around the room, and finally his gaze lighted on me, weighing me up. He walked across and stood behind me. 'The birds have flown, it appears,' he said.

'We have plenty of birds, sir,' I told him, seeking to divert him from his prey. 'They are not killed yet, but it would not take long to cook them.'

'If I stole a hen,' he said, 'do you know where I would hide it?' I remained silent. 'In a coop,' he said, answering his own question.

My heart sank, but again I pretended not to see where his argument was going. 'The coop is without, sir,' I said. 'Do you want a hen, then? I will send one of the boys to fetch one . . .'

'Ah,' he said, 'but which boy should we send?' He turned sharply and shouted at the small group, 'Line up, all you boys. I want to have a look at you.' The boys scrambled to get into an approximate line, but just as they were sorting themselves out he shouted out again, 'Kitchen boys over here, ostlers' boys over there, servants behind me. Move it, quick.'

I dared not look, but nothing I did would have made any difference. The boys began darting to where he had pointed, but Edward was transfixed, not long enough in the role to know what he was supposed to be. The hesitation was over in a moment, and he began to move to the area for servants, but the man had been looking for just such a sign, and as the boy passed him he reached out a hand and casually took hold of his shirt.

'You – stay still.'

Edward stopped.

'Servant, are you?'

'Yes, sir.'

'It would be a desperate man who would care to be served by a face like that. Ever serve the young princes?'

'No, sir.'

'Ever see them?'

'Occasionally, sir.'

For the first time the man looked at him. 'Occasionally,' he repeated, drawing out each syllable. 'Nice big educated word for a servant. Come closer, servant.' He pulled gently on the shirt and Edward took a pace nearer him. The man looked him over. 'Look around you, servant,' he said, 'and point out to me the two boys that you have seen "occasionally" – Edward's bastards.'

Edward must have reacted in some way to the last word, for the man did not wait for an answer. He delivered a backhanded slap to the prince's face and then shoved him so that he fell to the floor.

'How dare you!' Edward shouted at him, and all was lost.

The man walked across and grabbed one of the other serving boys. 'Tell me a lie and you die,' he said to him conversationally, and then pointed, 'Is this Edward, son of Edward, King of England?'

'Yes, sir,' the terrified boy said.

'Do you know that for a fact?'

'Yes, sir.'

'How do you know?'

'Through serving him at table these last three months, sir.'

The man nodded, apparently satisfied, thrust him back into line and poked his finger into the face of the next boy. 'Lie and you die,' he said. 'What's your name?'

'Peterkin, sir.'

He moved his finger slowly from the boy's face until it was pointing directly at Edward. 'Well, Peterkin, do you know who that is?'

'Yes, sir.'

'Who is it?'

'Edward that was a prince, sir, and was to be king.'

'How do you know this?'

'I attended him at stool, sir, and took away his turds.'

'Did you also deal with the turds of his brother Richard?'

'I did, sir.'

'Point to him.'

The terrified boy raised a finger and pointed at Edward.

'Not at him,' the man said, seemingly patient. 'Point at his brother, Richard.'

The boy looked around.

After a very long time he said quietly, 'He is not here, sir.'

The man put his face close to the boy's, their noses almost touching. 'Look again,' he said, 'and look carefully. If you lie, you die.'

The child, no more than ten or eleven years of age, began to shake violently, filled with the terror of death. He looked desperately round the room, his head shaking slightly from side to side as he considered each face in turn. Finally he said, 'I do not see him here, sir.'

The man straightened up and took a step backwards. He pulled the boy forward a pace and said, 'Stand there,' before turning his attention to Edward again.

'You are Edward, son of Edward the king?' he said.

'Thou hast said it,' Edward said, but the reference was lost on his tormentor.

'Point out your brother.'

'My brother is not here,' Edward told him. 'He was taken hence two days ago, before my lord Brackenbury left to fight for the king.'

'Now, I know that that is not true,' the man said. 'I have information that he was here this morning, and my information is never wrong. Therefore point him out to me.'

'I have told you,' Edward said, 'he is not here.'

The man turned to face the rest of the boys. His fingers went to the bag at his belt, and he withdrew a golden noble, which he twirled in his fingers before placing it on the table. 'A noble,' he said. 'More than you will earn in a year.' He tapped the coin, and then said, 'It belongs to whoever points out to me the boy who is Richard, brother to this boy Edward.' He pushed the coin along the table with one finger, and said, 'There it lies, awaiting only someone to claim it.'

The boys looked eagerly about, but the babble of excitement died down when they realized that the others had been right, and finally the room fell silent.

Silently, the tall figure withdrew another coin and placed it beside the first. Then he looked up, allowing his gaze to rest on each boy in turn. Still there was silence.

He let the silence lengthen, and then nodded. 'Very well,' he said, and prodded Edward in the chest. 'Come with me.' He guided the boy through the door and out of our sight.

'What shall I do about these?' one of the other men said to his retreating back.

'Let them go,' the man's voice said. 'Oh, except one.' He put his head round the door and pointed. 'You, turd boy, come with me.'

The lad walked to him and waited for him to stand aside, but the knight neither preceded him through the door nor made room for him to pass, but roughly dragged him across the threshold. The other men started to herd the remaining boys towards the outer door. I sauntered behind them, but the rough voice stopped me. 'Not you,' he said, pointing his finger directly at me.

He looked directly at his knights, and said, '*Et lui,*' his eyes flicking from them to me. He stepped back, so that he was hidden from me by the door, but I saw his reflection in a large brass plate which stood on a shelf at his shoulder, and I saw him draw his hand across his throat in a gesture which could not be misinterpreted. I heard him speak, too: '*Tuez-le vous-mêmes. Pas ici. En dehors.*'

I looked away, anxious that none of them should see that I understood.

'Why do you want the turd boy?' one knight asked.

The answer was a laugh, a short and humourless bark. 'I need two,' he said, and looked at the other man. 'Too bad about the princes,' he said. 'They were dead before we got here.'

I felt the shock run through me, but knew not to react. One of the other knights beckoned to me. 'Come on, you, outside.'

'What for?' I asked. 'I thought his lordship said we were to go.'

'Not you. Little job for you first. You'll be gone soon enough.' His companions smiled at their joke.

'Where do you wish me to take you, sir?' I asked, instantly the obedient servant once again.

'Just outside, in the fresh air,' one of them grunted.

I led them up a flight of steps and out onto the battlements above the river. Someone had remembered to light the torches so that people would not fall. 'Will this do?' I asked.

'Perfect,' said one of them, and as one they made to cluster round me, their hands moving towards their sword hilts. I knew Edward could not be saved, so I made my decision. The foremost of the men reached out a hand to take my shoulder, but I was ready for him. I took a step backwards and then put my right foot on top of one of the low crenellations and simply sprang out, into the air. I twisted as I fell and saw their faces for the slightest moment, and then I crashed into the water feet first. I came up gasping, and the four of them were staring over the parapet at me.

The tide was coming in, and I swam away from the shore and allowed the current to carry me upstream. It would take time for them to report what had happened and then find a boat, if they decided to follow me at all. They were, after all, knights in full armour, who are understandably nervous about water. All the same, the sooner I was back on land the better.

I struck out across the river and then let the incoming tide carry me to the Southwark shore. I shot under the bridge and then dragged myself ashore just above it. Fortunately it was a warm night, and my clothes soon began to dry. Thus I excited no comment as I made my way west through the alleys to the printing shop at Westminster, thanking God every step of the way for my lifelong habit of a daily morning swim in the canals of Bruges.

Richard was waiting there, having spent the afternoon helping Caxton and Wynkyn to print pages of a new book. Caxton asked no questions but gave us shelter, and a few days later I was able to contact Sir Edward Brampton, who, faithful to his king, made arrangements for me to take the boy aboard a Flemish ship and transport him to Maximilian's territory. I went home at the last, but not in the way I would have wished, yet it was a peaceful voyage, untroubled by Tudor or his agents.

Back in Bruges I kept the boy at my house for some weeks, and when Maximilian was next in the city I obtained a private audience and told him what I had done.

'We cannot acknowledge him,' he said, ever the political realist. 'The continuation of the English war would be to no one's benefit, and it appears that this Henry Tudor sits secure for now. It were best we provide for the boy and keep him safe; he can make his own decision when he comes of age.'

'You cannot provide for him here, sire,' I said. 'He will become a focus of disaffection.'

'Unless we disguise his identity.'

'Surely, sir, your stepmother-in-law would know him.'

'No,' he said. 'She would not; she mentioned to me that she has never seen either of her brother's children – she left England before they were born. On the other hand, a young boy running around the palace speaking fluent English might excite some comment. It were best perhaps if she knew nothing of this matter for the moment.'

'I could take him into my home,' I said. 'One more boy would not make much difference.'

Maximilian shook his head. 'You are known to have been in England,' he said. 'If they come looking yours will be the first house they search, and a boy of the right age speaking good English but no Hollandish will stick out a mile. No, it will have to be somewhere else.' He rubbed his brow. 'I wonder.' He paused, made a decision and went on, 'There is one of my officers who might be induced . . .' He stopped again. 'I do espy a kind of hope.' He stopped again, and then reached a decision. 'Listen, Hans,' he said, 'I was recently in Antwerp, where one of my sea captains was desolate. He had lost his boy, a twelve-year-old, in an accident.'

'You want to replace his boy?' I began. 'But his friends, his neighbours would ask questions.'

'Not if they didn't know the boy. There is a vacancy to be filled, as controller of the port of Tournai. If he took both the post and the boy, no one need ever know until the time was ripe.'

Thus it was that the next week, acting as his lordship's messenger, I travelled with the boy to Tournai, where he was to join his new parents. The father, Jehan de Werbecque, was a bluff, straightforward man, but obviously subdued as a result of his loss; Richard took to him immediately when he was offered regular fishing trips out to sea. The mother, Catherine, looked drawn, but was gentle, and folded the boy in her arms; it was clear that the son they had lost had been much loved. After a hug of inordinate length, she held Richard at arm's length and perused him. 'He even looks like my own,' she said. 'What is your name, my boy?'

'It were best you do not know it yet,' I told her, 'and you must speak to him only in Flemish. Give him a name of your own choosing.'

'Our boy was called Pierrechon,' she said. 'Would that do?'

'Pierrechon,' I said. 'In English, that would be Peterkin. Yes. It is a most appropriate name.'

Of the Evil that Men Do

(late 1485)

The words ring in my ears until this day – 'They were dead before we got here.' Not so, but the princes were dead from the moment Richard III fell at Bosworth. Dick underestimated the evil of Henry Tudor. A bastard's bastard himself, Henry knew that bastardy was no bar to the throne, as long as the bastard in question had the will and the power to do that will. But he knew too that if one such as he could take England, then it could be snatched back by one with a better title. If Edward and Richard were legitimate and alive, then they were the rightful heirs. If Edward and Richard were illegitimate, alive or dead, then Henry, whether or no he married their sister, had no claim. The only way Henry Tudor could claim the throne of England was if the boys were legitimate and if they were also dead. Henry was given his two bodies and then, predictably, the boys were legitimized once they were known to be dead and Henry safely married to their sister, the rightful monarch of England.

The story was put about that they had been killed during Richard's time. It was known that they were seen playing in the gardens of the Tower until his reign began, and it was said that no man saw the two princes alive after the summer of 1483. Certain it was that no man saw both of them unless he was within the Tower. Edward was too ill to go abroad and too melancholy to play; that is why he was not seen.

The rumour-mongers were looking for two princes; had they used their eyes they might have seen one prince, alive and well and happy, wandering the streets of London with his tutor or, more often, slaving over a printing press at Caxton's and carrying newly printed books back to his afflicted brother at night – but it would not have suited Henry Tudor to have such a thing known and broadcast.

All the same, no Tudor agents bothered me, then or since, but Henry Tudor has had his revenge. My portrait of Dick was destroyed, and inferior copies circulated, doctored to show Dick as the Tudors wanted him to be, rather than as he was. His bunched muscle was turned into a hump and his face repainted with thinner lips and narrowed eyes, presumably to show cruelty and suspicion rather than the warmth and openness I found in him.

But what Henry did to Dick's portrait was nothing compared to what he did to his character.

Dick – loving, gentle, loyal, honest Dick – became a creature to frighten children with. The stories were legion. He had killed Henry VI with his own hand and murdered Henry's son, Prince Edward, we were told. He forced his wife to marry him even though she hated him, he bastardized his brother and nephews, branded his father a cuckold and his mother a whore, he stole the throne of England and finally he murdered the two little nephews he was sworn to protect. And not a single word of it was true.

If you looked upon his portrait you saw his twisted body, a reflection of the twisted soul that lay within. He was evil personified; never had such a monster been seen in England, and it was the will of Heaven that Henry Tudor should come and rescue the land. So goes the Tudor legend, fed and watered by Henry Tudor himself, and again, not a single word of it is true.

The first act of Henry Tudor's reign was as ignoble as it was unfair, and set the tone for his kingship. He declared that his reign had begun the day before the battle at Bosworth Field, and thus Dick and every man who had fought for him against Tudor was branded a traitor.

It is the most complete of ironies – that Dick should be considered a traitor – for the truth is that King Richard III was the best and finest of men, the flower of English chivalry and a man who unfailingly lived by his motto, '*Loyauté me lie*' – 'Loyalty guides me' – and I love and honour his memory this side idolatry.

CODA

Of the Unexpected Visitor

(May 1491)

I had been commissioned to do an altarpiece for the conse-
cration of a new chapel at Lubeck, and was working,
ironically enough, on the Resurrection of Our Lord when he
came unannounced into the room, having told Simonelle to say
nothing. I looked up from my work, and for the space of two
heartbeats I did not know him, and then I went on one knee
and kissed his hand. 'Your Grace,' I said, and then bethought
myself, and amended, 'Your Majesty, you are most welcome
to my house.'

'There can be no formality between us, Hans,' he said, and
raised me up. 'No man who has boxed my ears as often as
you have can possibly be expected to treat me with total
reverence. But I thank you for the title – you are the first man
to acknowledge my new status, and haply will not be the
last.'

He had grown considerably – the healthy diet and life in the
open air with his new father had seen to that, and his skin had
weathered and coarsened, but there was no mistaking whose
son he was. 'Are you on a visit here?' I asked. 'Do your parents
accompany you?'

'I must be about my father's business, Hans,' he said. For a
moment I thought he was referring to the matters of the port,

but then he added, 'My real father. I am almost eighteen years of age, and must set about claiming my patrimony.'

'Has it come so soon?' I breathed.

'You do not keep as abreast of goings-on in England as I do, I imagine,' he said. I showed him to a chair and shouted to Simonelle for some wine.

'Not any more,' I admitted.

'Are you aware that some time ago, Henry Tudor reversed the Act of Illegitimacy against my brother and myself. You know what that means?'

'That you are, as we always knew you to be, the rightful King of England.'

'Exactly,' he said. 'If Parliament recognizes it and Henry admits it, then I must claim it.'

'Henry will not have done this out of any goodness of heart or desire to see the truth revealed,' I said. 'He simply wants to ensure that his own claim to the throne, through your sister, is strengthened. He gives it out that you are dead, and so can be safely legitimized.'

'But when he sees me, and sees that I am not dead . . .'

'He knows full well you are not dead,' I told him. 'Do you not know that he has recognized your late brother as king, and calls him Edward V?'

'I do know that, and thus he must admit my claim too.'

'Why do you think he recognized Edward?' I asked.

'Because it is true, surely?' He looked bewildered.

I shook my head. 'It is because he knows Edward is dead,' I told him. 'He is Edward V, and safely dead, but no man has ever called you Richard IV. And Henry could never do that, because he does not know for certain that Richard, Duke of York, is dead. If he recognized you as your brother's heir he would have to recognize you as king, and that he will never do.'

'But when he sees me . . .'

'You surely do not think he will recognize you?'

'But I am the living image of my father, am I not?'

'No, sire, you misunderstand me,' I told him. 'Of course he will see who you are, but he will not admit it or accept it. He will not simply hand the throne over to you. Surely the events after Bosworth must have convinced you of that? He will label you an impostor and have you at best imprisoned or, more likely, killed.'

He was crestfallen. 'Even though he is sworn to uphold the law of England?'

'Henry Tudor is the law of England,' I told him as Simonelle came in with the wine and a plate of small cakes. I cautioned him with a look, and said, 'But can we leave politics while we enjoy the wine, and you can tell me of your mother and father.'

'But you know that my father died eight years ago,' he said.

'Forgive me,' I said, 'I mean, of course, of your adoptive parents. I did not mean to insult you.'

'Nor did I think you had,' he said, smiling. 'They are both well, thank you, and ask to be remembered to you. For some reason, they consider that handing me over to them was a kindness on your part.'

I smiled in reply, and the problems of monarchy were forgotten for a couple of hours while we talked. Richard had not stayed all the time in Tournai, but had been to Portugal as page to Sir Edward Brampton, the man who had ferried us from London to Bruges in 1485 and who, despite his name, was a Portuguese Jew. Then he had attached himself to a Portuguese grandee and voyaged down the west coast of Africa as far as the kingdom of Jalof before returning to Flanders to begin his quest for the crown.

Richard stayed with me that night, and the next morning I went to the Burg and requested an urgent audience with

Maximilian, who was in town for the Procession of the Holy Blood later in the week. His secretary at first claimed that no time could be made for me, but on my insistence, and given that he knew how well Maximilian thought of me, he eventually agreed to fit us in the following morning.

As we walked through the city to the appointment, I tried to convince Richard that his dreams of being King of England might not be as immediately realizable as he seemed to think. He struck me as being a most naive young man. 'You are leaving yourself open to a sentence of death for insurrection,' I told him.

'I am already dead,' he smiled. 'I have packed a great deal into my short life, Hans. I was Earl Marshal of England at five and Lord Lieutenant of Ireland before I was six, and a Knight of the Garter on my seventh birthday. Earl of Nottingham, I was, and Duke of Norfolk as well as Lord of Seagrave, Mowbray and Gower. Six or seven other titles, too, I had. Did you know I was even a married man?'

'No,' I said.

'In that life, not this,' he smiled. 'I was married at four.'

I knew that marriages at such an early age were not uncommon among the nobility, but I shook my head. I had not known of this.

'Indeed I was, to Anne Mowbray. I remember only that she was unfriendly, and would not share her wedding breakfast sweetmeats with me. She was an older woman, of course.' He smiled down at me. 'Six years old at the time. Of course the marriage didn't last.'

'No?'

He shook his head. 'She died at nine years old. I was widowed at seven, isolated from the world at nine, and, as far as the world knows, murdered at twelve. So, my dear Hans, whatever Henry Tudor decides to do with me has already been done. I am already a dead man, and nothing worse can happen.'

I was not sure that I was able to agree with him, but by that time we were at the Burg and I led him inside for his audience.

Maximilian had never seen Richard, of course, and did not recognize him when we were ushered into his presence. 'You are welcome, Hans,' he said, 'as is, of course, your young friend here.'

'You are acquainted with my young friend's story, sire, even though you have not met him previously.'

He cocked an eyebrow.

'This young man is known to you as Pierrechon Werbecque.'

Obviously the name had slipped his mind.

'The son of your port controller at Tournai,' I prompted.

Light dawned. 'This is the boy that you brought from England?'

'It is, sire.'

Maximilian rose and knelt to his guest. Richard raised him up, and Maximilian grasped his hand. 'You are truly welcome, Your Majesty,' he said, and stepped to the door. 'Find the dowager duchess and ask her to attend upon us at her earliest convenience,' he said to the unseen servant who was waiting outside. 'Stress to her that the matter is of some urgency.'

Returning to his seat, he said, 'May I ask what Your Majesty's plans are?'

'To regain my kingdom, of course.'

'Indeed, Your Majesty, but exactly how do you mean to achieve this?'

'I thought I might write to Henry Tudor and tell him that I am still alive, and ask him to hand over the kingdom to me.'

Maximilian's face was a picture. He glanced at me, made as if to speak, composed himself, and then said, 'Well, yes, the direct approach sometimes works, but may not necessarily be the most effective one, and is rarely the most diplomatic.'

'I could always just go to London and see him,' the boy suggested, 'and let him see me.'

'I think it unlikely then that you would return,' Maximilian said, 'for Henry's response is unlikely to be as positive as you hope. For one thing, you have no proof of who you really are, and for another, even if Henry were to believe you, he is unlikely to wish to divest himself of the kingship. Power is an addictive drug; once tasted it is difficult to relinquish.'

'But surely, once he knew the truth . . . ?'

'Reality is the only truth,' Maximilian said.

'And truth itself no more than a matter of perspective,' I put in.

Maximilian nodded his agreement. 'Look at it from the people's viewpoint,' he said. 'Henry has been king for six years; his realm is peaceful, and he is accepted as king. You will find that his people, like all peoples, prefer peace and stability to eternal squabbling. What does it matter to them who sits on the throne? All they want is a quiet life, and time for grandfather to die before father, and father before son. That is the truth – England is Henry's, and it will not be a task easily accomplished to prise it from his grasp.'

Clearly, even after what I had told him, the boy had not expected such a response. 'So what do you advise, sir?'

'The truth?' Maximilian asked, and on receiving a nod from Richard, said, 'Go home, back to Tournai. Take up your father's post of port controller.'

'May I remind Your Grace that my father's post was King of England.'

'We must be realistic,' Maximilian said. 'Do you want to throw England, and perhaps Europe too, into another bloody war? We have had a quarter century of instability in England, and at last it is over. Can you take upon your shoulders the responsibility for starting up the war yet again?' He held up a hand to forestall Richard's enthusiastic nodding. 'And there is another question, too, that is pertinent. If you were to win the war you started, could you rule as well as Henry? He may not be the rightful king, but he is an effective one, and that is what people want. You could crown a dog King of England, and it would not matter as long as people were able to get on with their lives unimpeded. The truth is that it does not matter who rules a country – it is how he rules the country that is important. In effect, that man, whoever he might be, is the true king.'

He looked at the young man's face. 'I am sorry to speak to you like this,' he said, 'and perhaps to dampen your ambitions and dash your hopes, but these are questions that will be asked by every person to whom you go for help – and there is no doubt that you would need help. And therein lies another problem. Those who offer to help you will do so for their own reasons. If France helps you, it will be in order to destabilize England; Scotland and Spain will have their own priorities, as will any other state.'

'But you know who I am,' Richard said. 'You will recognize my claim, surely?'

'Recognize it, perhaps,' Maximilian said. 'Act upon it, never. You are welcome to all that my court may provide in terms of food and accommodation. You shall be my honoured guest, should you so desire, but I will give you no funds or armies. I make you no false promises. Like every other ruler in Europe, I will keep you safe, but it will be for my ends, not yours.' He shook his head. 'No, if I were you I would return to Tournai and dwell in peace. It is best to stay at home; you are young, and so are perhaps unaware of the inestimable value of a quiet life and a restful night's sleep.'

At which point the servant announced the arrival of Margaret, dowager duchess of Burgundy, Maximilian's step-mother-in-law and Richard's aunt. We all rose to greet her, and she swept into the room, a question on her lips which was destined never to be asked. Her mouth dropped open and her eyes widened as she looked upon the young man before her.

'Edward,' she said, and dropped onto a stool.

I had seen Richard's father for the first time when he was thirty. She had been brought up with him and had hardly seen him at all since his mid-twenties. I remembered the bloated sot I had last seen eight years before; she remembered the tall and beautiful young man of her own youth. I looked at Richard through her eyes, and saw the young Ned before me.

He spoke to her in English. 'Not Edward, madam, but his son Richard, formerly Duke of York, who now craves your blessing.'

He knelt before her, and she reached out to touch the mop of blond hair. 'You are so like him,' she said. 'For a moment it was him. They told me you were dead.'

While Richard sat and held his aunt's hand, Maximilian explained the subterfuge and why it had been necessary. Unlike her stepson-in-law, Margaret was enthusiastic about Richard's restoration. 'Of course, we must help him,' she said. 'We must remove the usurper and restore Richard to his throne.'

'Madam,' Maximilian said. 'Neither Burgundy nor the Empire is in a position to antagonize England.'

'Then the French will help.'

Maximilian sighed. 'I have already explained that any help the French offer will be designed to further French interests, not your nephew's,' he said, 'and the same goes for anyone in

Europe. If they can see an advantage, they will take it. If not, they'll do nothing. They may recognize you, Richard, of course, and give you a place in court and a title, but there is no one who will help you out of a love for truth, justice and the concept of primogeniture; anyone who helps you will do so only out of political self-interest.'

'Including you?' asked the disappointed boy.

'Absolutely,' Maximilian said. 'As I said, I have no intention of helping you. In any case, my son is about to inaugurate Henry VII, Henry Tudor as you call him, as a Knight of the Order of the Golden Fleece, and I have no intention of disturbing relations between our two countries at such a time. I will house and feed you for a few weeks while you visit your aunt and decide what to do next, but if you want a secure future then my advice to you remains the same. Go home.'

Richard shook his head. 'I cannot,' he said. 'I have been a king now for but a couple of days, but I see that it is a better destiny than the life of a port controller, and holds the promise of even greater things to come. I cannot give it up, but must take the road that has been mapped out for me. You said it yourself, sire. "Power is an addictive drug; once tasted it is difficult to relinquish."'

This from the boy who had enjoyed being a free bastard in Yorkshire. I felt sorry for him.

Margaret made the appropriate noises of protest, of course, but Maximilian was adamant, and that was where I left matters and came home. I had had enough of the ways of the great. Richard followed a few hours later. He stayed with me but a few days, thinking through what to do, and finally he was received into the household of his aunt Margaret, who told Maximilian that in her own domains she would act as she pleased, think as she pleased and recognize whomsoever she pleased.

One evening Richard had taken some of my special black chalk and drawn a sketch of himself; partly for me, partly for practice. He had not essayed a drawing in some years, and to a certain extent he had lost the skill, although there were hints of ability here and there. By accident, I presume, but all too possibly by design, he had drawn his face at the king's angle, looking down and to the left, as if bestowing a kind word to one lower in esteem than himself. By design possibly, as I said, although I recall that he observed his face in a mirror on his left-hand side. No matter, I suppose.

Facially, the drawing much resembled the portrait I had done of his father – Ned, I mean – all those years ago, but I forbore to mention the fact. I looked for the sketch after he had left, but it was nowhere to be found.

Although I did not witness the event, I am told that some weeks later Richard did indeed face Henry in person when the king came to Bruges for the Golden Fleece ceremony. He asked Henry to relinquish the crown, but 'Master Tudor', as Richard insisted on calling him, laughed in his face and threatened to hang, draw and quarter him if he should turn up in England.

Insulted, Richard pointed out that such a method of execution was reserved for commoners, not nobles, to which Henry replied, 'Precisely,' and walked away.

Some months later I learned that Richard had returned to Portugal, where he felt that he might gain some support, and I have heard since that he landed in Ireland in a Portuguese ship. I have heard nothing of him since then save for the occasional rumour that he is wandering from monarch to monarch in Europe, looking for some support in his quest for truth and justice. Poor boy; I fear no good will come of it all.

Of Framing

As a young man necessity forced me to make my own frames, and I became adept at it, taking pride in making the various joints and fitting the whole together snugly around the picture.

As I became more prosperous, however, I grew out of the habit in order to concentrate on the painting, and only after it was finished did I have the panels mounted in the frame by a joiner. This went well enough. At the height of my powers I was able to employ a carpenter for two days of every week for the making of frames to my specifications.

In later years I took to making them myself again, as a form of relaxation. On these occasions I made sure to sign it; I am still proud of my joinery.

Mostly the frame is separate from the picture it contains, a discrete creation in its own right, but I sometimes made the frame an integral part of the painting. This can be done in two ways.

One is by painting the frame into the picture, so that the portrait itself seems at a second remove. This technique I employed when I wanted to use trompe l'oeil lettering, painted to look incuse, along the edge of the border.

The other way is the reverse, to add depth by spilling

characters or material over the edge of the picture. This adds reality, the subject seeming to obtrude into our world and to become three-dimensional, and lends perspective to what lies behind. Some purists felt that this was unacceptable, and that a painting's very flatness is one of its virtues.

I did not let this stop me. If a sitter's hand reaches out and lets a fingertip enter our dimension, or if a fold of cloth or a page of a book spills over the edge and cascades into our world or a shadow falls from the picture's world into ours, I can see no objection. It breaks through into the real space beyond the picture frame and thus adds to the image and to the illusion.

There is a third way, when the painted object is of the portrait but not in it. It is diverting to watch a patron reach out, trying and failing to brush a perceived fly from the canvas, unaware at first that the fly which seems to have perched on the frame exists independently of both our own world and of that of the portrait, and is a two-dimensional representation of a three-dimensional object which inhabits the zero-dimensional world between our world and the plane of the portrait. It is an enigma, a joke that I like to play on patrons sometimes.

Not all of the painting needs to be confined to the frame. The truth sometimes lies outside.

Of the Last Things

(August 1494)

O nly truth remains.

It is late. Family and servants are all asleep, but there is no sleep for me any more. The canker that is growing inside me will not allow it, and I feel more than ever the insistent presence of death, waiting here, hovering just out of reach, attending upon his moment. I think I may survive this night, for 'tis almost dawn, but I do not look to see many dawns after this one. I can see no water from my room, so there will be no last blue for me.

I remain unshriven. I can tell no man my sins, not even a priest; there is no forgiveness possible for such as me.

Nonetheless the secret cries aloud to be told – this paper must suffice, then, and truth take its chance whether it shall be revealed in time to come.

I have been befriended by seven princes, six of them ruling, and one landless. Some are dead; Charles and Ned I could do naught for – their deaths came to them through their own actions. Dick and young Edward died at the hands of the usurper, and there was naught I could do for them either. Maximilian lives yet, a prosperous prince, and so does Richard of York, or Perkin as some would call him, though who knows for how much longer, as he goes to face the murderer of his uncle and brother.

It is the seventh of whom I must now reveal the truth, the real truth, and to relate this truth, I must venture once again into that forest at Winendaele in 1482. At the last, agonizing though it is, I must return in my mind to that day in the forest. I have written before about that day, and written deceit, for while what I wrote was all true, it was not all of the truth.

There remains this to tell.

When I dismounted from my horse, things were not as I have said before. Not unconscious and lying on the ground, but conscious and sitting did I find her, the princess. Her horse had run into a deep but dry stream bed and was standing quietly nearby, its head level with my feet. Marie looked up at my approach and said, 'Oh, Hans! The horse bolted with me.' Her face was white, but her eyes were clear.

'It is Hans now, is it?' I asked. 'You must be in desperate need of my help, my lady, or I would still be a mere Mynheer Memling to you.'

'Why so bitter, Hans?'

I held out my hand, and she took it so that I could raise her from the ground. 'I am bitter because I was given hope,' I told her, 'and then had the cup dashed from my lips. I see you are not too proud to take my hand now. Are you hurt?'

She ignored my first question and answered the second. 'A little shaken. He threw me.' She smiled faintly. 'It appears that a horse may say "You may not" to me, at any rate.'

I was not to be appeased by a jest. I faced her, alone, for the first time in five years, with five years' worth of unspoken resentment within me bursting to come out. 'I loved you, Marie,' I said. 'I would have done anything for you.'

She brushed herself down, flicking away stalks of grass and

bits of dried leaf as casually as she had a painter's dreams. 'It would not have been enough, Hans. Nothing you have would ever have been enough for me, not after what I had been brought up to be. Do you not see – did you not see even then, that there was nothing in that cup you thought you tasted from – there was never any hope, Hans.'

I held out my hand to lead her, hoping to remount her on my animal and take her from the forest, but she faltered, her speech halting and troubled. 'It was all a game, Hans – a girl playing at being in love, and pretending, and teasing you. It was not real, none of it.'

I spun round. 'Not real?' I said incredulously. 'Not real? It is the only real thing I have ever known in a life filled with facsimiles and fakes.'

She did not reply, but stood watching me.

I stepped towards her, angry and tense. 'How can you say it was not real?' I snarled. 'What can you know of reality, hidden away in your palaces and fortresses, cosseted from the world by courtiers, living a fairy tale?'

She stood looking at me, compassion and pity in her gaze. 'Don't be angry with me, Hans,' she said. 'I meant no harm or insult to you.'

I waited, feeling the resentment well up within me. Marie took a step towards me. 'I was a child, Hans,' she said. 'A mere child.'

She came closer, her arms raised. I think she meant only to reassure me, to soothe my torment, but I was not yet calm – my anger, violent and sudden as it was, had not quite spent itself in that brief outburst – and I resisted. 'No,' I said, 'don't touch me; don't pity me.'

I pushed her away, more violently than was necessary, my arms extending to their fullest. Off balance, she tried to step back, and her heel caught on a projecting tree root. She staggered, took a half-step backwards and then toppled slowly over the edge of the stream bed. There was an unbridgeable gap between us; before I could reach out to correct what I had done, she fell. I saw the look on her face.

It was not a great fall – little more than the height of a man – but a dead tree lay athwart the bed and her back landed right across it. I waited, thinking that she must be winded, but she made no sound, and I realized that the blow had knocked her unconscious. Oddly, my first thought was that I could not now manage to get her on my horse unaided; she must perforce lie there until help arrived.

But there was no help at hand, and no man in that forest glade but me. I jumped down from the bank into the bed and looked at her where she lay, with that extraordinary beauty. Her hair was a wilderness, escaped from her cap and spread around her beautiful face, and below was the gentle swelling of her belly, with another life there within for the prince.

Beneath the dripping boughs in that sunken tunnel she lay still, face up. I dropped to my knees beside her, and saw that she breathed yet. Her body was arched, head and shoulders hanging over one side of the fallen tree and her legs on the other. I reached out to try to lift her gently to the ground, but I could not move her; something was preventing me. Then, beneath her waist, I saw blood thick on the ground, and more dripping from her back.

I ran my hand beneath her and found a protruding branch, standing proud from the tree and as cruelly pointed as a dagger. This limb had entered my lady's body, and my hand came away red with her blood.

The heart beats; the heart is the centre of all feelings and emotions which may last for ever, but the heart is only a muscle.

I lifted her clear of the branch and placed her on the bed of the stream. Along the path I could hear the sound of voices, and hooves drumming, and the approach of courtiers, too late. I rose and called to them, although I could not see them nor they me, and telling them what was the closest I dared go to the truth: 'Here! Here! My lady is grievously hurt! She has been thrown!'

They forced their way through the bushes, the first few leaping one by one into the dry bed. One of them went to collect her horse. Each tongue was stilled as her people crowded onto the bank and saw, those at the rear peering through the throng to get a glimpse, some kneeling on the edge. No man saw me as anything but one of them, one appalled, like them. And appalled I was, not only at what I saw, but at the knowledge that I alone had caused it to happen.

She died beautiful, and I gave her that; it was I, Hans Memling, who had power over her at the last, power to say 'You may not' and power to end the sentence with 'live', and it was I who determined the fate of Burgundy – I loved her, and my love killed her, and worse, her last thought was that I had killed her deliberately. Worst of all, I knew that she thought it, and have carried the guilt and shame of that knowledge with me.

It was in truth an accident, but I could tell no man of it, for no one would have believed me, and I have never expected anyone to do so. A boy overbalances with an easel; I give a girl a push – how insignificant and trivial they seem at the time, these accidents that are of themselves nothing, but that change lives, end lives, bring down princes, transform a continent and condemn otherwise good men to Hell.

I am not proud of my secret knowledge of the terrible power that lies hidden and uncontrolled in a broken heart, and so no man shall ever know of it. This paper can join the others.

Brugge, 9th August, Anno Domini 1494

Author's Afterword

All of the main characters who appear in *The Master of Bruges* are historical, and lived, worked in or visited Bruges between 1465 and 1494. Only minor characters have been invented. Similarly, almost all of the scenes in the story are real events, although sometimes characterization and motivation have had to be surmised.

Almost all of the paintings or drawings mentioned in the story are extant paintings by Hans Memling, many of them on view at the Memlingsmuseum in Bruges. The major exceptions to this are the small sketch of Marie as a child, which is fictional, the portrait of Charles the Bold which Memling claims to have worked on and which is attributed to 'the studio of Rogier van der Weyden' and is in the Staatliche Museen zu Berlin, and the *Portrait of a Lawyer* which Memling claims was stolen at the time of Rogier's death. This last is in the National Gallery in London under the title *St Ivo*, where it is attributed to Rogier. It is, however, the only painting ascribed to him which has a landscape view through a window behind the sitter, which was to become almost a trademark of Memling. I have taken a liberty in calling the sketch of Perkin Warbeck a self-portrait.

For those interested in Memling's life and career, the Memlingsmuseum and its near neighbour the Groeningenmuseum are the obvious starting points. Many of the buildings (although not his own house) which Memling mentions are still standing in Bruges. The Procession of the Holy Blood is still held annually on Ascension Day, and every five years the wedding procession of Charles the Bold and Margaret of York is enacted in the city's streets. The Order of the Golden Fleece still thrives. Edward IV was the first Englishman ever to be inducted; the last was the future Edward VIII, inducted in 1912.

For his art, the best reference work is Dirk de Vos's *Hans Memling: The Complete Works* (Ludion Press, Ghent, 1994), to which I am greatly indebted.

Select Bibliography

Borchert, Till-Holger, *Memling's Portraits*, Ludion Press, Ghent, 2005

Coleman, Sally Whitman, *Empathetic Construction in Early Netherlandish Painting: Narrative and Reception in the Art of Hans Memling*, unpublished doctoral thesis, University of Texas at Austin, 2003. (University Microfilms International (UMI), available through Dissertation Abstracts International) (University Microfilms no. DA3110764)

Commynes, Philippe de, *Memoires* (published 1524), translated by Professor Michael Jones (Penguin, 1972) and available at Fifteenth Century Texts – www.r3.org/bookcase/de_commynes/decom_2.html

Costain, Thomas B., *The Last Plantagenets*, Doubleday, New York, 1962

de Vos, Dirk, *Hans Memling: The Complete Works*, Ludion Press, Ghent, 1994

Fields, Bertram, *Royal Blood*, ReganBooks, HarperCollins, New York, 1998

Kendall, Paul Murray, *Richard the Third*, Allen and Unwin, London, 1955

Weir, Alison, *The Princes in the Tower*, Pimlico, London, 1992

Wroe, Ann, *The Perfect Prince*, Random House, London, 2003